What people are saying about

Cloud Warriors

I want a book that will take me someplace I've never been before. Rob Jung does that with *Cloud Warriors*...a fast-paced, exotic suspense novel into the heart of darkness.
Steve Thayer, *New York Times* bestselling author of *The Weatherman*.

A story that includes encounters with the spirits, a powerful magical potion that could change the world, and a clash between ancient and modern civilizations that places Professor Castro at the heart of one of the biggest discoveries (and potentially the most dangerous changes) humanity will ever face. Readers of thrillers that incorporate scientific discovery, deadly special interests, and confrontations between ethical and moral purposes will relish *Cloud Warriors*...well-written, replete with surprising twists and turns, and hard to put down; especially recommended for thriller readers who look for the kind of high-octane action, complex plots and powerful characterization mastered by such big names as Michael Crichton, H. Rider Haggard and Philip Kerr.
D. Donovan, senior reviewer for Midwest Book Reviews, reviews *Cloud Warriors*

Cloud Warriors

Cloud Warriors

Rob Jung

Winchester, UK
Washington, USA

First published by Roundfire Books, 2018
Roundfire Books is an imprint of John Hunt Publishing Ltd., No. 3 East St., Alresford, Hampshire SO24 9EE, UK
office1@jhpbooks.net
www.johnhuntpublishing.com
www.roundfire-books.com

For distributor details and how to order please visit the 'Ordering' section on our website.

ISBN: 978 1 78535 918 7
978 1 78535 919 4 (ebook)
Library of Congress Control Number: 2017961313

A CIP catalogue record for this book is available from the British Library.

Design: Stuart Davies

Printed and bound by CPI Group (UK) Ltd, Croydon, CR0 4YY, UK

I dedicate this book to my brother, Phil, and my sister-in-law, Joan, without whom this would not have been possible, and to Denise Brockman, my first beta reader whose battle with cancer ended before she got to see the finished product.

Acknowledgments

No book is written in a vacuum. Many people have a hand in it and I'd like to thank some of them: Phil, Joan and Denise to whom this book is dedicated. To my long-suffering wife Kathy, whose patience and advice is appreciated more than she'll ever know. To Dr. Jon Wogenson for his counsel related to all things medical. To Shelley Mahannah, Kelly Langdon, Bret Farley, Jessica Mueller, Anna Lissiman and Melissa Kaelin for their editing and encouragement. Uber agent Barbara Poelle whose rejection letter gave sound and welcome criticism. To Steve Thayer. Sorry about the lunch. There are many more who gave encouragement and support. Thank you all.

Chapter 1

They emerged from the dense undergrowth without the rustle of a leaf or stirring of the humid air, three hunters warned by instinct that something was not right. They stopped less than fifty feet from Professor Terry Castro's camouflaged observation post, completely naked except for the ochre paint covering their faces and the bows strapped to their backs.

He studied the three men: all well over six feet tall with light-colored skin, dirty yellow hair, and ice-blue eyes. Sinewy muscles stood out like ropes under taut skin. Gnarly hands and large feet, flaccid genitalia, bodies nearly hairless; only flared nostrils and darting eyes moved as they sought the source of discord in their jungle.

Castro checked the four students with him in the narrow observation post, each handpicked to be part of the Berrie University summer anthropology program. They sat still as statues with mouths agape, staring at the clearing. When Castro looked back the hunting party had melted into the jungle. He prayed that the remote cameras had been working.

They exhaled in unison, smiles beginning to spread across their faces as they realized they had just been firsthand witnesses to history. Tom Wise, the only underclassman in the group, began to rise. Castro raised his hand, palm out, to signal stop.

S-s-s-THUNK!

Feathers quivered inches from Castro's right ear, attached to a short shaft buried in a tree trunk that was part of the back wall of the observation post.

"Get down!" Castro shouted as he dove for the dirt floor.

Fear mingled with sweat from the heat and humidity. His clothes stuck to him like a second skin as he waited for the next arrow. The acrid smell of urine permeated the air. Castro turned his head slightly and saw a wet stain spreading on the back of the khaki shorts worn by a student he had thought would become the leader of this group. A muffled whimper escaped from another student as she tried to keep her terror under control. They all lay against the back wall, instinctively curled in fetal positions with their arms and hands covering their heads. One student's shoulders convulsed as he sobbed silently.

A minute passed. Two. Musty dampness seeped into their skin from the earthen floor. The fetid odor of decaying vegetation mixed with the smell of urine and fear as the five inhaled the primordial soup that one hundred percent humidity created. An eternity passed, it seemed, until the chirrup of a bird broke the quiet. A monkey chittered. Castro became aware of the buzz and hum of insects. The jungle slowly regained its rhythm.

Carefully he rose to one knee and peeked through a crack in the wall of vines and bamboo. The clearing was as it had been, no sign of the strange white-skinned hunters. Slowly the four students gathered their courage and stood. Castro motioned them to evacuate the blind. Once outside, they turned and began a measured retreat to their Toyota Land Cruiser, single file with Castro in the rear, afraid to look back; scientists no longer, just survivors.

Castro had warned the students that the trip could be dangerous, but he had meant disease or injury. Nothing in his experience suggested that the inhabitants of the Peruvian Amazon would be hostile. The central Amazon basin had its alleged headhunters, but that was a thousand miles to the east and a century ago. Yet he couldn't shake the thought: *I should be dead. They must shoot flying birds and running animals for survival.* Six-foot-three, two-hundred-fifteen-pound, stationary Dr. Terry Castro should have been an easy target.

"The arrow!" he blurted.

They stopped in mid-stride at the exclamation. He ordered them to continue to the truck and wait for him. He was going back for the arrow.

Castro cautiously retraced his steps to the observation post, his eyes darting as he strained to see through the dense curtain of foliage on both sides of the path. Only vines, bromeliads, orchids, ferns, bamboo, and bugs suspended in shafts of sunlight sifting through the green canopy a hundred feet overhead returned his gaze. The hunters, if they were there, were invisible.

He slid into the back of the observation post, wiggling between two palm trunks. The arrow was still there. It seemed small, even frail. He unsheathed his knife and began digging into the tree, careful not to cut the shaft of the arrow. The tree wood was soft and it took only a few minutes to free the arrow.

Castro cradled it in both hands, marveling at the primitive artistry. The head was three inches long and not more than a half inch wide, barely wider than the shaft itself. It appeared to be made from pounded metal and had streaks of a dark, varnish-like substance covering it. It was set in a smooth wooden shaft, split to accept the arrowhead, which was held in place by a thin piece of hide tightly wrapped and covered with a transparent red substance. Castro rubbed the head with his thumb to see if the dark streaks would rub off. To his surprise two thin lines of red, and then droplets of blood, formed on his thumb. He looked back at the arrowhead and discovered microscopic razor-sharp ridges on the flat sides, running the length of the head.

Odd, he thought as he sucked the blood off his thumb. *What's the purpose?* He turned to leave.

Standing in the clearing was one of the hunters, the tallest of the three at over seven feet, a blowpipe held by a long angular arm pressed to his mouth.

Castro froze.

It's not an arrow. It's a dart!

Slowly he removed his thumb from his mouth and raised the dart with both hands so that it was in full view of the hunter. Carefully he slid it into one of the observation portals that faced the clearing and balanced it there. Then he spread both arms, palms out, to show he was holding nothing. He made a slight nod toward the dart. Only the hunter's eyes moved.

Slowly Castro backed up, taking his eye off the hunter for only a split second to find the opening in the wall behind him. When he looked back, the hunter and the dart were gone. He wedged himself out of the observation post, took a few tentative steps, then broke into a run. He reached the truck gasping for air.

"Get in the truck," he croaked at the frightened students.

Chapter 2

Amaru Topac sat on his long, bony haunches, chewing seeds of the Devil's Trumpet. He removed the small pouch of prongbuck hide from around his neck, pulled open the drawstring and dumped the contents in front of him. Circled by the adult male members of his tribe, all watching silently, Amaru carefully arranged the talismans in a pattern intended to summon the spirits of his forefathers.

Long, tapered fingers caressed each talisman: a bone from the ear of a cougar to hear the wisdom of the spirits, flanked by two tiny feathers from the wing of an Andean condor to carry the spirits to this place. Seven tiny freshwater pearls were positioned below the cougar bone in the shape of the head of a dart, the point aimed directly at Amaru so that the spirits could find their way to him, and, finally, an orb of pure gold, two centimeters in diameter and polished by centuries of use, delicately laid at the point of the pearl dart so that they would know that he, Amaru Topac, was one of them.

Now he needed only to wait for the Devil's Trumpet to take effect; to conjure the spirits. He closed his eyes and rocked back and forth on his large feet as the plant's drugs fused with his mind.

* * *

Amaru had returned from the hunt with a story that were it not for his stature as shaman and chieftain of the two hundred remaining members of the Chilco tribe, would not have been believed. He had seen the people who were the color of clouds; those who, according to legend, had destroyed the great Incan empire and forced the Chilco to flee their mountain home. Yet he, Amaru Topac, had faced those whose skin was fairer than his own and had single-handedly defeated them. No shaman in the history of the Chilco could make that claim.

There was much rejoicing when the story spread among the clan and a great outcry for celebration, but Amaru's wisdom spanned centuries and he was greatly troubled. He bade them wait until he had consulted the spirits.

* * *

Colors of green and blue and pink, flowing interchangeably but never blending, began to form on the inside of his closed eyelids, projected there as the Devil's Trumpet took control. Amaru began to hum, and then to chant in a low monotone *"um, um um,"* beseeching the spirits of past shamans to come to this place and share their knowledge, the wisdom of the ages, with him and this remnant of a once great nation.

As always, the vision came first: flames gnawing at a thatched hut, smoke filling the single room. A wraith-like figure scrabbled on the dirt floor, his bony fingers snagging leather cords tied around the necks of gourds scattered about the hut, gasping for air. It wiped away burning tears with the back of its hand, but the smoke roiled thicker as fire broke through the roof.

Amaru felt the heat, the pain, the tears as if he was the figure in the dream.

Fighting against the searing heat, coughing, refusing to let pain dominate him, the figure crawled toward the doorway, doggedly clutching the leather thongs. The gourds bounced along the dirt floor behind him. Blisters formed on his face and his lungs gasped frantically as the fire consumed the oxygen. Just as he prepared to surrender himself to the flames, he tumbled headfirst out the door of the hut into the midst of a massacre. Screams and shouts, grunts, running feet, the crackle of fire and thunder from the long sticks filled his ears as he crawled away from the hut, fighting to breathe the smoke-filled air.

Strong hands lifted him and began to drag him.

"Stop," he gasped. "The seeds. We must save the seeds."

Through burning eyes Amaru watched the arc of a broadsword descending, cleaving nearly in half the young warrior who had lifted the crawling figure. A red spray of blood colored the dream as the chain mailed arm of a conquistador wrenched a broadsword from the gaping wound. But the withdrawal stopped at midpoint. The dark, Spanish eyes below the iron helmet grew large and round, and then vacant. A second Chilco warrior appeared in the dream, towering over the Spaniard, twisting his lance violently, then jerking it from just below the breastplate of the attacker. Amaru watched the dead conquistador, blood spewing from his gut, fall face-first at the warrior's feet.

"Come, Great One. We must leave," the warrior said with no trace of emotion.

"But we must save the seeds," the figure repeated through burnt and disfigured lips.

"Go. Run." The warrior pointed in the direction of the river. "I will get the seeds."

Amaru and the figure hobbled as one toward the river. A line of tall, fair-skinned Chilco, armed with blowpipes and slingshots, valiantly tried to hold back the conquistadors' advance on the river as others frantically untied large, clumsy dugouts. A young boy ran toward the metal-clad invaders, spinning a sling over his head, but his missile never left the leather strap as a Spaniard on horseback cut him down. The belching smoke from the Spanish guns mingled with the smoke from the burning village as Chilco after Chilco fell before the onslaught of musket balls and steel. A young woman of the tribe, armed only with a hoe, crumbled under the feet of another sword-yielding horseman, her yellow hair and fair skin gone in another gush of red.

Suddenly Amaru could not move, his ankles tangled in the leather cords he was still clutching. Although he had experienced the vision numerous times, Amaru felt the fear, expecting at any moment to be struck down. He was now the figure in the dream.

A strong hand under his armpit lifted him, propelling him toward the river.

"I have them," the warrior shouted, shoving a seed-filled gourd into Amaru's hands as his long strides carried them the last yards. Amaru felt himself being lifted into a dugout already overflowing with people. The warrior leaned his broad shoulders into the canoe, pushing it away from the shore. As it broke free from the sandy bottom the warrior shouted, "Go," but the shout was cut short by the deafening roar of a long stick. A musket ball pierced the warrior's throat.

The long arms of men and women frantically pulled on the oars, maneuvering the lumbering dugout into the strong current where it slowly picked up speed, separating itself from the carnage. Another dugout reached the river's current, and then another. Amaru looked back to the shore. The two remaining dugouts were still tied to their moorings. The slaughter on the riverbank was nearly over. The once-mighty Chilco had fallen. The nation of towering, fair-skinned, yellow-haired people that lived high in the Andes Mountains among the clouds, whom the entire Incan nation knew were blessed by the gods, were no more.

The first bend in the river muffled the sounds of the waning battle, and Amaru could hear the roar of whitewater in the distance as his spirit rose from the boat, floating upward. The figure, still seated in the dugout, lifted his burn-ravaged face toward the heavens in prayer while still clutching the gourds that contained the herbs and tinctures and seeds from which curare could be made, and by which the Chilco might survive.

Chapter 3

Amaru looked toward the village and saw the fire grow until it engulfed the entire vision.

One by one they came out of the fire, shrouded in brilliant orange, glistening silver, diaphanous black, ever moving; their faces materializing only when they spoke; their man parts engorged in readiness to again assure the perpetuation of the Chilco. Amaru rocked faster on the balls of his feet, raising his voice in singsong praise and gratitude for their coming.

"Oh, wise fathers," he intoned. "It is I, Amaru Topac, shaman of the mighty Chilco, survivors of the great scourge, who seeks your counsel. Please look kindly upon the remnant of your progeny and your humble servant."

"WE HAVE COME," the voices, coming from all directions, boomed in Amaru's head. He stopped rocking, pitched forward on his face, and began to twitch. His tribesmen made no move, watching.

I have seen the people who are as white as clouds, like the ones in the vision. They were only a few, and they ran from me, but I feel a stirring of dread. I seek your counsel for I have lived on this earth only one hundred years and have no wisdom in these matters.

The five spirits shimmered before him. The eldest, his face grotesquely scarred from burns, congealed and then thrust forward on a scrawny, elongated neck.

Young Amaru, you have been wise to call upon us. Only the wisdom born of grief and pain can guide you in such times. Remember the vision and learn its lessons well.

The neck recoiled and a second face, decimated by disease, emerged.

Your darts and your poison cannot defend you against these people for they bring disease and deceit. Even the great Inca Atahualpa was no match for them. Ten thousand fell to their three hundred.

A third face projected forward, this one aflame in brilliant orange and yellow. Only dark hollow eyes and a mouth were visible amid the flames.

The might fortress of Kuelap fell. The citadel of Vira Vira and Huayabamba were no match for them. Only a few at the beginning, they kept coming and coming, multiplying like mountain chinchilla.

The fiery visage receded into the miasma of the spirits, and a fourth face, deeply lined and pockmarked from parasites, manifested itself.

Even Cayo Topac, our own ancestor who was the greatest shaman of all; who was to lead us back to glory as when the Chilco were the greatest tribe in the Chachapoyas federation and when even the great Inca, Tupac Yupanqui, feared us, could not withstand the onslaught of the transparent people. Though their skin is whiter than clouds, their hearts are blacker than that of the traitor, Guaman, whose treachery caused the destruction of Chachapoyas by the devil, Pizzaro.

The face of the fifth shaman, this one smooth and unlined, replaced the decimated face of the fourth spirit.

I have lived longer than all, having trod the earth for nearly two hundred years. Hear my wisdom, and that of our forbearers, my son. Since my passing you have been a great leader, keeping the Chilco nation alive despite great famine and disease. Now your number is small and you will be ravaged by exposure to the whiter-than-clouds warriors. They will come in greater numbers with weapons that you cannot imagine. You must lead the Chilco deep into the Montana where no transparent person has ever set foot. You must become like the oil bird, only to be seen or heard by night. It is time to train your son, the blessed one, as the next shaman for your days are numbered and he is the future of the Chilco.

The last shaman receded from Amaru's vision. The fire subsided, and the colors in his head grew dim, then disappeared as the effects of the Devil's Trumpet wore off.

He lay on the ground for a few more minutes, then rose and shook himself like a dog.

"Come," he said. "We must leave."

Chapter 4

The criollos, the white people.

The words burned in Castro's mind as he pushed the Toyota, too fast, down the ruts that led back to base camp. Castro had thought the locals' references to *criollos* had been about others like him: tourists, adventurers, educators who had come to experience the Amazonian rainforest. It hadn't occurred to him that they might be referring to a local tribe of giants with fair skin, blue eyes and dirty yellow hair.

He drove the hour-long trip back to camp in less than forty minutes, his mind pummeled by the events of the last few minutes and the hazards of traversing a winding jungle trail at high speed.

"We'll talk at dinner about what happened," Castro said when he finally parked the truck. He needed time to concentrate on exactly what had just happened, and to concoct a plan to handle it. He watched the four students, silent throughout the pell-mell escape from the observation post, wander zombie-like toward their tents, still in shock.

His own legs felt as if they weighed two hundred pounds each as he dragged himself back to his tent. Exhausted, he peeled off his sweat-soaked shirt and tossed it in the corner where it clumped next to a rolled-up sleeping bag. Thoughts tumbled through Castro's mind as he sagged into a canvas chair that was the only piece of furniture in his tent.

What now? There's still four weeks left. What do we do now? Will the kids want to continue? I've got to go back and get the cameras. He stared blankly at the small slice on his thumb and wished he had stopped at the mess tent for an antibiotic and a bottle of beer.

His thoughts were interrupted by the sound of splashing water from the camp's tree shower, a rubber membrane suspended in a forked branch, filled each morning with water and heated by the sun during the hot afternoons. One of the students stood without moving as water streamed from the showerhead, plastering his hair to his skull. A tree shower was one of the most enjoyable parts of camp life, and the most luxurious, but this student wasn't standing like a statue under the running water for luxury or enjoyment. He was washing away the stink of fear. Castro needed to do the same.

After his shower, a bottle of beer in his hand, Castro dragged a canvas chair to the fire ring. One by one the students joined him, making small talk and waiting for their professor to indicate that it was okay to talk about what happened at the observation post. A camp staffer delivered cups of bitter tea, giving them each something to hold and stare at so they didn't have to make eye contact.

Finally, over a dinner of stew and bread, Castro told them what had happened when he went back to get the arrow, including his discovery that the arrow was, in fact, a dart. He intentionally omitted any mention of the mental connection he sensed between himself and the hunter when he placed the dart in the observation portal. He feared the students would think he was weird or delusional, not understanding that his gesture was meant, and apparently accepted, as a peace offering.

He also didn't mention the cut on his thumb. It didn't occur to him that it was significant.

"What now?" they wanted to know.

"If they were truly hostile I'd be dead...twice," Castro said. "On the other hand, they apparently aren't keen on us mucking around in their jungle. Tomorrow we...I...will go retrieve the cameras. If they captured photos of the white hunters I'm thinking that we should visit some nearby villages. Maybe the locals can give us more information about these people if we can show them a video. A few years ago a couple of people we interviewed spoke of the *criollos,* which translates into 'white people'." Castro made air quotes with his fingers. "The people we saw today may be the *criollos.*"

"Do you think that they could be the descendants of the *Chachapoyas*, the cloud people?" one of the students asked.

"That was the first thing I thought when I saw them," said another.

"But the *Chachapoyas* were mountain dwellers," argued a third. "That's why the Incans called them that, because they lived in the mountains up in the clouds. They weren't jungle people."

The debate continued into the evening until Castro excused himself, saying he was feeling "a bit out of sorts." He stopped at the supply tent to get a pack of antibiotic pills from the first-aid supplies. He ripped off one corner of the packet, swallowed the two pills, and thought about how this would impact the anthropology department and the summer program. Once the diocese heard about the incident it would bring great pressure on the university to shut down the program. Even though he could now verify the existence of the lost tribe, the concern for safety would drown out any argument for scientific research. Dead students—even dead faculty—were not good for the university's image. These thoughts worried him as he bent to open the flap of his tent.

The next morning they found him sprawled face down, half in and half out of his tent, fully clothed. His sleeping bag was still rolled up in the corner.

Chapter 5

His breathing was shallow and erratic, but his pulse was normal and his heartbeat strong. He was cool to the touch, indicating no fever. The only thing out of the ordinary was his breathing; that and he was unconscious—with his eyes wide open.

Word spread quickly. The students assembled in a semicircle around the entrance to Castro's tent while the chief steward searched for bruises, insect bites or any evidence that Castro was attacked by some beast, either four- or two-legged. He found nothing.

Castro's staring, unblinking, blank eyes unnerved the students.

"Is he dead?"

"I think he's dead."

"Don't be stupid. He's not dead or he wouldn't be breathing."

As the students babbled among themselves, the steward attempted, without success, to revive Castro with smelling salts. Without wounds to bind or bug bites to swab, the steward had run the gamut of his medical expertise. He placed a call by satellite phone to the outfitter in Cajamarca. Within fifteen minutes the head of emergency services at Nuevo Hospital Regional de Cajamarca called back. The doctor listened as the steward told him of the situation and the symptoms. After a long pause the doctor said he would have to call him back.

The return call finally came an hour later. The hospital was not equipped to do a medi-vac nearly five hundred kilometers away, but they had arranged a helicopter evacuation with a medical air service out of Pucallpa, only ninety kilometers from the camp site. They would be there within the hour and would take the patient to Hospital II de Pucallpa-Essalud in Pucallpa.

The doctor was no help in diagnosing Castro, admitting that a discussion among the emergency room doctors there had provided no insight into what might be the problem.

The students, facing a crisis not of their own making for the second time in two days, descended upon the steward. "Does Professor Castro have a disease?" "Is it communicable?" "What will happen when the helicopter arrives?" "Will it be big enough to take all of us?" The steward, no stranger to panicky travelers, handled the questions with the aplomb of a five-star concierge. "Professor Castro showed no symptoms at dinner. There was no way of knowing if he has a disease until the paramedics arrived. It is unlikely the helicopter would be big enough for all of them. No, he had never seen anything quite like this in his twenty-two years as a camp steward. Yes, he was sure Professor Castro would receive very good medical attention. Yes, the university is being contacted. He was sure the university would send instructions on what the students were supposed to do next."

Eventually the students ran out of questions and shuffled off to their tents, comforted by the steward's calm demeanor, if not by his answers to their questions. They drew numbers to see who would be first to get on the helicopter.

* * *

The *whup, whup, whup* of the helicopter came suddenly over the treetops. The pilot made one pass, then turned and slowly landed the BK 117 Kawasaki, blowing sand and debris throughout the camp site, toppling two of the tents.

An EMT, bulky medical pack over one shoulder, ducked under the swirling rotors and, shielding her face from the dust, made straight for the steward. He pointed toward Castro's tent. Minutes later the helicopter pilot and the steward emerged from the tent carrying Castro, strapped to a stretcher. The EMT, a short woman with broad shoulders and lines in her face from too many emergencies, approached the students. The nameplate on the pocket of her blouse read "Valentina Garcia, Emergency

Medical Technician."

"What can you tell me about what happened?" she asked, motioning toward the stretcher. The students babbled, recounting the events of the previous day in a jumble until EMT Garcia stopped them with a curt "one at a time." After restoring order she listened, taking a few notes, then turned toward the helicopter after concluding that there was nothing more to be learned from the nervous group.

"Is there room for us in the helicopter?" one of the student blurted.

"No. There's only room for the pilot, the patient and me," she said. "The copter has room for one more passenger, but extra weight uses fuel and we're about at the end of our range. The pilot said no extra passengers."

Hope and their shoulders sagged.

* * *

Castro regained consciousness amid a howling wind, a *whup, whup, whup* sound, and the sensation of movement. An extremely bright overhead light bored into him, but he couldn't close his eyes or turn his head to avoid it, adding to his confusion. He sensed someone sitting next to him, and he could hear shouted conversation as people tried to communicate over the noise. He wanted to ask them what was happening, where was he, but he couldn't form words or make any sound come out.

"Is he going to make it?" the pilot shouted over his shoulder as the helicopter gained altitude.

"Touch and go," Valentina shouted back.

It registered in Castro's brain that they were talking about him.

"What are his vitals?"

"Heart rate is 45. Blood pressure 75 over 38. Respiration is down to nine."

Castro was no medical expert, but those didn't sound like good numbers.

"Any idea what happened to him?" It was the pilot shouting again.

"From his symptoms I'd say it might be poison. According to those kids back there, they had a run-in with a tribal hunting party. That would suggest it might be curare poisoning, although I've never seen a case of it in my twenty years of doing this."

"Never heard of it," the pilot replied.

"I remember it from my training. It paralyzes the victim and they die of suffocation. I doubt that's what this is, though. My recollection is that curare works pretty fast. This guy's been in this condition since some time last night; probably fifteen to eighteen hours. I think he would have been dead a long time ago if this was curare."

A head leaned over and blocked the bright light. Castro had just enough time to realize it was the woman who had been doing the talking before the head moved and the bright light once again blinded him. He felt pressure on his right forearm and then a sting.

She must be drawing blood. What the hell is curare? What the hell is going on! He wanted to scream. He fought the panic rising within him. *Think. Think. I must be in a helicopter. That sound can only be a helicopter. How did I get here? Where am I going? Is this a dream?*

Castro felt his shirt being unbuttoned. He felt a hand move lightly over the hair on his chest and his flat, hairless stomach; then his belt was unbuckled and his shorts unbuttoned. Strong hands rolled him on his left side and his shirt was wrenched over his shoulder and left elbow. His pants were pulled down over his left buttock. The silhouette of the woman moved in and out of his line of sight. He was rolled to the right and his shirt was completely removed. His shorts and underwear were pulled down so he was bare to his knees. He felt her touch on his side, back and butt: here a light touch, there a little firmer, a little longer. He again was rolled on his left side and the same inspection took place. His shorts were pulled up, but left unbuttoned. He felt her hands move down his legs, and then his arms, hands and fingers.

"Nothing." Valentina shouted at the pilot. "I don't see any bite or a cut or anything like that. If he was poisoned is must have been something he ate or drank."

It came back to Castro in a flash: *I'm in Peru. I'm leading a team of…oh, shit…the white warriors. We found the lost tribe. The dart. The razor ridges. There's a cut on my thumb. She missed it! I'm going to die.*

Chapter 6

But Castro didn't die.

He could hear. He could see. His mind was clear. He could feel pain. It's just that he couldn't make his body respond. He wanted to lift his hand and show her the cut on his thumb but it was as if his muscles, and his voice, were caught in a vise. For all outward appearances, except for his barely perceptible breathing, he was dead.

Lying in a gray, antiseptic hospital emergency waiting room, Castro listened as Valentina briefed the ER doctor. Castro recognized the word *veneno*, the Spanish word for poison, used multiple times. The ceiling, or what he could see of it, started to move and Castro caught a brief glimpse of a metal rod and rings holding a curtain. He could feel himself being lifted from the gurney as unseen hands grasped the sheet he was lying on and transferred him to an emergency room bed. There was more conversation and movement. He could hear the rings being slid along the metal rod. Then there were only two voices, and neither was the voice of Valentina. Apparently the emergency medical evacuation team was gone.

He felt a blood pressure cuff being placed around his right bicep and a warm hand, female he thought, held his forearm, palm up. He felt two fingers on his wrist. They were taking his vitals again. A woman's face appeared in his scope of vision. She lifted his head and placed a mask over his nose and mouth. Castro could feel air being forced into him. Then he felt a sharp sting on his right shoulder. His muscles jerked reflexively. She had injected him with something.

Then, as you would with a dead person, she closed his eyelids.

Panic flooded him as sight joined the lengthening list of Castro's lost senses.

* * *

It may have been two or three days later, Castro couldn't be sure, when he heard the familiar American voice of Father Paul Wyman. Castro had not heard anyone enter the hospital room, but now the pleasant modulation of Father Wyman's voice and smell of his ever-present Old Spice cologne, brought Castro's remaining usable senses to full attention. Father Wyman was talking to someone who spoke English with a thick, syrupy Spanish accent.

"Our tests confirm that he was poisoned, probably some variety of curare," the heavy accent intoned. "We administered physostigmine and put him on a ventilator, but his condition hasn't changed. Ordinarily it only takes a few hours, or at most a day, before the poison wears off and the patient is back to normal. Your Mr. Castro has something else going on."

"What is physostigmine?" Father Wyman asked.

"The antidote for curare poisoning."

"What, exactly, is curare poisoning?"

"Curare is a substance that destabilizes the neurotransmitters by impacting the muscle sole plate..."

"Excuse me," Father Wyman interjected. "I'm just a simple priest who doesn't understand medical terminology. Can you make it simpler for me?"

There was a pause, then: "Curare is a poison used by certain primitive tribes for hunting. It paralyzes the animals or birds they hunt, which die of asphyxiation. Because the poison is effective only if it is introduced into the bloodstream, the natives can eat their prey immediately without the curare adversely affecting them."

"So somehow this poison got in Dr. Castro's bloodstream?"

"Yes. According to the reports we received when the patient was admitted, he had come in contact with a tribal hunting party within twenty-four hours of the onset of his condition. We don't know precisely how it got into his bloodstream, but we assume it happened then."

"But you're not sure?"

"This case is very unusual. First of all, use of curare as a poison is almost unheard of these days. It was more common fifty to a hundred years ago. As civilization came to the local tribes they learned of easier ways to gather their food. This is the first case of curare poisoning I've heard of in at least ten years. More importantly, curare usually acts quickly. Its victim either dies of suffocation within a few hours, or if artificial respiration is provided, the poison usually passes through the victim's system within twenty-four hours and the patient fully recovers without any aftereffects."

"Are you sure the poisoning is from this curare?" Father Wyman asked.

"Reasonably sure. Keep in mind that curare is not a single substance. It is made out of tree bark and other plants, and according to what I've read, some varieties include poison from snakes or bats or insects. Every tribe had its own recipe, so we can't be exactly sure what is in this particular version, and we don't have the technology here that might help us find out. We will have to transfer him to Lima."

"Is he capable of traveling?" asked Father Wyman. "I mean, would travel put him in further jeopardy?"

"His condition is stable," the doctor replied. "Moving him shouldn't put him at any increased risk."

Castro wanted to shout his disagreement. His condition had changed. His sense of touch on his skin when the nurses attended to him was less acute, he could feel his heart beating faster and he had a nagging, dull pain in his chest. He was not stable!

"Don't transfer him to Lima." It was Father Wyman again. "I will arrange to have him taken back to the United States."

Those were the last words Castro heard as the two left the room; words that gave him hope.

* * *

Father Wyman returned to his hotel, happy to shed his suit jacket and find respite in the air-conditioning. He collected one of the two crystal low ball glasses from the well-stocked bar in his suite and poured a scotch, neat. He sat at the desk, swirling the amber liquid, then took a single swallow and picked up the phone.

"I'd like to place a call to the United States," he said. He would attend to the arrangements for Terry Castro later, but first he needed to talk to Leon Day.

Father Wyman hadn't seen Leon Day, or his lovely wife, Mahogany, in over a year. They had attended the annual alumni dinner at Berrie University where Father Wyman served as Provost. The Days were the university's biggest contributors, having provided the funds for a new basketball field house, state-of-the-art training facilities for the entire athletic department, a complete renovation of the venerable old football stadium and many lesser projects.

Sanjay, the Days' houseboy, answered the call and went to get Mr. Day. Father Wyman envisioned Leon in a golf shirt and khaki shorts, sitting barefoot on the veranda, cocktail in hand, looking out over San Francisco Bay, watching the ferry pull into Sausalito harbor. He's leading the good life, the priest thought. They've earned it, and it couldn't happen to two nicer people.

"I have some bad news," he said after Leon came on the line. "Something has happened to Terry Castro. He's in a hospital in Peru. I'm here with him. They think he may have been poisoned."

"Why would someone poison Terry Castro?"

That thought caught Father Wyman off guard. "I...I don't think anyone intentionally tried to poison him," he said. "At least no one has raised that possibility. Apparently he came in contact with a local tribe, and because of that, the doctors think he got something called curare poisoning. Personally, I don't think they really know what is wrong with him. I'm arranging to have him transported back to the States."

Leon didn't hesitate. "Father Paul, I'd like to have him brought to San Francisco, UCSF Hospital. They have some of the world's top experts on exotic diseases. If anyone can figure out what's wrong with him, they can."

"I know his parents have passed, and I don't believe he has any siblings, so that should not be a problem." Father Wyman said, intentionally omitting any mention of Castro's marital status, still a sore subject at the university. "I can arrange transportation for him directly to UCSF. Can you make the arrangements with the hospital on your end?"

"Of course," Leon responded, and then, "What prompted you to call me?"

"I know what goes on at my university," Father Wyman replied with a lilt in his voice, a wry smile crossing his lips. "I've known all along that you were funding Castro's summer programs."

"How..."

"Never mind," he said with a chuckle. "I have my sources and they shall remain anonymous."

"Someday," Leon chided Father Wyman, "I'm going to have my friend, Dan Brown, write a book about conspiracies at Berrie University. I think it will be called 'The Wyman Code'."

The two friends laughed in unison.

Chapter 7

Three thousand five hundred miles away, and six months earlier, at the north end of Petaluma, gateway to California's wine country, Vikter Glass sat across the desk from his boss, Leon Day, explaining why Day Pharmaceuticals was headed for financial trouble.

"The last trial was a failure," said Glass, the company's trusted chief financial officer. "We're years away from bringing another product on board, and the patents on our two biggest sellers expire in eighteen months. There are already at least four companies getting generics ready. You know what that means."

"We'll develop our own generic and have to cut prices," Day responded with a shrug.

"By three hundred percent!" Glass's agitation was evident. "And our overseas sales have dropped for the third straight quarter. We need to start doing some belt-tightening. We might start by withdrawing support for that wild goose chase in the Amazon every year. That, alone, would save half a million dollars annually."

* * *

Day Pharmaceuticals was located in an upscale industrial park just off U.S. 101. Leon and Mahogany Day looked upon the company like it was their firstborn child. The Days had no actual children. Leon had been in his early fifties and Mahogany only twenty-three when they married twenty years earlier, so the expectation of children was present, but none came. Now, with advancing age and Leon's declining health, an heir was extremely unlikely. To complicate matters, Leon had become hooked on prescription narcotics, prescribed in the course of psychiatric treatment related to his brother's death, and his interest in the company ebbed.

Initially all of this had alarmed Vikter. Leon's dwindling involvement, and his refusal to hand over the day-to-day reins to anyone, was beginning to affect the bottom line, and the bottom line was, after all, the focal point of Vikter Glass's existence. The broad expanse of manicured lawn that stretched before him, the glistening two hundred thousand square foot building in which he sat, and the Porsches and Bentleys and Benzes that populated the parking lot, all attested to the wealth that was being generated within the walls of polished aluminum and mirrors. To watch this erode was excruciating for Vikter.

As he sat staring out the one-way glass that made up one entire wall of his spacious office, watching shadows created by puffy clouds scud across the lawn, he began to see how the situation actually might create an opportunity for him.

Despite his seven-figure salary, his personal fleet of expensive cars, his mansion in San Rafael, his yacht in Paradise Cay, a trophy (second) wife, and the title of chief financial officer of the largest privately owned pharmaceutical company in the United States, Vikter felt unappreciated. In fact, he felt betrayed.

Two months earlier Glass had approached Leon with a proposal to take Day Pharmaceuticals public.

"You can take millions out of the company and still retain an ownership interest big enough to leave you in control," Glass had said. "In fact, if we coordinate the public offering with the announcement of FDA approval of the new drug that we have in trials, your interest in a publicly traded company could be worth more than the entire company is worth right now."

Leon wasn't interested.

"Mahogany and I have reaped the benefits of the business during our lifetimes," he had said. "We've treated our employees very well, but they should reap the full benefits of being owners after we're gone. Mahogany and I don't need to take another big chunk of money out of the company. We'd rather leave the equity in it so there is a healthy company for the employees to inherit."

He went on to explain that he and Mahogany, with the help of outside advisers, had worked out a formula so that every employee would receive ownership in the company, the percentage dependent upon length of service and salary level.

"You'll end up being the biggest shareholder," Leon proclaimed proudly.

Glass tried to look pleased, but he was stunned. That he had not been included in the planning for transition of the company was a blow to his ego, but beyond that, the concept of not needing or wanting more money was as foreign to him as was the idea of giving away a billion-dollar company. As the realization of how Leon's plan would actually work sunk in, Glass became more and more upset. He would be sharing ownership with four hundred other employees, many of whom, he knew, didn't like him very much. At best, he would end up owning only five percent of the company's stock. With four hundred employee stockholders, all of whom thought they knew how to run the business, it would be chaos, and he could easily find himself on the outside looking in.

He had worked at the company from the time he had emigrated from Russia more than twenty-five years ago. *This was how I am going to be rewarded? My loyalty is worth five percent?* He was barely able to contain his rage.

Over the next several weeks Glass thought of quitting, of starting a lawsuit, of destroying the company, of numerous other destructive acts, but, driven by his natural greed and refined by the fire of his anger, a scheme began to take shape. As was his practice, he thought through every contingency, every nuance, every risk until he was sure that it was viable, but no matter how he framed his plan there was always one major obstacle. He had to convince the Days to take the company public.

It was that obstacle Vikter contemplated as he gazed through the glass wall. Lost in thought, he leaned forward on his chair, took a lemon drop from the candy bowl on his desk, and popped it into his mouth. He winced as the sugar and acid combination came in contact with one of the canker sores in his mouth, a chronic condition. *Our next research project should be how to get rid of these damn things,* he thought, as his tongue gingerly massaged the open sore in an attempt to alleviate the pain.

He rocked back in his chair and resumed his contemplation, his left hand mindlessly stroking his hairless temple; a habit when he was deep in thought.

Perhaps the new drug trial shouldn't turn out successful. Maybe the company isn't on such sound financial footing. And Leon's health could get worse.

A crooked smile crossed his thin lips as his plan to overcome the obstacle began to take shape. His ice-blue eyes, glistening with satisfaction, did not participate in the smile.

* * *

Vikter had attended the wedding of Leon Day and Mahogany Lewis on June 1, 1992, thinking, as did most in attendance, that she was a gold-digging cheerleader out to get Leon's money.

Thirty years younger than Leon, with breathtaking beauty that turned the heads of both male and female, and a sudden rise in influential social circles, fed the rumors among the gossipmongers for the first years after the wedding. When she became the co-chair of one of the Bay area's major charitable events, a local talk show host decided she would take this upstart gold-digger down a peg, but Mahogany handled the snarky live interview with humility and grace, making the TV host look contemptible and avaricious.

When Mahogany rose from the couch at the end of the interview, took the host's proffered hand in both of hers, and said in her most gracious tone: "Rita, you should never go into a battle of wits unarmed," the studio audience rose and applauded. Rita lasted less than a month at the television station.

Since that interview no one had underestimated Mahogany Day. Vikter wasn't about to be the first.

"I'm really more concerned about Leon than I am about the company," he said over coffee at a local Starbucks. "As long as there is someone there to make the day-to-day decisions the company will be okay, but Leon seems to be less and less engaged. Is this thing about his brother affecting him that much?"

It wasn't the first time Vikter and Mahogany had discussed Leon's health. He had become, over the years, more than just an employee whose economic interests aligned with theirs. As he rose through the ranks at Day Pharmaceuticals Vikter became part of the inner circle. By the time he was named Chief Financial Officer he was considered a good and trusted friend by both Leon and Mahogany and was a frequent visitor at their home in Tiburon.

Mahogany nodded, confirming Vikter's statement about Leon's brother. "That, and his neurological issues. I think he's hanging on to day-to-day control because it's the one thing that gives him normalcy," she said.

"But he seems so stressed when he's at the office."

"I know," she continued. "I think it's because he knows that he's not doing a good job of running the company even though he feels compelled that he has to."

Vikter shook his head slowly in apparent empathy. "What can I do to help?" he asked. The conversation was headed exactly where he had planned.

A week later Leon made it official: Vikter Glass was named Chief Operating Officer of Day Pharmaceuticals to go with his CFO title. Leon would remain as Chairman of the Board, but day-to-day operations were now in Vikter's hands.

The next day Vikter called a meeting of the legal and accounting teams, directing them to start investigating the possibility of taking Day Pharmaceuticals public. When the meeting concluded, Vikter made a phone call to the Russian Consulate in San Francisco.

"Uri?" he said, speaking to an assistant secretary to the counsel general, "I think it's time we had that meeting with our friend from Moscow. There's money to be made here."

* * *

Two weeks later Leon made his first trip to company headquarters since putting Vikter in charge. The meeting had not gone well.

"It's not your fault," Vikter said. "You've been under a lot of stress, and the expiring patents and failed trial are not something either you or I could have controlled. I'm just saying we've got to start tightening our belt around here."

"It won't be at the expense of Berrie University," Leon responded. "You know that money comes out of my foundation and not out of the company."

"I'm aware of that, but the time may be coming when the funds from the foundation may be needed to keep the company operating."

"As long as I'm still vertical and taking nourishment the endowment for Berrie will not be touched," Leon said. "And that includes the money for Terry Castro's summer program."

Chapter 8

Berrie University was one of those rare institutions of higher education, a liberal Catholic school in a conservative Midwestern city. The desire of Father Wyman to stretch the academic curriculum to allow the mingling of science and religion in a parallel path to wisdom often put the university and the archdiocese in conflict, but Father Wyman's charisma and vision, not to mention his considerable fund-raising skills, kept him at the helm of the university and its fifteen thousand students and staff.

Teaching at Berrie was the only job Terry Castro had ever held. He received his PhD from DePaul University in 2004 and had been hired by renowned archaeologist, Dr. Adam Starling, dean of the Berrie Archaeology and Anthropology Department, because his doctoral thesis had caught Starling's attention. In it Castro drew parallels between two unique cultures: the Nemadi, desert dwelling nomadic hunters who inhabited the West African country of Mauritania, and the Nuristan, mountain dwellers of eastern Afghanistan, both of which shared common traits of blue eyes, light skin and blond hair while surrounded by cultures where dark skin, black hair and brown eyes were predominant.

Professor Starling was an internationally recognized expert on the Incan empire, and Castro's thesis was of particular interest to him because of a single line in the sixteenth century writing of a Catholic monk who had accompanied Francisco Pizarro in his conquest of the Incas. It spoke of a fair-skinned, blond-haired tribe that lived in the higher elevations of the Andes Mountains in northern Peru. The Incans called them *"Chachapoyas,"* the Cloud People.

Each year Starling led a group of students and faculty to Peru or Ecuador to study Incan culture. The annual six-week adventure had discovered several minor sites of Incan ruins, and had been the subject of a National Geographic film. An invitation to the program was highly coveted. Usually Starling asked a notable professor from another university to join him as a co-leader. In 2005, one year into Castro's tenure as an associate professor of anthropology, Starling surprised everyone, and disappointed many, by inviting Castro to be co-leader.

The invitation, quickly accepted, came with an unexpected cost: Castro's marriage.

Castro's athletic body, leading-man good looks and confident demeanor had been an attraction for the opposite sex since high school, but his romances ordinarily didn't last long. Jealousy, or "lack of commitment," ended most of his relationships because of his breezy, flirty style with women that threatened the expectations of possessive or needy partners. But his honest and empathetic nature usually resulted in his exes continuing as friends after the flame had died. That had served him well until he met Holly in his last year at DePaul. She was a graduate student in criminal justice, and within a week he knew that she was the woman he wanted to spend the rest of his life with. They had been married six months later after graduation, but two years after moving to Ohio, with his passion for his wife as strong as ever, amid discussions about starting a family, he had faltered in the face of temptation.

It started with a knock on the door of his small, cluttered office, a common occurrence in the life of an associate professor. Castro was revising a course outline, his desk awash in papers and books, and time had slipped away from him. It was late afternoon and the winter sky was rapidly turning to dusk.

"Come in," he said, and she did, closing the door behind her.

"Have a seat," he said without looking up, motioning to the chair on the opposite side of his desk. She ignored the chair, moved the sign that read "Professor Terry Castro" out of her way, and sat on the corner of his desk, all golden hair, big eyes and pouting red lips.

Her name was Suzanne Beatty, a student in his Anthropology 201 class. He had noticed her on the first day of class. Her looks were an A, and she had gone out of her way to engage him in conversation after class, but her scholastic performance had been unexceptional. He had given her a C- on her midterm exam.

"I need to go on the summer trip to Peru," she said. "I need it to get into grad school." She made it sound urgent as she slid toward him, her already short skirt riding up her thighs.

"I believe all the spots on the trip have been committed," Castro said, struggling to keep his eyes on her face. "And I'm not sure your academic performance would qualify you to go." The moment he said it he knew that he should have phrased it differently.

"I could perform some extra credit," she purred, with an emphasis on "perform." She leaned toward him, putting her warm hand on his. He found himself looking directly at a button on her blouse that was straining to contain two large and perfectly formed breasts. Her nipples pushed hard against the thin material. She took his hand and slid it up her thigh until it touched her naked, cleanly shaven cleft.

A little "oh" escaped from her lips as he touched her. She opened her thighs, rubbing his hand hard on the wet lips of her vagina, then slid off the desk, straddling his lap as she worked at his belt. For Castro any common sense or semblance of resistance was gone.

He thrust up hard inside her, bringing a sharp cry and "uh, uh, uh" as they banged together. She frantically rode him, unbuttoning her blouse to let her breasts free. He was momentarily mesmerized by their bouncing, then he lifted her and laid her on her back on the desk top, kicking the chair out of the way and sweeping papers and books off the desk, sending them crashing onto the floor. His rock-hard phallus reentered her to a long, low moan. Her legs were thrust straight in the air, spread to their maximum, as she grasped his ass with each hand

and tried to pull him in deeper as she lifted to meet his thrusts.

"Take me from the rear," she gasped.

He pulled out and she rolled over, bent over the desk. He spread her cheeks and let the head of his cock massage the gaping lips that now formed a perfect "o."

"Fuck me! Fuck me!" she urged, and Castro slammed into the cushion of her ass again and again until she screamed. The sound of her orgasm made him come. He collapsed over the desk on her back, sliding one hand under each breast. They rhythmically rocked back and forth, still coupled, as the tremors of orgasm coursed through them.

They lay that way, limp, as their breathing returned to normal.

Castro disengaged from the plump pink ass. Suzanne stood, tugged down her skirt and, with a bemused look, exited his office.

"I'm an A+ in extra credit," she said over her shoulder. "Just in case you change your mind and want someone to keep you warm on that Peru trip."

Castro looked around at the mess that was his office, a perfect preview of what was to become of his life.

The disgrace that arose from the noisy copulation cost Castro his marriage and nearly his job, but he had survived thanks to his honesty in reporting the incident, Christian forgiveness and an investigation that disclosed that one Miss Suzanne Beatty was in the habit of collecting trophies in the form of faculty conquests. She was asked to leave the school.

While the school had forgiven him, Holly had not. She could not live with the daily specter of her husband going off to teach at a university filled with aggressive, nubile young women. She knew this would not be the last time he would be tempted, and she couldn't trust him to resist. Castro wanted to persuade her that it wouldn't happen again, but, honestly, he couldn't do it because he didn't trust himself. The divorce was quick and quiet, at least as quiet as it could be in a small Midwestern city.

Castro buried the ache in his heart from the loss of Holly by burying himself in his work, but acting normal in the classroom or at a department meeting was difficult. He became distant and terse, and in doing so, unintentionally drew more attention to the failure in his personal life. Following a weekly staff meeting in early April he was summoned to Dr. Starling's office. He expected that his services might no longer be needed, but Starling wanted to talk about preparation for the summer program.

Chapter 9

That was the year they discovered the footprints.

Castro and three students were hiking a nearly invisible trail twenty kilometers east of the Ucayali River in northeastern Peru, hoping the path would lead them to a village named San Roque.

"Let's take a break," Castro said as they came upon a spot where the trail widened slightly. He slipped the straps of his backpack off his shoulders and dropped it on the edge of the path. They had been on the move since they broke camp four hours ago, and their clothes clung to them from perspiration. Two of the students sat wearily, scratching bites, while the third ventured off to relieve himself.

Castro dug through the outside pocket of his backpack in search of an energy bar, and then took a bite of the limp biscuit. "If Dr. Starling's calculations are right we should be in San Roque in about three hours, provided this trail holds up," he said. "If we have to cut our own path, we may not get there until tomorrow."

"Thank God for GPS." A student with a dirt-streaked face offered up the prayer.

"Amen," Castro responded just as the now-relieved student pushed his way through a curtain of platter-sized rhododendron leaves and rejoined the group.

"I heard," he said. "Three hours. I sure hope they have a shower there."

"Probably not," Castro replied. "This village is tiny, less than a hundred people, so I'm guessing it's grass huts and a bath in the Ucayali tonight." He swatted away a bug as the students groaned in unison.

The Berrie University group had split that morning when they left their overnight camp. Starling had taken three of the students on what appeared to be the most direct route to the village. He was anxious to get there to confirm information he had gathered on a previous trip about Incan ruins in the San Roque area. He had sent Castro and the other students on a more indirect route, telling them to "keep their eyes and ears open."

He wants to get there so he can take full credit for any find, Castro thought. He had learned quickly that he was playing a poor second fiddle to the famous archaeologist. Starling, mild-mannered and self-effacing on campus, morphed into a little Napoleon once the trip began, frequently making it clear that he would get the credit for any discoveries or artifacts they gathered regardless of who actually found them. That's probably why none of the guest professors come back a second year, Castro thought. Occasionally, like this morning, it rankled Castro, but his pique was always brief, remembering that he was part of the summer program and was still employed by Berrie University, thanks primarily to Dr. Starling.

Castro's team had stumbled upon the trail less than half an hour after they left camp. He was in the lead, hacking through undergrowth, when they came upon the thin strip of smooth earth walled by ferns, massive tree trunks, thick vines and broad leaf rhododendron. The dirt was packed hard from constant use. It appeared to angle toward the northwest, the general direction of their destination, and Castro, already fatigued from swinging the machete, decided to take the path of least resistance and follow it. Periodic checking of his handheld GPS proved that his decision had been a good one. They were headed in the direction of San Roque.

They hoisted their backpacks into walking position and resumed their single file trek through the bugs and the heat and the humidity. An hour later the party came upon a bog that interrupted the trail.

"I knew it was too good to be true," Castro said, motioning to the expanse of water about the length of a football field. He checked both sides of the trail, but it was clear that the bog extended far into the underbrush, making any attempt to go around it chancy at best.

"Well. Let's see how deep it is," he said, trying to sound upbeat. He hacked off a six-foot piece of sturdy vine to use as a plumbing rod and waded out into the bog, poking the vine in front of him to test the water's depth. His team hesitantly followed him.

Luckily there were no snakes, and the bog never reached more than knee deep. As they sloshed their way toward the other side, Castro stopped.

In front of them, in the mud and soft earth where the trail emerged from the water, were at least a dozen footprints, wide, flat and long; size 16 or bigger Castro guessed. In an area where a full-grown man rarely stood more than five and a half feet tall, the size of the prints were enormous.

The students, following Castro's lead, carefully made their way around the footprints on to dry land where the impressions disappeared as the trail reverted to its hard surface. Avoiding any disruption of the site, Castro unpacked his camera and took multiple photos. He supervised as the students made plaster casts of the footprints. By the time they were done it was late afternoon. In the ninety percent humidity they would have to wait overnight for the plaster to harden.

Castro wasn't sure what they had found, but he was sure the footprints had not been made by local villagers. Whoever or whatever they were, they had huge feet and the prints were reasonably fresh, less than a week old.

The next day they reached San Roque. Excitedly they told Starling and his team, which had arrived the night before, of finding the footprints. "Interesting," was Starling's less than enthusiastic response. He was far more interested in planning the next day's search for Incan ruins. Castro couldn't help but think that if Starling had found the prints, it would have been a big deal.

* * *

In the years that followed, Starling invited Castro on other the summer trips. Whenever he had the opportunity Castro inquired of the locals about the footprints, trying to connect them to an existing tribe. His search included villages near to, or on, the banks of the Huallaga and Maranon rivers, as well as the Ucayali. He found villages of people who claimed to be direct descendants of the tribes that had inhabited the region at the time of the Incas: the *Chayma* and the *Bracamoros*, but all of them disclaimed any connection to the footprints. These footprints were far too large to belong to them. They must, they said, belong to the *criollos,* the white people.

Then the unthinkable happened.

The archdiocese was besieged by claims of sexual misconduct. Funds previously directed to the university went into legal defense, and Berrie had to tighten its fiscal belt. Among the first things to go were summer programs. Within a year Starling left to pursue his research independently, the anthropology/archaeology department shrunk to two instructors, and Castro, the only PhD, was appointed head of the department, a nice title that was good for cocktail talk but it didn't include a raise.

He looked elsewhere for a position, but nothing materialized. Meanwhile he led the two-person department; fighting and scratching for enough of the school's budget to keep his department alive. And he continued to look at the photo of the footprints framed on his office wall; footprints that would have gone undiscovered if not for him. He knew there was something special there; the kind of thing that could make a professor's reputation.

He needed to go back to Peru and find out what it was... before Starling did.

Chapter 10

"That's quite a story, but why are you telling it to me?"

Leon Day fixed his deep brown eyes on Terry Castro and waited for an answer.

Castro had tried to find funds for the summer program: grants, government programs, the Smithsonian, but nothing had come to fruition until someone mentioned Leon Day.

Decades earlier Day had been an All-American fullback at Berrie; the first All-American in university history. He had played professional football after graduation but back then it was neither the lucrative profession it is now, nor were black athletes treated as equals, no matter how good they were. After four years of physical pounding and emotional abuse, he retired.

Day took a job in the pharmaceutical industry as a salesman. The same intensity, perseverance and passion for success that had served him so well on the football field were equally apt for his new occupation. In a few years he became vice president of sales, and within a decade chief executive officer of the small company. There his career hit a dead end. The company was owned by two brothers who were content with what they had built and the millions it generated for them each year. They didn't share Day's vision of pharmaceutical development or company growth.

After years of watching profits line the owners' pockets rather than develop new products, Day left to form Day Pharmaceuticals. Within five years he cashed out his financial backers, and a year later bought his former employer. Now, as he sat and talked with Castro, he was the owner and chairman of the board of the largest privately owned pharmaceutical company in the world with sales in the billions and scores of patents that guaranteed the billions would keep coming.

"I know your thing is athletics," Castro said, "but think of it as the scientific equivalent of a national football championship." He pointed at a large map of South America he had spread upon the desk that separated the two men. "We will be searching a region that has never been fully explored. If we can locate this lost tribe it would be the greatest discovery since Hiram Bingham discovered Machu Picchu. "

Castro knew he was laying it on thick, but Day was his last chance to resurrect the summer program and his search for the source of the footprints.

"And," Castro continued, "there's also the potential of finding new resources that could advance medical science." He had saved this for last, hoping it would be the carrot that made Day open his wallet. "We could include personnel from your company and from Berrie University in a parallel search for potential new resources for pharmaceutical development while my students and I search for the lost tribe."

"I presume," Day mused, breaking his silence, "that anything we might be lucky enough to discover could be jointly developed by Berrie and Day?"

Castro nodded in agreement even though his thoughts had not evolved that far. He knew he was stepping beyond his authority, but he was desperate and Day actually seemed interested.

Day leaned back in his recliner, part of a perfectly coordinated furniture suite that adorned his home office. Except for salt-and-pepper hair and a few lines at the corners of his eyes, Day looked like he could still play fullback for the 49ers. Through an open patio door Castro could hear the winsome sound of waves gently lapping on the Tiburon peninsula shoreline. San Francisco Bay was remarkably calm.

Day put the fingertips of his large, manicured hands together, hooked his thumbs under his jaw and let the steeple formed by his fingers rest on the bridge of his nose. "How much did you say you need?" he asked through his fingers.

"Approximately two hundred thousand a year. That covers

the expenses for a team of seven for six weeks. Of course, I would provide you a detailed expense projection in advance and follow-up reports." For the first time Castro thought that this might actually happen.

"I don't think that's enough money," Day said.

Castro's jaw dropped.

"People asking for money usually only ask for half of a much as they need," Day continued. "You haven't included any funds to record and catalog your findings, to do follow-up research or experimentation on anything you bring back, and you'll need funds to visit me after each trip to give a full report on what you've discovered.

"I'll have my CFO, Vikter Glass, work with you on a budget. Assuming the budget makes sense, I'll fund your program on the condition that you keep this confidential. If word gets out, every department at the university will be on my doorstep with their hand out. I'll funnel the money through my foundation. You can tell the administration that you were awarded a grant, which will technically be true, but if any of your colleagues show up here asking for funds, the grant will end."

That conversation had taken place five years earlier and, despite opposition from Glass, Day had been true to his word.

* * *

Dutifully Castro went to San Francisco each year to report on the results of that year's exploration, but by the fourth annual trip Castro began to get nervous. Although Castro included minute details in his reports to make them sound exciting, most of the summer trips were spent slogging through the humid, oppressive rainforest, or staked out in some secluded observation portal that overlooked a path or clearing that had shown signs of human activity. And swatting bugs: biting, buzzing, hounding bugs of all shapes and sizes. Always there were bugs. But most concerning of all for Castro: there were no discoveries of a lost tribe nor were there any significant pharmaceutical developments.

Leon Day did not seem to mind. He would sit with rapt interest and listen to Castro's reports. He would examine artifacts that were brought for perusal. He would inquire about plant and mineral samples that had been brought back for experimentation, and he never left Castro with any indication that he wasn't satisfied with his "investment."

But the meeting following the fifth expedition gave Castro a new reason for concern. Day looked old and tired. His seventy-three years, and the pounding he had taken from football, appeared to be catching up with him.

Ordinarily their meetings were casual and relaxed affairs that took several hours and multiple bottles of wine, but this one had been strained and cut to less than two hours. Day's attention wandered and twice he asked the same question just minutes apart. Mahogany, a tall, lithe woman, now in her forties, with skin the color of her name, had hovered nearby during the meeting.

"What going on?" Castro asked her on his way out. "Is Leon okay?"

"He says everything is fine," she confided, "but I'm worried about him. He doesn't have the same energy. His workouts are only half of what they used to be, and he forgets things. He just says he's growing older."

"Has he seen a doctor?"

"He's so stubborn," Mahogany said, shaking her head. "He says that unless a doctor can stop the aging process, there is no reason to see one."

There was an uncomfortable pause. "He won't see a doctor," she continued, "but he's seeing a medium."

"A what?"

"A medium. You know. One of those people who talks to the dead."

"What on earth is he seeing a medium for?"

"He has some things in his past that have to do with his late brother that he needs to resolve. I'm not exactly sure why, but after his sessions with this medium he seems to be more content and relaxed. If it makes him happier I guess there's no harm in it."

Castro decided to leave it there, not wishing to meddle further into the Days' personal lives, but on his way out the door he couldn't refrain from one last comment. "Be careful. He may just be after your money."

"The medium? It's a she," Mahogany replied." She's Vikter Glass's niece. I pay her one hundred dollars after each session."

"Sorry," Castro apologized. "I didn't mean to imply anything. Just concerned for you and Leon. If there's anything I can do..."

Castro offered his help the way people do when they don't know what else to say. On the way back to Berrie University he worried over Leon's health and wondered if he was going to have to find new sponsor for future summer programs. He was also troubled by Leon's resort to a medium and the recalcitrant Glass's role in providing one.

Maybe it's just a California thing, he thought.

Chapter 11

"I've been able to communicate with people in the late stages of Alzheimer's who can't talk," Carrie Waters said, tucking her mousy brown hair behind her left ear. "Maybe I could communicate with your friend."

Waters was in the middle of one of her sessions with Leon Day, but Leon didn't feel like dealing with his brother today. Instead, he wanted to talk about Terry Castro and what had happened in Peru.

"I thought you just talked to dead people, like my brother," Leon said.

"That's how it started," Waters said. "But when my mom was in the hospital with Alzheimer's she had a roommate named Irene who was in the last stages. One day I was with my mom and this voice suddenly is in my head saying, 'This is Irene and I need you to do something for me.' I probably should have been shocked, but I'm so used to voices going off in my head, I just thought, 'Okay, what do you want?'."

There was a pause as she shifted her bulk on the straight-backed chair she used during their sessions. Leon waited patiently. He had learned that Carrie Waters could not be rushed.

"She wanted me to tell her best friend that it wasn't her fault," Waters went on. She paused again, thinking about Irene.

"What wasn't her fault?" Day asked.

"I never asked," Waters said. "I called her friend and asked her to come visit Irene. Like most people, she was skeptical at first. I think she came as much out of curiosity about me as to see Irene, but when we were there, and I told her that Irene wanted to tell her that it wasn't her fault, she broke down and cried. Later, when we were out of Irene's room, she hugged me and told me how much it meant to her and how relieved she was."

"But you never asked what it was all about?"

"No. It really wasn't any of my business," Waters responded. "I'm just a conduit for communication. If they don't tell me what it's about I assume they don't want me to know."

* * *

It had been six months since Leon and Carrie began meeting because of Leon's continuing struggle with the death of his brother.

Louis "Sonny" Day was Leon's little brother. Five years younger, physically smaller, less intelligent and lazy, Sonny was little in every way when compared to his brother. The inevitable comparisons had made their relationship testy at best. In an attempt to patch up the rift between him and his brother, Leon had hired Sonny at Day Pharmaceuticals. It only served to estrange them further when Sonny failed at several jobs and Leon had to fire him. After that Sonny bounced from job to job between scrapes with the law. Until their father's funeral, it had been years since the brothers had spoken.

"Everyone at the funeral was real polite," Leon told Carrie at their first meeting. "Sonny and I actually reminisced a little about our dad, but when Dad's will was read after the funeral we both learned that Sonny had intentionally been cut out. Sonny went ballistic. He accused me of poisoning Dad's mind against him and threatened to get even."

Leon had offered him half of the estate, but Sonny, in no mood to be placated, ranted that he should have all of it because Leon was rich. Leon capitulated, offering to give him the entire estate of several hundred thousand dollars.

"I told him I'd give it all to him if he'd agree to let me manage it for him. Otherwise he would have pissed it away on drugs in six months."

But Sonny stormed out of the room, spewing vulgarities at his brother as he slammed the door.

A week later the police found him dead of a drug overdose, the result of a weeklong binge.

Repeated sessions with psychologists and psychiatrists had given Leon no relief from his guilt, but it did result in a plethora of drug prescriptions, including a powerful painkiller for recurrent headaches he was suffering. Despite the drugs Leon's emotional and physical condition deteriorated.

It was Glass who had suggested to a distraught Mahogany that using a medium to connect Leon and Sonny might be an alternative way for Leon to ease his guilt. He gave Mahogany the phone number for Carrie Waters. It took her several months to convince a reluctant Leon to meet with Waters.

Leon had expected a mysterious person dressed like a gypsy with tattoos, smoke and a crystal ball. What he got was a plain, plumpish, twenty-something dressed in slacks and a blouse off a ready-to-wear rack at JC Penney, with a friendly, unassuming manner. Her only tools were a pen, a spiral pocket notebook and a business card that said "spiritual consultant."

"How does this work?" he had asked.

"How do you want it to work?" she had replied.

"I want to contact my brother...err...ah...on the other side. We had some issues."

They were in his office at his home in Tiburon, Leon seated behind his massive writer's desk with Carrie facing him. She had declined the plush wingback guest chairs and had asked for a straight-backed chair, preferably with no padding.

"Will I be able to talk directly to him?" Leon asked.

"No," Carrie replied. "If I can make contact with your brother, he will communicate with me and I will relay it to you. Then anything you have to say to him I will communicate back to him."

"You mean you can talk to him, but I can't?"

"It's not like I'm talking to him in structured sentences," she said. "It's more like a sense of what is going on at the other side.

Sort of a 'disturbance in the force'." She made air quotes as she said it.

Day pondered this for several minutes.

"Are you in a trance during this 'communication'?" Day finally asked. His emphasis on the word 'communication' reflected his skepticism.

"Sort of, but not really," she replied, unruffled by his tone. "I'm totally conscious but I'm not really in control. The communications just come...or sometimes they don't."

"Mmm. Do I pay you if they don't come?"

"That will be up to you even if there is communication," she said, again matter-of-factly. "I don't do this for the money. I have been given an ability and I try to use it to help people."

She wasn't boasting or looking for a compliment. That impressed him.

"Let's try it," he said, his skepticism forgotten for the moment. "Do we need to sit holding hands around a table or something like that?"

"No," Carrie said. "We can just sit where we are. Can you tell me a little more about your brother: his name, when he died, how old he was?"

Leon gave her the facts.

"Now let me concentrate for a little bit," she said, closing her eyes.

It was the quickest Carrie had ever intentionally made contact with a spirit, and what she heard left her shocked. She opened her eyes and looked at Leon. He had been watching her, had seen her eyes roll under her eyelids and her body flex, as though recoiling.

"Whoa!" she said, shaking her head. "Your brother really wanted to say something to you."

"What did he say?" Leon asked.

"Do you want it verbatim, or should I paraphrase it?"

"Verbatim."

"He said, 'Fuck you, you sonofabitch.'"
Day did not seem surprised.
Carrie Waters now had his full confidence.

Chapter 12

Carrie ran her hand over the velvety leather and wiggled deeper into the expansive, plush rear seat of Day's ultra-stretch Hummer limousine as it wound its way through Golden Gate Park, down John F. Kennedy Parkway toward University of California-San Francisco Hospital. Charlie "Yardbird" Parker's sax quietly wafted from hidden speakers.

Leon, humming along with Parker's rendition of "April in Paris," studied his spiritual consultant from the opposite seat.

"Why do you insist on using a straight-backed chair when we meet?" he asked.

Waters shrugged. "I don't know, really," she said. "It's just that I remember sitting in a chair like that the first time I heard a voice in my head. And I think it helps me concentrate. If I was in a chair like these seats I'd probably fall asleep."

"When was the first time you heard voices?" Mahogany asked, recognizing that the "fall asleep" comment was Carrie's attempt at humor.

Carrie gazed out the window as the limo glided between Spreckels Lake and the polo field, trying to formulate an answer that didn't make her sound weird or defensive.

"I've heard them for as long as I can remember," she finally replied, looking nervously at her hands. "But the first time I really understood that someone was trying to communicate with me, and it wasn't just lot of jumbled voices, was when I was six."

Carrie leaned forward, unconsciously trying to emphasize the truthfulness of the story she was about to tell.

"My aunt, my mom's sister Margaret, had just died," she began. "We had just come home from the funeral, and we had a bunch of people at our house, eating and talking. I remember being angry at God because everyone was saying what a great person Aunt Margaret was, and I couldn't understand why God would take such a good person when there were so many bad people in the world. I went upstairs to my room to be alone with my anger and I heard a voice. I thought my mom was calling me, but I was mad and didn't answer. Then I heard the voice again so I went downstairs and asked Mom what she wanted, but she said she hadn't called me. When I went back to my room I heard the voice for a third time. This time it said: 'Carrie, it's your Aunt Margaret. Don't be mad at God. I was sick and I needed to see God. It's okay.' I remember it as if it was yesterday."

Mahogany's dark eyes had that oh-you-poor-child-I-want-to-put-my-arms-around-you-and-hug-you look.

"Didn't that scare you?" she asked.

"No. I wasn't scared, or even...startled...for that matter," Carrie said, gesturing with her hands as she searched for the right word to describe her state of mind twenty years ago. "I'd been hearing voices all along and I just thought that's how everyone was. I thought it was normal, but boy, did I learn differently."

Mahogany cocked her head, an inquiring, concerned look on her face.

"When I told Mom about Aunt Margaret she hushed me up and shooed me out of the room," Carrie continued. "She looked really embarrassed. I heard some of the other people say how I was under stress or was imagining things because Aunt Margaret was the first person I knew that died. When I tried to tell my cousins they made fun of me. You learn pretty quickly that you're different, strange. You learn to suppress it. You don't tell people about it. Sooner or later you start to doubt yourself; to think you're crazy."

They turned right onto Crossover Drive and then left on Lincoln Way. The green of the park gave way to small, stucco homes.

"Obviously you don't think you're crazy now," Leon said, getting a disapproving look from Mahogany.

Carrie didn't mind the assertion. "It took a long time," she answered. "I'd hear all these voices all the time. My brain was like a twenty-four-hour truck stop, the doors were always open and it was noisy. I couldn't tune it out and I couldn't tell anyone about them. I'd cry and I'd get migraines and end up in bed for days at a time, exhausted. The medical doctors couldn't find anything wrong with me so my parents finally sent me to a psychologist. I was seventeen. I think it was my sixth session, the last one I had with her, when I told her about the voices. She didn't even blink. She just said, 'I have a sister-in-law in California who's a medium. She hears voices too.' It was like someone lifted a million pounds off my chest. I wasn't the only one. There were others."

The limousine turned off Parnassus Avenue into the hospital drop-off area and stopped. The driver got out and opened the door, offering a gloved hand to Mahogany. She extended her slim fingers, adorned in Big Apple Red lacquer, allowing him to take her hand, and slid across the buttermilk-colored leather seat. Her calf-length designer skirt and blouse in striking monochromatic green contrasted elegantly with the seat. Louis Vuitton pumps, the soles matching her fingernail color, and a silk scarf in a multitude of complementing colors completed the ensemble. Except for her three-carat solitaire wedding ring no jewelry was necessary.

Even though she felt plain by comparison, in her denim skirt and white blouse, Carrie was in awe of Mahogany Day. It was not so much the money, or the beauty, but the way she related to people. She was caring, she listened and she was not afraid to let herself be vulnerable or show her emotions. *She is,* Carrie thought, *a beautiful person, both inside and out.*

The chauffeur's gloved hand was offered to Carrie as she followed Mrs. Day out of the limousine. Leon had exited through the opposite door, slowed by the cane he was now forced to use. The ladies waited for him on the sidewalk. As he stepped up on the curb he offered his free arm to Carrie. "Shall we go visit Dr.

Castro?" he said.

The three of them disappeared through the revolving doors, into the bowels of the University of California-San Francisco Hospital.

Leon was all too familiar with UCSF hospital. His own maladies, and now Castro's, had made him a regular visitor. Each time he had come away impressed with the level of care and the expertise of the specialists. Several years ago he had been asked to serve on the hospital's board of directors but declined, feeling it would be a conflict of interest because his company was, indirectly, a vendor to the hospital. Recently, he toyed with the idea of gifting a substantial sum, perhaps enough to build a wing dedicated to the research and treatment of head trauma caused by athletics. He suspected that some of his current problems, including the headaches, stemmed from his football days but he did not pass that suspicion along to anyone, not even Mahogany. He hadn't discussed the potential gift with her either.

Since Castro had returned from Peru, Leon had been to the hospital twice to see him, but there was nothing to do except sit beside the bed in room 1165 and watch the monitors attached to Castro by various tubes and wires. Today would be different, but even as Leon tried to be optimistic, this was an experiment that he only half believed in. He liked Carrie Waters but he still harbored skepticism about this "ability" she had supposedly been given "as a gift from God." Leon was no Bible scholar, but he did recall the gifts of the spirit in the Book of Ecclesiastes. They didn't include the ability to talk to the dead or, in Terry Castro's case, the unconscious. On the other hand, the communications Carrie had relayed from his brother, Sonny, certainly sounded like things Sonny would say, and she had never met Sonny.

Leon wanted to believe.

They entered room 1165 in single file, Carrie bringing up the rear. Terry Castro lay there, connected to a multitude of medical equipment. Mahogany walked to the bedside and took Castro's lifeless hand. It was the first time she had seen him since "the incident" as she and Leon referred to it. Her eyes welled with tears.

"He looks really good," she lied.

"Carrie, come meet Dr. Terry Castro," Leon said, gesturing toward the bed.

"Terry, meet Carrie Waters, spiritual consultant par excellence," Leon continued, addressing the inert body on the bed. "She has come here today to talk to you."

Carrie's first thought was: *he's beautiful,* quickly replaced by, *My God, he's in pain!*

"Um. Ah. I don't want to be rude, but can I have a moment alone with him," Carrie said. "I sense a need for urgency."

Leon and Mahogany looked at each other, puzzled. Then Leon nodded and they both left the room.

Carrie pulled up a chair next to the bed. Usually touch was not necessary to make contact, but she felt the need to touch Terry Castro. She took his right hand in both of hers and immediately felt the disturbance that she had learned to identify with pain.

Can you tell me what is wrong?

Moments later Carrie flung open the door of room 1165.

"I think you better get a doctor in there fast." she said to the nurse at the nurses' station, pointing toward the door of room 1165. "Professor Castro is in extreme pain."

Part II

Chapter 13

The line on the cardio monitor went flat, and he felt free, relieved of the body that had been the source of his pain.

Drifting upward, he watched the receding blue-clad figures moving in a laconic dance, choreographed to a constant buzz that rose and fell like surf. The lead surgeon, now the size of a smurf, turned, reaching for paddles held by one of the attending nurses. He grasped them in his rubber-gloved hands and methodically turned to the body on the table. Slowly he lowered the paddles, one on each side of the chest. His lips formed the word "c-l-e-a-r." There was a pause. The body convulsed and settled back on the table. The surgeon, paddles now suspended in mid-air, fixated on the monitor.

Castro felt nothing.

The surgeon, sweat beading on his forehead, again turned to the body. Again, he placed the paddles on the chest. Again, silent words were uttered. There was the anticipated pause. The body lurched. The line on the monitor spiked, fell back, then rose again...and again.

The room exhaled. Relief replaced anxiety in the eyes above the blue masks. Shouts of victory raised in silence, lost in the white noise. Death averted.

Castro floated above them, disappointed, once again feeling the burden of life, expecting to be pulled back. Instead the room grew taller; the surgical team smaller. He drifted upward, as if pulled by a lazy current, until they were only blue specks.

Chapter 14

The surgeon's meeting with Leon, Mahogany and Carrie lasted exactly fifty-seven seconds.

"The surgery was a success. We stopped the fibrillation and implanted a pacemaker. He's being moved to recovery. You can check with the nurse about when you can see him."

He started to leave, then hesitated and looked at Carrie, "Someone told me that you said he was in pain before surgery?"

Carrie nodded.

"How did you know?"

"She's a medium," Leon interjected. "Dr. Castro told her."

A derisive snort reflexively burst from the surgeon. He spun on his heels, dismissing them without uttering another word. They stood, marginalized, embarrassed, watching the hem of his white surgical lab coat flap down the hallway as he beat double time to get away from them.

"I'm sorry," Mahogany said to Carrie, chastising Leon with a withering look.

Carrie shook her head. "I'm used to it. You just learn to roll with the punches."

They checked with the nurse outside the surgical waiting room. He would let them know as soon as the patient could have visitors. They retreated to the drab waiting room and waited, Leon rethinking his philanthropic intentions toward the hospital.

It was Mahogany who broke the silence.

"Did Dr. Castro actually tell you he was in pain?" she asked Carrie.

"I've learned to identify some emotions...feelings," Carrie replied. "Joy and pain are the easiest. It's a sense that I get." There was a pause and Carrie, feeling the need to fill the silence, went on: "I'm not sure if Dr. Castro was communicating with me...I didn't have any voices in my head...I don't know. I just knew it, and it was a really elevated sensation."

They lapsed back into silence, until Mahogany, again, spoke. "You said something on the way here; about getting migraines and being exhausted. This must take quite a toll on you."

"It used to," Carrie said. "It was like my brain was an old-time switchboard and I was the operator, but all the lines were always open and I couldn't move fast enough and didn't have enough hands to deal with all of them. I'd cry a lot because I was overwhelmed."

Carrie took a breath and Leon used the pause to ask, "What changed?"

"A few weeks after my therapist told me about her sister being a medium I was flying out here to visit a friend and I saw an ad in one of those airplane magazines. It was a seminar about the after-life and spiritual counseling to people who had lost someone. When I landed I called the number and signed up for the seminar. It was the best thing I've ever done. I found out there were hundreds of people like me who hear things and see things that the world considers abnormal. Everyone in the seminar had to get up and talk about their experiences. It was the first time I remember talking about hearing voices without starting a sentence: you're going to think I'm crazy, but..."

Leon and Mahogany both smiled and nodded. A year ago they would have been among those questioning Carrie's sanity.

"I've gone to several of those seminars," Carrie continued, "I learned to master my emotions, not to be so intense and not to question everything that I was hearing or seeing in my mind's eye. I also learned that it was okay to say 'not now' when a voice gets too loud or there are too many. I've been able to turn down the volume, so to speak, although they never completely go away."

The nurse stuck his head into the room interrupting Carrie's story. "Mr. Castro is in recovery. You can go see him now."

* * *

Castro drifted on air currents created by a ceiling fan, watching a man in blue scrubs mop the operating room floor, wondering: *Am I, or am I not, dead?* Though the monitor had shown his heart beating when they wheeled his body out of the operating room, the fact that he was no longer tethered to it left him confused, destabilized. Was he sentenced to spend eternity in this operating room in a state of astral suspension? What had he done to deserve this? Was this purgatory? Were there others in this state? Was this punishment for all his sins?

Questions without answers raced through his consciousness with escalating rapidity until he willed them to stop.

Hello?...Hello?

There was no response to his cerebral call. The operating room was devoid of humans and, apparently, of spirits.

There has got to be some explanation for all of this. I can't be the only person who has left this operating room in this state. The thought calmed him, but left him wondering how the others, if there were others, got out of this room?

His first attempt to physically move shocked him. He had no arms or legs. He thought that blowing might create a jet-like propulsion, but he had no lips to pucker, no lungs to exhale. It was his first, stark realization that he was, indeed, separated from his physical body.

I wonder where they took my body?

Instantly he was looking down upon a gurney being wheeled down a corridor. It turned into a room. Two nurses attended to the body for a few minutes and then left. He was looking down at himself. His body, itself, held little interest for Castro. His amazement centered around the instantaneous change in location that had occurred without any sense of movement. He again found himself instinctively trying to move non-existent arms and legs.

Think! How did that happen? Think!

He studied his body, attached to tubes and wires; watched the blinking monitors and the drip, drip, drip of the intervenous tubes. It gave no clue. He tried to retrace everything that had happened. He knew that he had been poisoned by the dark substance on the dart, but why he had ended up in the operating room, or in this state, was a mystery. If I could just ask the doctors, he thought. *I wonder where they are?*

"I'm still not convinced he was poisoned."

Dr. Deepak Subbiah, the hospital's leading exotic disease expert, was sitting in a drab, windowless room with Castro's primary physician, Dr. Naomi Graff, and the lead surgeon. Castro was now hovering above them, listening to the debriefing.

That's it. All I have to do is think and I'm transported to where, or who, I'm thinking about! Wow!

"According to the records from Peru there were traces of Strychnos toxifera and Menispermaceae in his blood, but his symptomology does not comport at all with curare poisoning." Dr. Subbiah was continuing his analysis. "If curare was the cause he would have been dead in the first twenty-four hours or, more likely, would have completely recovered. It's what? Five, six weeks?"

"I've spent a lot of time going over this case," Dr. Graff said, as if to emphasize the validity of what she was about to say. "The patient has Gilbert's Syndrome, and tests show that his liver has a very low metabolic rate. There were also significant amounts of Neomycin in his system. He must have taken it shortly before he became unconscious. Either, or both, could explain why curare poison may have stayed in his system longer than usual."

"But five or six weeks?"

"There are several possible scenarios that could extend it for that period...and longer. For example, he was given Physostigmine shortly after he was admitted to the hospital in Peru. That's the standard antidote for curare, but in my research

I found that in the rare circumstance where the curatization is caused by depolarization, Physostigmine has the reverse effect. Instead of reducing the effect of the curare, it would enhance it. Poison dart frogs are indigenous to the area where this happened, and the toxin from those frogs is a depolarizing agent. If the maker of this particular curare used that toxin, the use of Physostigmine may have exacerbated the interruption of the neurotransmitters. It's also possible that the patient has early-onset myasthenia gravis. That, alone, would explain why the paralysis has lasted this long."

I had no idea that I had so many health issues, Castro thought. *Gilbert's Syndrome? A bad liver? Myasthenia gravis?*

"None of that explains the ventricular tachycardia," the surgeon snapped, interrupting Castro's thoughts.

Heart attack! For the first time Castro understood why he was in the operating room.

"Maybe it does," Dr. Graff responded, refusing to succumb to the surgeon's petulance. "If this particular curare, with its life extended because of the patient's metabolic malfunction, and made more robust by the Physostigmine, included an agent such as Sarin or Atropine, it may have totally blocked the neurotransmitters, disabling the vagus nerve and causing tachycardia."

"That's a lot of speculation," the surgeon snorted. His interest in the case was gone. The surgery was over. The patient survived. His job was done and this debriefing was a waste of his time. Plus, the people with the patient were idiots.

"You're right," Dr. Subbiah agreed. "Without the actual substance to test we are really just making educated guesses. What I do know is that this doesn't seem to fit curare poisoning, nor does it comport with any known tropical disease."

If only I had kept the dart, Castro thought. *But, then, I probably would have died in the observation post.*

"So what is your post-surgery prognosis?" Dr. Graff pressed

the surgeon.

"He was in a coma when we started surgery, and he was in a coma after the surgery," was the surgeon's terse reply. "I have no idea whether he will come out of the coma, but at least he's still alive."

"If this is a case of curare poisoning, as I suspect it is," Dr. Graff corrected, "he is not in a coma but a state of paralysis. If not for the anesthetic, he would have been able to feel everything that went on during surgery."

"Well, whatever it is, his heart is still beating," the surgeon snapped. He stood and swept out of the room, being careful to slam the door behind him to emphasize his disdain for being admonished by a general practice doctor, and a woman at that!

Castro had never had a particularly high opinion of Western medicine, and the conversation he had just observed did nothing to enhance it, but at least he had learned some things about his condition. More importantly, he had learned that he could change locations by just thinking.

I wonder what would happen if I tried to reenter my body?

Instantly everything was black. He felt restricted, confined. He could hear the hum and whir of the machines monitoring his vital signs. *Shit!* He hadn't anticipated that. *I don't want to be trapped in this body, in this blackness!* He fought to control his rising anxiety, forcing himself to focus on how he had first become separated from his body, but it didn't help.

He lay contained in the blackness wondering why he could no longer see. *Of course,* he reasoned. *The surgeon was right. I am in a coma. My eyes can't see. Only my soul can see and that is now stuck back in my body. I wonder if I could escape my body by just thinking about it?*

There was light and space and a feeling that his shackles had been removed. He was again looking down at his body.

The relief he felt was interrupted as the hospital room door opened. Leon and Mahogany walked in, followed by a young woman, plain in appearance, but surrounded by an aura of something. *Light? Energy?* Castro watched and listened. Small talk. Inconsequential, except that it confirmed that he'd had a heart attack and now his body was functioning because of a pacemaker. Castro also realized the pounding pain in his chest was gone. Was it because he was no longer in his body? He didn't remember the pain when he had been trapped there just seconds earlier.

Perhaps the operation did accomplish something.

After several minutes Leon and Mahogany left the room. The young woman they called "Carrie" sat down beside the bed and took one of his hands, pressing it between both of hers.

He couldn't feel her touch but he did feel something, an intrusion of some kind, a not-unpleasant tingling. She didn't speak but he could hear…no feel…bits and snatches of words disrupted and made unintelligible by the disturbance she created in his consciousness. The aura that surrounded her undulated and changed shape, like flames in a fireplace. Castro was mesmerized.

After several minutes the aura grew faint and he could no longer hear her. He watched her gently stroke his hand, then lay it back on the bed beside his body. She left the room.

Castro felt like he had missed an opportunity.

* * *

Nothing had changed. The tubes were back in place, the numbers bobbed and weaved on the monitors to affirm that Castro was, indeed, still alive by medical standards, but he lay there as before, unresponsive.

They stood around the bed and awkwardly made small talk until Leon asked Carrie if she wanted some individual time with Castro. She nodded, and Mahogany and Leon left the room.

Fifteen minutes later Carrie entered the waiting room and sat down next to them.

"I couldn't make contact with him," she said. "I felt something, but I couldn't identify it. The body is there, but it's like his essence is gone. Maybe he just wasn't ready."

The ride back to the wharf, and the ferry ride to Tiburon, were done in silence. Carrie was worn out. She opened a Pixie Stix and downed the sugary contents, then took a second one from her pocket and did the same. She saw Leon looking at her quizzically. "For energy," she said. "Trying to replace what was depleted today." Leon nodded, not quite understanding. But he was sure that the day's experiment had been a failure. Carrie may have saved his physical body, but Terry Castro was gone.

Chapter 15

Amaru held up his hand, signaling the column to stop. To his left water bubbled from the depths, clear and cold, seeping from beneath dank foliage to form a pond in a depression the size of a child's wading pool. The overflow from the pool coalesced into a tiny stream that disappeared and reappeared and disappeared in the undergrowth. Still holding his hand aloft, Amaru moved forward, alone, until he saw the water again. Now the stream was slightly wider, about the length of his foot.

He motioned the others to follow.

Silently they took up the march again. It was the twenty-third day after Amaru had summoned the spirits. The Chilco, and the small mules they used to carry the few things that were essential to their lives, had been marching for twenty-two of them. They had traveled nearly four hundred miles but neither distance nor manmade borders were of importance to them. They knew that when their shaman found the safe place he would know it and would tell them, and there they would stop and live until the next time a forced march was required for survival; the way of the Chilco for the past six centuries.

Amaru followed the stream, joined by another trickle, and then another, until it became wider than a man was tall. The water remained clear. Amaru knelt, cupped his hands and lifted the water to his lips. It was sweet and good. His nod brought the others to the water's edge, filling their gourds, swilling just enough to satisfy their thirst, dipping a hand into the stream and wiping their face and necks with the fresh water.

"We will stay here tonight," Amaru said. He summoned four young men, sending them in teams of two to hunt for food. The rest of the tribe melted into the jungle. In less than five minutes there was no sign that two hundred people and thirty mules had just been there.

Amaru summoned the spirits again that night. The next morning he announced: "Today we will find our safe place."

Since they had fled their mountain home in the clouds high in the Andes, the Chilco had been stoically following their shaman from safe place to safe place, just as they had earlier obediently followed their warrior chieftains into battle after battle. Starting with their futile war to avoid domination by the Inca; then the Incan civil war between brothers, Atahualpa and Huascar; the short-lived but deadly resistance to the Spanish conquistadors of Pizarro; and, finally, the rebellion against the Spanish led by Manco Inca, whom Pizarro had appointed Inca after the fall of Cusco: in each case the Chilco had been on the losing side.

Over half of their population had either been displaced or died in the constant warfare. Disease and battles with lowland tribes upon whose territory they encroached during their transition from mountain dwellers to jungle inhabitants decimated the remaining population. Now only two hundred remained.

Amaru pondered these things as he chopped a narrow passage through the ferns and the vines covered in orchids and fuchsia five hours into the day's march. They had been paralleling the ever-expanding stream until it came to a place where it joined with another to become the Rio Curuçá River. There Amaru stopped. This was the safe place the spirits had promised. It would be, he hoped, the place where his people would find peace, would flourish and procreate.

Deep in his heart he knew it would not be so.

The Rio Curuçá began one hundred fifty miles from where it emptied into the Rio Javari, and two hundred seventy miles from where the combined rivers, and many others, joined just east of Tabatinga to become the mighty Amazon.

Amaru and the Chilco did not know they had crossed the Peruvian border into Brazil, did not know that none of the whiter-than-a-cloud people were within one hundred miles of where they stood, nor did they know that if they spit in the

Rio Curuçá their saliva would travel more than fifteen hundred miles to the Atlantic Ocean. It was not important to know these things. The spirits had told Amaru this was the safe place. That was all they needed to know.

Amaru chose a spot, close to an open area large enough so that many could gather, but invisible from the open area. There he and his family would live. The remaining families would scatter around the shaman's place, each invisible from the other but within hearing distance. The young men and those not of a family would form an outer ring around the families in the same manner. There were no permanent dwellings, only lean-tos that could be dismantled and loaded on the pygmy mules in seconds. They were virtually invisible, only large enough to protect the family and their mule from the frequent heavy rains. They slept in the trees, in hammocks of fiber winnowed from the vines that hung from every tree, or simply propped in a fork. They ate what they could hunt, fish or harvest.

With rare exception, they were invisible to those who might venture into the area, or if discovered, only one person, or, at most, one family, would be seen. The rest would be warned by a sound that mimicked the oil bird, a nocturnal creature with feathers as black as its name. Within minutes the Chilco could destroy any sign of their camp and disappear into the rainforest to survive another day. Never, in Amaru's reign, had they stood and fought an intruder.

* * *

Urco, oldest surviving son of Amaru, had lived for nineteen years; about half the normal life span of a Chilco man. He was born with a purple birthmark on his left cheek and neck; a rare gift from the Gods that foretold of greatness. He had fulfilled this prophecy when he killed his first jaguar at age eleven. At age fourteen he was mated for life with a female of the tribe as was the custom of the Chilco. He and his mate had three children, an inordinately large number for a Chilco family, which also brought him honor and respect. He had caught and trained a dwarf marmoset, displaying the same patience and persistence that he had shown with his children. It had become his constant companion, usually found perched on one of Urco's muscular forearms with its long tail wrapped around his bicep, or sitting on his shoulder. Other than the mules, it was the only animal allowed in the Chilco encampment.

Urco was surprised when his father walked up to his lean-to. Ordinarily he would be summoned if a conversation was needed.

"Come, my son," Amaru said. "It is time to teach you some things."

Urco knew, barring a fate similar to that which had befallen his two older brothers, that he was the next to be chief and shaman of the Chilco, but his father was healthy and robust. He had not expected his time to learn the ways of the shaman to come this soon.

As they left the camp area Urco gave a soft whistle, and the four-ounce monkey scampered across the clearing and leaped onto his outstretched arm.

They walked for a time without making a sound, the gaunt seven-foot frame of Amaru leading, his eyes searching for the proper place. Urco, several inches shorter and broader, with chiseled muscles that bespoke of incredible physical strength, followed. They both saw the snake at the same time the marmoset chittered a warning.

Amaru used his walking stick to worry the nine-foot emerald tree boa coiled in the branches of a fallen tree until the snake slithered off the branches and into the underbrush. The two men sat on the tree's trunk and gave thanks to the spirits for putting the fallen tree in their path and to their serpent brother for marking it as the place where wisdom could be given and willingly received. Amaru removed the four gourds that had been hanging from prongbuck cords around his neck and placed them carefully on the ground between his feet.

With sad eyes he looked at Urco.

"These vessels hold the fate of our tribe. The curare," he said, nodding toward the gourds. "The curare provides food and long life and fertility. Without the curare, the Chilco would not survive."

Urco nodded, although he did not fully understand. He knew that only the shaman made the curare. He knew that when he went hunting he painted the heads of his darts with it, and that it paralyzed his prey even if the shot was not true, but he knew nothing of the other things of which his father spoke.

"I must teach you many things for soon you will become shaman of the Chilco," Amaru said. "The gift you bear," he continued, reaching out to touch the birthmark on his son's face, "has been an omen of your prowess, but you will be tested in ways you have never imagined. A heavy burden you will carry, and you will carry it for a long time."

"But father," Urco protested, "you are strong and healthy. You will be shaman for many more years. Your own father lived twice as many years as you have been on this earth. Surely you will live as long as he."

"We do not know when our time will come," Amaru replied, waving away his son's protest. "Only the Great Spirit which is the essence of every animal and every plant and every insect and of the clouds and the mountains and the rivers, knows when it is a man's time, but it has been foretold by the spirits of the shamans that my days on this earth are few."

They sat in silence.

"Do you know when...how...your time will end?" Urco finally asked.

"No. It has not been foretold."

Again, there was silence, broken only by the buzz of insects and the sounds of the rainforest. The marmoset, now apparently convinced the snake was no longer a threat, jumped down and scurried into the brush, easily avoiding the vicious thorns that could rip a man's skin open with the slightest touch.

"You must hear and remember this story, my son," Amaru said, breaking the silence. "For it is the history of our people. Through it you will learn of the great and terrible burden you must bear, and you will pass it on to your oldest son when you are an old man and can no longer be shaman."

And so he began. The jungle fell silent, even the buzz of the insects, to show respect.

"We arose from the eyebrow of the mountains at a place called Ceja: the Chilco, the Revash, the Hirito and many other clans whose names of been lost in time. We sprung as plants from the sparse soil and rock, reaching for the warmth of the pale sun, until the Great Spirit pulled us free, one by one, and turned our roots into legs. We, the Chilco, of all the clans reached the highest and so we became tall and bleached by the sun's rays." As he spoke a single ray of sunshine found its way through the dense canopy to the fallen tree upon which they sat. Amaru lifted his face in a silent prayer to the giver of life.

"We were the most numerous of the clans, at one time numbering in the tens of thousands, and the Great Spirit looked most kindly upon us, promising long and abundant life," he continued after a moment. "For hundreds of years the clans lived peacefully, high in the clouds where the sun rarely visited. We built cities such as Vira Vira and great citadels, like Kuelap, where we worshiped and traded with the tribes from the rainforest on the eastern slope of the mountains. The shamans of all the clans were humble and honorable and wise, and great prosperity was among us, but the evil one who brings lightning and storms and avalanches was always watchful, waiting for a time to destroy us, as he does to all civilizations.

"In the south a great nation called Inca was forming. They

were greedy and warlike. At the right time the evil one, in the form of a harpy eagle, attacked our shaman, Yawar, and bit off his nose and scratched out one of his eyes. He infected Yawar with evil. When the Inca war hordes climbed our mountains Yawar told them of the places of safe passage and led them into our midst before we could mount our defenses. Although fierce warriors, our federation of clans fell with little resistance, and Yawar was rewarded by the Incas with much wealth. The Incas failed to recognize that we were many clans and called us all Chachapoyas—Cloud People. The Inca ruler, Tupac Yupanqui, imposed "mitmaqcuna" disbursing all clan members of childbearing years, and all young people were taken from the mountain clans and were seen no more. They killed all the shaman, except Yawar, and for a hundred years we forgot who we were. The Great Spirit deserted us because of the evil that Yawar had brought upon his own people.

"Our numbers grew small as fighting between clans became common, and brother fought brother. When the Inca pretender Atahualpa massacred seven thousand of our warriors, a new Chilco leader arose, Guaman, but he was not a shaman so he could not see the future. He promised that the Spanish devil, Pizarro, would save the Chilco, and pledged the Chilco's support in the great battle of Cusco. The Chilco fought bravely and Guaman was made a general in the Spanish army, but greed and avarice overtook him and he forgot his brothers. The Spanish devil murdered our shaman, Cayo Topac, and named an Inca, Manco, to rule the Chilco.

"There was, at that time, a young boy of purest heart, and a soul that reached back to the time when the Chilco were strong and mighty. His name was Hatun Cayo. He constantly prayed to the Great Spirit, and his prayers were answered.

"'I have seen you, Hatun Cayo, and have heard your cries for your people,' the Great Spirit said, 'because you are as pure as fresh snow and there is no fault in you, I will answer your prayers and once again look kindly upon the Chilco. You shall lead your people from the scourge of the Inca and the deceit of Pizarro. You shall take them from the mountain into the rainforest of the Montana where you shall find peace. I shall give you wisdom and shall guide your feet, and I shall teach you how to make a curare that will assure survival of the Chilco and enable you to live long on the earth. But this will come with personal sacrifice and a heavy burden. You shall be disfigured by fire and your face will bear the disfigurement for all your years which shall be many.

"The wisdom I give you is for you alone. Others will be envious and angry because of your knowledge, but you must stand firm and find ways to keep peace. Your humility will be your greatest weapon. And, most painfully, you will live more than twice as long as any other Chilco. You will watch your friends and family die, and their friends and family die, while you continue in life until the only thing you have left is your wisdom and your humility. Then, and only then, will you be able to pass on the wisdom I shall give you. You shall pass it on to the oldest of your sons who is living. You will know, when the time comes, to teach your eldest.

"'If you use your wisdom for personal gain or wrongful purposes, or fail to pass on the wisdom, or you share your wisdom with the wrong person, the Chilco shall no longer procreate and shall, upon the death of the youngest person living at the time you fail, cease to be.

"'Are you, Hatun Cayo, willing to take on this burden and save your people?'

"Hatun Cayo fell to his knees, overcome by the presence and the words of the Great Spirit who knew the answer to the question before he asked it.

"And, having learned the secret of the new curare and many other things from the Great Spirit, Hatun Cayo led the Chilco out of the mountains and into the Montana.

"Hatun Cayo was your grandfather five times removed. The disfigurement of his face, suffered as he led the Chilco through the fire to freedom, has reappeared six hundred years later in you, my son. You will be the seventh and greatest shaman."

Chapter 16

Amaru snagged the prongbuck cords with his bony fingers and unfolded his lean frame from the snake tree. The four gourds clacked together as he hoisted them over his shoulder.

"Come," he said to Urco.

They walked silently until the occasional sun's ray slanted at a sharp angle through the tree canopy. Amaru stopped intermittently, listening, tilting his head, flaring his nostrils. Once or twice they left the footpath but each time returned and continued onward, away from the encampment where the Chilco had ended their trek two days earlier. Urco, judging by the direction they were traveling and the waning light, knew they would be spending the night in the jungle. They would, as they had each night during their twenty-three-day trek, sleep in the trees high above where night insects flew or jaguars climbed, for it was not safe, even for the Chilco, to challenge the fangs and stings of the night-feeders after dark.

As light faded, and with their senses on high alert, Amaru and Urco came to a halt in a bamboo thicket on the edge of a clearing. In the middle of the clearing was a sink hole, no more than ten feet across, filled with water and edged by a mud apron marked by hundreds of tracks the provenance of which could not be determined from their vantage point. Amaru scanned the clearing and sniffed the air, then closed his eyes and listened with intensity. Satisfied that the clearing was safe, he stepped out of the copse. He signaled Urco to wait and began walking the perimeter of the clearing, stopping on the opposite side at a towering brazil nut tree whose base was deformed. Remnants of fallen fruit, some as large as Amaru's head, lay at the base of the tree. He began a three-note, singsong chant; words Urco did not recognize. He realized how little he knew of the ways of the shaman.

"Heuy ha muy NAHA NU hoya oyah," Amaru's chant rose and fell as he half-danced, half-marched around the clearing. Reaching the spot where Urco waited, he signaled him to follow and they continued around the clearing until reaching the nut tree that had been partially hollowed by fire, used by earlier travelers to cook their meals or fend off night predators. There Amaru ended his chant.

"This is a place where life is sustained. Here we shall cook the curare," Amaru said.

But they did not cook curare that night. Instead, the two warriors slipped out of the clearing and waited among the lush bromeliads and cascading orchids; hidden in both sight and scent from the animals that would soon come to the watering hole in the waning light.

The sounds of the jungle began to take on their night timbre, and an adult kinkajou scurried out of the jungle toward the water. Urco's dart cut short its hurried journey.

Urco skinned the honey bear while Amaru started a fire in the base of the brazil nut tree. Urco threaded the meat onto two freshly cut saplings and laid them in the fire, then scraped the fat and tissue off the inner side of the thick honey bear pelt and stretched it across a framework he had fashioned from extra palm saplings. He stuck the framework in the ground close enough to the fire to take advantage of the heat, but far enough so that neither the hide nor the double layered hair would catch fire. The honey bear pelt would make a luxurious pillow for his wife and him.

As Urco worked on the pelt Amaru turned the meat-laden skewers so the meat would cook on all sides. When they had been thoroughly blackened, he took them out of the fire and handed one to Urco. The two, leader and future of the Chilco, sat on their haunches and ate. Not a word had been exchanged since they had melted into the jungle to await the arrival of their dinner.

Dead branches were added to the fire to keep the nightly water hole visitors at bay for a few more hours. When the new kindling had caught and the flames licked up the tree trunk, Amaru, his face aglow from the flames, squatted among the four gourds and summoned Urco.

"The survival of the Chilco is in these vessels," Amaru intoned. "They contain the seeds of the plants from which the curare is made. Tomorrow I will ask the spirits of the shaman where to plant the seeds at our new home so that the plants will thrive. We have seeds to plant and enough extra to make curare, but we must gather the golden frogs before we can cook."

"I have heard you say, father, that the Chilco cannot survive without the curare," Urco said in one of the few times that his patience failed him. "Surely we can hunt without the curare on the tips of our darts." He had thought this many times but, until this moment, had not given words to his thoughts.

Amaru stared at his son, saying nothing.

"Our brother kinkajou would have provided us dinner even if there had been no curare," Urco said, to make his point.

Amaru's expression did not waiver. He held Urco's gaze as he knelt and picked up the largest of the gourds. He pulled the stopper from the gourd and poured a few seeds into the palm of his hand. "These are the seeds of the woorari," he said, showing them to Urco. "They must be planted next to a tree, for the woorari grows a vine that will only thrive if it can climb the trunk of another plant. It winds around the other plant like a boa encircles the body of its prey. You have heard the women talk of the snake vine. This is that vine. Women do not know the purpose of this vine, finding it only useful for the beautiful white flowers it sprouts which they put in their hair, but the bark of this vine is poisonous. Without it the curare could not help us hunt our food. The root provides the poison, and the flowers provide beauty for the animals the poison kills. It helps them remember the beauty of their life on this earth as they pass on to the next world."

Still ignoring his son's question, Amaru took a second, smaller gourd, dark red in color. He poured out a few of the seeds in his hand and handed them to Urco who looked at them with exaggerated interest, aware that his earlier question had been seen by his father as impertinent, exposing a flaw in his character. Urco hoped that his careful examination of the seeds from the red gourd would help return him to his father's good graces.

"This," Amaru said, "is the seed of the taja bush. It must be planted where it can see the sun. When the bush is grown to the height of a man's knee the bark must be stripped from the branches of the bush and added to the curare. The bark of the taja bush makes the animals bleed until all their blood is gone. Because of taja bark the spirit of the animal, contained in its blood, can pass into the great beyond and nourish those who have gone before us. When the spirit leaves the animal we are allowed to eat it."

Amaru held out the gourd to Urco who dutifully poured the seeds back into it. Amaru picked up the third gourd, this one a golden yellow. The seeds in it were of the same color.

"These are the seeds of maca," he said to Urco. "The root of the maca plant is added to the curare so that the animals will be well nourished when they pass into the great beyond. You have seen maca for the women use it to flavor our food, but it is the root that must be saved for the curare. If we do not honor the gods by putting it in the curare our brothers of the forest who the gods have placed here to sustain us, will abandon us and we will starve."

Amaru set the golden gourd aside and picked up the fourth and final gourd, ivory in color.

"This, my son," Amaru said, holding the gourd with gentle reverence, "is the fulfillment of the promise made by the Great Spirit to the Chilco. This was given to me by my father, and it was given to him by his father, and so on, and so on. At the right time I will give it to you, but you must remember above all things I have told you today, that this holds the future of the Chilco within it. There are many forms of curare. Each tribe has its own. But only the Chilco have ashwagandha. You must protect these seeds with your life, harvest more from each crop, and pass them on to your eldest son, along with the story I have just told you, and all the other things I will teach you in the coming days, at the right time; a time which will be made known to you. If the seeds are destroyed or lost, or they do not grow, or you fail to pass them on to your eldest son, the Chilco will disappear from the face of the earth and be no more."

Amaru hesitated, remembering the burden he had felt when the leadership mantle had been cast upon him by his own father; the longest-living of all shaman. He had been unprepared, but in time patience and wisdom grew, and, although he had not been a great shaman with no great events marking his time (except, perhaps, adding the golden frogs to the curare recipe) his leadership had been fair and cautious. It had allowed the tribe to survive, albeit in ever-dwindling numbers.

The words also weighed heavily upon Urco. How could someone as impatient and impulsive as he, become shaman and leader? How could he be trusted with the ashwagandha seeds and the very existence of his entire tribe?

His thoughts were interrupted as Amaru opened the white gourd and took from it a single, unexceptional seed; ivory in color and no larger than the eye of a fly. He gently took it between his thumb and finger and held it up for Urco to see. He did not offer to let him hold it.

"When the Great Spirit told Hatun Cayo that he would save the Chilco, he told this story," Amaru said. "'In a faraway land where only snow and ice exist there is a plant called ashwagandha. I will cause a great flock of birds to eat the seeds of the ashwagandha and migrate to your mountain where they will deposit those seeds in their dung. From the plants that grow from those seeds you will harvest leaves and add them to your curare. It will help preserve the flesh of your quarry from decay, and, as you taste the curare for potency, it will also extend your life and virility ten times more than all the men of your tribe and will lead you to great wisdom and great humility.

"'But there will come a time when you will have to flee your mountain home and the birds will come no more, so be vigilant when you harvest the leaves to be sure that you do not kill the plants, for they must grow until they produce seeds. Collect the seeds and keep them dry and safe so that when you are forced to find a new home you may grow the ashwagandha.

"It is this seed, my son," Amaru continued, "that is the answer to the question you so impetuously asked." Urco stared at the ground in embarrassment.

"Our curare is more than a poison to feed or protect ourselves. Because of it the great shamans, your forefathers, were able to live hundreds of years and lead the Chilco through the ordeal that has been our existence since we were forced to flee the mountains."

The firelight flickered, and the grousing of a big cat, kept too long from its watering hole, came from just outside the clearing. Urco was anxious to ascend to the upper reaches of the brazil nut tree, but Amaru was not done.

"It is the promise of the Great One, delivered in the form of this seed, that enables us to survive. As with me and our forefathers, our curare will give you long life and virility, and the wisdom and patience to fulfill the promise of your birth; to be the greatest leader of the Chilco. The one who will lead us back to the mountains and the greatness that is our destiny."

Amaru extended his hand and touched the seed to the birthmark on Urco's face.

Chapter 17

Carrie sipped a perfectly chilled glass of Chablis, sheltered from a stiff breeze off the bay by the corrugated siding of Le Garage, a tony waterfront restaurant. She watched the sailboats bobbing in Sausalito Harbor. The azure sky was cloudless and the sun felt good as she waited for Uncle Vikter. She hoped he didn't mind sitting on the deck.

A waiter, clad in a faux auto mechanic's uniform, with collar-length hair and a terrible French accent, asked her if she wanted to wait for her luncheon companion before seeing the menu. "*Oui,*" she said, inwardly smiling at the waiter's momentary pause as he mentally processed her answer.

"Would you like another glass of wine while you wait?" he asked, dropping any semblance of the accent.

"*Non,*" she said, wishing to exude a sense of mystery for the over-matched waiter. He backed away, nodding, and Carrie went back to enjoying the wine, weather and the view, taking pleasure in her little deception. She had splurged on a new dress, and then decided she needed a new hairstyle to go with it. She was feeling very European.

"How's my favorite niece?"

The words, and the hand on her shoulder, caused Carrie to jump.

"Uncle Vikter. You startled me." She rose to give him a hug, adding, "I'm your only niece."

"Aahh, but even if there were more you would still be my favorite."

"Smooth as a baby's butt, just like his bald head." That's what her mother always said about Uncle Vikter.

Vikter, and Carrie's mom, Katrina, had emigrated from Russia together in 1990. Katrina had gotten pregnant, married, got a minimum-wage job as a grocery store checkout clerk, and divorced, in that order. Vikter had gotten a job as a bookkeeper at Day Pharmaceuticals and had risen quickly through the ranks. They seldom saw each other, but when they did it was painful. Vikter exuded new wealth: cars, clothes, jewelry, a trophy wife, but he never offered to help his sister financially, and she was too proud to ask even though she and Carrie lived in a series of roach-infested flats, subsisted on pancakes and ramen and rode public transportation.

Carrie only knew Uncle Vikter as the bald rich uncle she saw once or twice a year and about whom her mother talked bitterly. Vikter didn't know Carrie at all, completely ignoring her until recently. Carrie, who had never known her father nor had a male role model in her life, was grateful for the newfound attention despite her suspicion that Uncle Vikter's real interest revolved only around her counseling with Leon Day.

Today he was resplendent in a perfectly tailored Italian cut sport coat, navy blue with brass buttons, over a starched white open-collared linen shirt and matching pocket handkerchief. Sun glinted off both his head and his highly polished black shoes.

Not surprisingly, Vikter insisted that they move inside the restaurant, and, after being reseated twice, he found a location he liked with his back to the wall facing a broad expanse of windows looking out on the harbor.

They traded small talk, with Uncle Vikter doing most of the talking, until the waiter came. In his usual manner, Vikter ordered something vegetarian that was not on the menu. Carrie knew that it was going to be another lunch where Uncle Vikter was unhappy with his food. She ordered a side salad with fat-free Italian dressing which brought a comment from Uncle Vikter about how "out of character" that was for her.

"New boyfriend?" he asked.

"No. No boyfriend."

"Prospects?"

That brought a scowl from Carrie. The innocent, single word

question had confronted Carrie with something she hadn't wanted to admit to herself. She was infatuated with a man in a coma.

They sat in uncomfortable silence while they waited for their food, Carrie struggling with her guilt while, at the same time, envisioning the strong hands and ruggedly handsome face of Terry Castro. Even lying in a hospital bed, unable to move or to speak, he stirred something in her.

Vikter broke the silence by broaching the subject of her "gift," as he called her spiritual consultation business. She knew he would eventually get around to asking her about her sessions with Leon. It made sense, she guessed, since Leon was his boss, and since Uncle Vikter had gotten her the job as Leon's spiritual counselor, but it made her uncomfortable when he asked.

"Any interesting new clients?" he asked.

But before she was confronted with the aspect of lying, or discussing Terry Castro with her uncle, the food arrived and changed the direction of the conversation.

"Why can't anyone find a chef who can make a decent vegetarian cassoulet?" Vikter imperiously inquired after taking a tiny bite of his entree. The heads of the other diners swiveled in their direction, then returned to their own plates, looking down in a futile attempt to ignore the vulgarly loud complainant. The young waiter came and offered to replace the offending dish, but Vikter waved him away with a derisive backhand, and then proceeded to grumble throughout the meal.

Carrie had learned to put up with her uncle's embarrassing behavior. After all, he was her only uncle and she appreciated his interest in her, not to mention she got to eat meals at places she couldn't afford. Today, however, she had lost her appetite. Was it Uncle Vikter or Terry Castro that was the cause? She wasn't sure.

She pushed her salad plate away.

After Vikter had picked his way through most of the cassoulet the waiter cleared the dishes and, careful to avoid any eye contact with Vikter, asked Carrie if there was something wrong with her salad. Before she could answer, Uncle Vikter, looking at his diamond Rolex, said: "I think we have time for an aperitif."

The waiter returned with espresso for Carrie and a glass of 2008 Fonseca LBV for Vikter.

"Any progress in dealing with Leon's brother?" Vikter asked.

There it was. The real reason for the luncheon meeting.

"I think you'd have to ask Mr. Day about that," she replied.

"He doesn't come into the office much anymore, so I don't often get a chance to talk to him. When I do it's usually limited to business. Is he doing all right?"

"I think he's doing okay."

"Mahogany says his headaches are more frequent." It was a lie, but Vikter wanted to get his niece talking in more than monosyllables. "Has she said anything to you about that?"

"He seemed all right the last time I saw him," Carrie said. "Although he is using a cane now."

The minute she said it she wished she hadn't.

"Hmm." Vikter tried to show concern, but Carrie detected a flicker of something else. Elation? Excitement? Satisfaction? She couldn't be sure.

He paid the bill and they left the restaurant.

Carrie got in her dilapidated Honda while Vikter settled into a Bentley convertible that made throaty sounds as it accelerated out of the parking lot. Carrie looked at her watch and decided she did not have enough time to go see Terry Castro before she had to be at work. Damn. New hairstyle and a new dress wasted. She had tried to convince herself they were for her lunch with Uncle Vikter, but he hadn't even noticed, and deep down she knew she had been lying to herself.

* * *

Vikter sped north on Highway 101, the gleaming Bentley emitting a muscular purr beneath his right foot. He turned right on Tiburon Boulevard and left onto Pacific Glen, heading for the home of Leon and Mahogany Day. He was not expected.

"Mr. Glass. So nice to see you," Sanjay, the Days' houseboy, said as he answered the door.

"Is Leon at home?"

"He is either napping or on the back deck. I will check."

"I'll wait in his office," Vikter said as Sanjay turned to go and search for Leon.

Vikter waited until Sanjay was out of sight, then removed a tiny plastic square from his jacket pocket, peeled off the backing and stuck it on the top of the door molding. He took several steps into the room and stood on his tiptoes. He could not see the transmitter. He stopped in the kitchen long enough to plant another, then went into Leon's office where a third transmitter was placed on the underside of the base of Leon's desk lamp. Each transmitter included a chip that recorded any sound within twenty feet. The online advertisement said the devices would last at least three months before new batteries would be needed. The recorded conversations, it said, could be accessed by mobile phone.

He sat in one of the leather wingback chairs, waiting for Sanjay. A month earlier he had arranged for Leon and Mahogany to get new "upgraded" mobile phones; phones that allowed him access to all of their conversations. To his disappointment, they seldom talked "business" on their mobile phones unless they were talking to him. It did help him keep track of their schedules, though; most importantly Leon's medical appointment schedule. He was hopeful that the bugs he was planting would provide a more steady stream of helpful information.

"Mr. Day asks that you come out on the deck, please," Sanjay said as he entered the room.

Vikter followed the diminutive houseboy through the formal

dining room, and the living room that never got used, scoping out more hiding places for transmitters.

"I was having lunch with my niece in Sausalito and thought I'd drop in to see how you're doing," Vikter greeted Leon as he walked through the French doors onto an expansive limestone-tiled deck. "A social call, rather than our usual business meetings."

"I appreciate that," Leon said, struggling to his feet to greet Vikter. "Mahogany is at one of her charity meetings and I was getting tired of staring at the boats. Want a drink?"

"I would have a glass of wine, viognier if you have it."

"Of course I have it." Leon smiled. He knew Vikter was very aware of the scope of Leon and Mahogany's wine cellar. He had often been a benefactor of its finer offerings. Sanjay was sent to fetch a bottle as Vikter joined Leon on the plush, pumpkin-colored sectional. To his left lay San Francisco Bay and a view of the Golden Gate Bridge; to his right Sausalito Harbor with the city behind, the buildings flowing up the steep hillside toward Highway 101.

"I never get tired of this view," Vikter said.

"I didn't think I would either, but sitting here day after day is getting to me. I need to get back to work."

"What's this?" Vikter changed the subject, pointing to a cane propped against Leon's right leg.

"Getting old," Leon said, shaking his head. The conversation was now trending in a direction more to Vikter's liking.

"Bull. You look like you could still play for the 49ers," he said.

"And you need your eyes checked," Leon replied. They both chuckled.

"You okay?" Vikter asked, again referring to the cane.

"Doctor recommended it if I'm walking on an uneven surface. That would include these flagstones," Leon said, pointing at the patio surface. Vikter nodded.

Sanjay returned with two Riedel viognier glasses and a chilled bottle of 2014 Penner-Ash. "May I?" Vikter asked holding out his right hand to Sanjay, who set down the ice bucket and obediently displayed the dripping wine bottle on a white towel.

"Oregon?"

"Better than the recent French offerings," Leon responded. "Best I've had since the Rosenberg brothers had that one spectacular vintage back in the late nineties." He nodded at Sanjay to pour the wine.

The two men sipped the wine, enjoying the layers of citrus, smoke and nutmeg.

"Incredible," Vikter said. Leon nodded, smiling. They relaxed against the cushions and watched the boats, mainsails reefed, tack back and forth across the bay.

"Well, isn't this a lovely scene." Mahogany, resplendent in a navy and cream diaphanous silk pant suit, walked onto the patio.

"A social call," Vikter said, standing up as Mahogany walked to Leon and, bending over, gave him a kiss on the cheek.

"You look marvelous, as always," Vikter said, admiring the cut of her trousers and the curve of her butt from behind his Gucci aviator sunglasses. She straightened up, saying, "It's good to see you, Vikter," then bent slightly to hug the shorter man.

"How was your meeting? Would you like a glass of wine?" Leon asked, not waiting for an answer. "Viognier." He raised his glass to show her.

"I would love one, but I need to change into something more comfortable," Mahogany said. "Vikter, can you stay for dinner?"

"No. I really should be going. I need to stop at the office before heading home."

"Oh, please stay for a bit more so we can share a glass of wine. It's so seldom we get to see you unless it's about business."

Vikter capitulated and, as they waited for Mahogany to return, Sanjay brought a phone out on the patio. "It's for you, sir." He handed it to Leon.

"Who is it?"

"Father Wyman, from Berrie University."

Leon mouthed the word "sorry" to Vikter and took the phone. Vikter gave the "should-I-leave" sign and Leon shook his head.

"Father Wyman! To what do I owe the pleasure?"

Leon's half of the conversation was mostly "uh-huh" and "that's great."

"I'd be very interested in seeing them," he was saying just as a barefoot Mahogany, in skinny jeans and a bright pink and turquoise halter top, came back on the patio. Leon wrapped up the call with Father Wyman.

"Who was that?" Mahogany asked, accepting a glass of wine from Sanjay, who had materialized out of nowhere.

"Father Wyman," Leon answered. "They have recovered videos from when Terry was in the Amazon. It appears that he may have really found a Lost Tribe. They're sending us a copy."

"Do they show what happened to Terry?" she asked.

"The cameras were focused on what they were watching, not on the watchers, so, no, according to Father Wyman they don't show Terry at all, but they do show what appears to be a hunting party of light-skinned, very tall and completely naked natives."

Mahogany raised her eyebrows in mock horror at the "completely naked" statement, and they all laughed.

"I'd like to see the videos when you get them, if you don't mind," Vikter said, "perhaps with a group from our creative marketing team. Maybe we can get some return on your investment in this project."

"Let's look at them before we get marketing involved," Leon replied. "I'm not so sure we should exploit Terry's misfortune." Mahogany nodded.

Vikter, who had never been in favor of sending company biologists to the Amazon on a "treasure hunt," felt rebuked, but he controlled himself and maintained a pleasant demeanor.

"Of course," he said, trying to sound affable. "You know me, always looking out for the bottom line."

"For which we are eternally grateful," Leon responded with a reassuring smile.

"Where would we be without you," Mahogany added. They all raised their glasses in a silent toast to Vikter and his stewardship of the Day Pharmaceutical bottom line.

"You know, I had Carrie try to communicate with Terry," Leon said. "She wasn't successful, though. I'm afraid we've lost him."

Why hadn't Carrie mentioned that, he wondered? He didn't like it when things went on that he didn't know about. That was why the eavesdropping bugs were necessary. He shook his head, putting on his best disappointed face.

Vikter drained the last few drops from his glass. "I've really got to be going," he said, rising from the sectional. "I can show myself out," he continued as Leon struggled to stand. "Don't get up."

He extended his hand to Leon, and bent over to kiss Mahogany on the cheek, leaving behind another unseen transmitter, tucked neatly under the curled back of the wicker chair in which she was sitting.

"I'll stop by at our usual time on Monday," he said to Leon, "when it will be back to business as usual."

Vikter would have liked to plant his last transmitter in the dining room, but Sanjay followed him through the house to the front door.

The Bentley rumbled to life and Vikter turned left out of the circular driveway. Two blocks away, out of sight of the house, he pulled to the curb and stopped. He tapped the app on his phone and four icons appeared, one for each of the transmitters he had planted. He tapped the fourth icon, the one on the patio. "It was really nice of Vikter to stop in," he heard Mahogany say. "It was a pleasant way to spend the afternoon," Leon replied.

Clear as a bell. Perfect.

Vikter switched to the transmitter above the front door and listened to the recording of Sanjay and himself saying good-byes.

He swung back out on 101, north toward Petaluma, feeling quite pleased with how the day had unfolded. The lost tribe was just the thing to keep Leon and Mahogany busy so they wouldn't interfere. Maybe he would persuade them to go there; get them out of his hair altogether.

He smirked at his little joke as he ran his hand over his bald head.

Chapter 18

How had she let herself get so flabby? The spinning dial came to a stop between her bare feet: 163 pounds. Ugh!

Carrie stepped off the scale, and examining her face in the medicine cabinet mirror, applied a new lipstick, something called "Nude Pink." She tilted her head, thinking, maybe it's okay. She brushed through her hair, wishing she knew how to make it look like the stylist had done two days earlier. I need someone to teach me how, she thought. Shit, I need a complete makeover.

The makeover, however, was outside of Carrie's budget so she did her best with foundation, eyeliner and mascara. She slipped on the same dress she had worn to lunch with Uncle Vikter, a knee-length floral sheath that drew attention to her bust and away from her waist. She stepped back from the mirror, wishing her bedroom was big enough for a floor-length mirror, and surveyed the results.

This is stupid. I'm going to see a man in a coma and I'm worrying about what I look like. What is wrong with me?

She left her apartment, locking the door behind her. The creaky old Honda wheezed to life, and she headed for UCSF Hospital, hoping that Terry Castro had no other visitors.

As she inched her way up Mission Street Carrie's thoughts took her back to Irene, her mother's roommate in the Alzheimer's ward. It was the only time she had ever made spiritual contact with someone who was still living. To be accurate, Irene had made contact with Carrie. She had walked through the door of Carrie's always-open brain cafe and announced her presence. Would this be the same way, Carrie wondered? Would Dr. Terry Castro simply walk into her brain and tell her what she wanted to know?

In fact, what did she want to know?

That thought occupied Carrie for the next twenty-five minutes until she pulled into an open space in the UCSF Hospital parking ramp. Even then she sat for a few minutes wondering if, and how, she could actually make contact with Castro, and questioning her own motives. She was no longer doing this at the request of Mr. Day. He had given up on what he called "the experiment." No, she was doing this totally on her own. Was it the challenge of proving that Irene was not a fluke and that she could communicate with the living as well as the dead? Or was it the chance to explore how far her God-given ability would take her into this other time dimension her mind seemed to regularly occupy? Or was it just lust?

She didn't want to think about the latter. It was creepy, perverted, but there she was, in makeup and a new dress about to visit a man in a coma. Carrie vacillated between leaving and staying; then with a sigh of resignation, she got out of the car, locked the doors and entered the hospital.

Tears welled on the brim of her lower lids as she stood in the doorway of room 1165. There he was, the most gorgeous human she had ever seen, lying inert, comatose. As the tears slid down her cheeks an observer, had there been one, would have assumed they were tears of sadness, but Carrie knew that they were caused by a different base emotion, revealed by the lurch in her heart and warmth in her groin when she walked into the room. She felt flushed.

Thank God no one is here, she thought.

It took a moment for her to compose herself before dragging a chair to the side of the bed. She sat and tenderly took Castro's right hand between hers. She felt no pain this time. She looked at his face and imagined him without a beard. Had he always had a beard or had it grown since he was airlifted out of the Amazon? She guessed the latter, because he was also in need of a haircut. She wondered about the color of his eyes, how he had gotten the small half-moon scar that intersected the end of his right eyebrow, and whether his biceps had been more muscular before the "incident." But none of it mattered. He was, in her eyes, perfect.

She rubbed his hand softly against her cheek, then kissed its palm, then cupped it again between both of her hands and held it to her lips, all the while never letting her gaze drift from his face. Her breathing slowed and the flush left her cheeks. The world in room 1165 receded until only Castro and Carrie were there. She leaned forward.

Where are you, Dr. Castro? How did you get in this coma? How can I help you? The thoughts had barely formed in her head when a nurse burst into the room.

"Is there something wrong?"

Carrie jerked back from the bed and realized she had leaned on the call button built into Castro's bed. She felt like a teenager caught making out with her boyfriend. Heat radiated from her face as it turned red. The annoyed look from the nurse added to her embarrassment. The nurse left in a huff. Carrie lingered in the room, hoping she wouldn't have to pass by the nurse when she left.

She looked at Castro. Her clumsiness had destroyed the moment, but the room was unchanged. Castro still lay in the same position with the same non-expression. She thought about trying again to make contact but instinctively decided against it. She was sure she had felt a spiritual connection in that briefest of moments before the nurse charged into the room, and she was now equally sure that Terry Castro hadn't judged her for her faux pas. That was enough for now.

Carrie went into the bathroom and relieved herself. Finished, she pulled up her panties, then looked in the mirror to make sure she was no longer blushing, checked her makeup and tucked her hair behind her ears. She stepped back into the room. "See you tomorrow," she said to the prone figure on the bed, then straightened the skirt of her dress, threw back her shoulders and walked out of the room.

* * *

Just before noon the next day Carrie reappeared in room 1165, toting a bag filled with paraphernalia. She had maxed out her Visa account to buy a barber kit. She laid out scissors, combs, clipper, an electric razor on the table beside Castro's bed, and then proceeded ever-so-carefully to shave his beard. She quickly learned that she had to cut off the beard with scissors to get it down to scruff before the electric razor would work without continually getting clogged. Methodically she ran the razor over his face until Castro's cheeks and jaw were smooth. She toyed with the idea of leaving him with a mustache, but decided against it.

When she was done Carrie removed a bottle from her purse, uncapped it and poured a small amount of liquid into the palm of her left hand. She rubbed her hands together and then massaged the aftershave gently into Castro's face. She sat up to admire her handiwork, then slowly leaned over and buried her face in Castro's neck and shoulder, deeply inhaling the spicy aroma of the aftershave that blended with the natural scent of his body.

After two or three minutes, Carrie forced herself to sit up.

She picked up the scissors and took a lock of Castro's hair between her fingers, then decided that there was no way that she could cut his hair while he was lying down. She would ask the nurse if the hospital had someone who could do that. She checked her watch and realized that she had been there for nearly two hours. She was going to be late for work. Quickly she packed away the grooming tools and, as if it were the most natural thing in the world, leaned over and kissed Castro on the cheek, then turned and left the room.

Thank you.

The words stopped her in her tracks.

"Terry? Dr. Castro?" She said the words aloud.

There was no response.

She retraced her steps back to room 1165. The scent of aftershave permeated the room but nothing else had changed. Had she imagined it? She didn't think so.

"I'll be back," she whispered softly.

* * *

Castro watched her as she walked down the corridor, got into the elevator, descended to the main level of the hospital, and walked through the lobby and into the parking ramp. He realized it was the first time he had been outside the hospital building.

Since his surgery, and the separation of his consciousness from his physical body, his existence had become tedious. Time, he realized, was a complex concept. For him it had always been forward or backward in a straight line. People's minds and bodies age over this lineal progression. An event is planned to happen in the future, and once it occurs, it is in the past. But, in his current state, the tools that humans use to measure time—a clock, a calendar, phases of the moon—were of no significance. Only light follows dark follows light provided any sense of progression and since he spent most of his "time" in a well-lit hospital, even the earth's revolution gave him only sporadic glimpses of the passage of time.

At first he had shadowed Doctors Graff and Subbiah, hoping to learn more about his medical condition. He found that he was no longer a priority. Except for one visit by Dr. Graff, spent talking to the nursing staff to confirm that there had been no change in his condition, they had moved on to more pressing matters. At best, he realized, he would become a chapter in a book by Dr. Subbiah on undiagnosed tropical diseases.

He observed two surgeries in the same operating room in which he had died and been revived, but found his lack of anatomical knowledge made them little more than interludes in blood and organs he couldn't identify. He watched grieving people but felt no grief himself, and saw the relief and happiness when a loved one recovered, but did not share those emotions. He even watched a doctor and a nurse having frantic sex in a supply room but had none of the exhilaration or sensations that he remembered from that activity.

His astral condition definitely had shortcomings.

He also learned that time was a fiction. There were no minutes, hours or days of the week. It was all one long, infinite progression, like railroad tracks on the prairie plain that go on until they disappear in the horizon and then go on from there. Nor was Castro's power of observation dependent upon light or its absence. Night or day, it was all the same, as if seen through a hazy soft light, like morning's first light on a foggy morning.

His existence had become free-floating and sterile except for one thing that kept him tethered to his body. Regardless where he was floating at the time, whenever he was touched he could sense it and, if he chose, could return to his body and become part of it. He did this the first few times the nurses came, but the novelty of having your diaper changed, your ass wiped or your body sponged with soap and water soon wore off. Besides, unlike before, the feelings and sensations were diminished, as if he was numb.

Castro had stopped returning to his body each time the touching sensation came upon him, but then it changed. The first time he had nearly missed it, a new and different feeling that his body was being touched. Curiosity propelled him back to his hospital room just in time to see the woman the Days called Carrie leaving. She appeared upset.

He had not given it further thought until later when he felt that same touch again, stronger this time. He returned to his room to find Carrie's face buried in the neck of his body. The beard he had grown was gone and a razor and scissors were on the bedside table. The aura which surrounded her the first time he had seen her had returned.

He watched her pick up the scissors with her left hand and take a lock of his hair between the first two fingers of her right hand. She hesitated, then let go of his hair and put the scissors back on the table. She put the scissors, an electric razor, a comb and a bottle in her bag, then leaned over his body and kissed him on the cheek. It was not a kiss of passion, but kind, gentle, loving. It felt soft and warm. Her aura grew brighter.

"Thank you," he thought, just as she left the room.

Chapter 19

"So who's the new guy?" Carrie's best friend, Julie, asked from her cubicle across the aisle.

"What?"

"The new guy. This is the second day in a row you're all dressed up," Julie continued. "Jewelry. Your hair's been fixed. Must be a new guy."

"Uh...no," Carrie stammered. "Just trying out a new look."

"Oh." Julie was clearly disappointed.

So, oddly enough, was Castro.

His escape from the confines of the hospital had left him surprised and a bit giddy. He had followed Carrie without thinking about where he was going, and had toggled back and forth between the inside of her car and hovering above it. While being in the car with her was pleasant, he found hovering above her black Honda as it made its way from the hospital to the office building where she worked gave him a sense of freedom that he hadn't realized was missing. Although there was no perception of movement or speed, nor did his consciousness record anything but Carrie's Honda, he instinctively knew there were other vehicles, the streets of San Francisco, houses, trees, the sky. Like the first time he rode a bicycle, or was handed the keys to the family car, he experienced true liberation.

That's why, as he listened to the exchange between Carrie and Julie, it surprised him when he felt...*what?...disappointed, rejected, jilted?...*by her denial that she had a new beau. Her actions back at the hospital had certainly indicated she was attracted to him. To hear her say that there was no new man in her life was a blow to his ego.

"So, then, you're trolling?" Julie brightened, trying a new tack in her interrogation of her friend.

"Um...uh...yes. You got me. I'm trolling." Carrie's response was less than convincing.

"Want to go out Friday night and see if we can score?"

"Uh…no…I have a family thing Friday night," Carrie said, immediately regretting she had lied to her friend and surprised by how easily it had come.

But the lie made Castro feel better.

Abruptly the young women turned their attention back to their computers and an older man came into Castro's view. Overweight and sloppily dressed, with five or six hairs futilely trying to achieve a comb-over of his bald head, the man stopped between the two cubicles.

"Dressed to the nines again," he said to Carrie, giving her a too-long visual once-over.

"Just trying to raise the standards of the company," Carrie responded icily.

The fat man smirked and moved on.

"Asshole," Julie whispered after he had moved out of hearing range. "Sonofabitch is always trying to look up my skirt or down my blouse."

Carrie nodded.

Castro bristled. *Motherfucker oughta be castrated.*

Like a freight train it hit him: he was the fat man. Students, other faculty, women in random settings: he had looked at them all as sex objects. Short skirts and exposed cleavage had given him license to leer and fantasize and make suggestive remarks to women that, because he was young and attractive, had been tolerated and, sometimes, even encouraged. Had he been sixty, bald and fat he would just have been lewd, and probably sued for sexual harassment.

Jesus, what a hypocrite I am. He drifted away in a miasma of self-loathing.

* * *

Like an inchworm the day bumped along for Carrie. Tender thoughts of Castro, her ogling boss, lying to her friend, and, mostly, questioning her own motives, kept her from focusing on her work. She hated the digital clock on her desk: 6:15, 6:17; 6:21; minute by minute it made its way toward quitting time.

Finally, it came. She gathered her things and left, walking past the office of her leering, sweating boss. "Good night, Carrie," he shouted after her in a syrupy voice. "Can't wait to see what you're wearing tomorrow."

Carrie hurried to her car, checking behind her to make sure that he wasn't following. As she drove home it kept rolling over in her mind: who's the bigger pervert, him or me?

The next day, and the next, she stayed away from the hospital, determined to prove to herself that she was not a pervert, that she was not falling in love with a man in a coma, but Terry Castro was never more than one thought away. On day three she gave in, convincing herself that she would try again to contact Dr. Castro. It would be strictly a professional call.

Carrie toweled off after her morning shower, then tried to redo her hair in the configuration her stylist had conceived a week earlier. She took her favorite pair of black pants off the hanger—the pair she hadn't fit into for a while—then put them back on the hanger and started to hang them back in the closet. She stopped, took them off the hanger again and tried them on. They were snug but not uncomfortable.

Curious, she took them off and stepped on the bathroom scale: 157. She had lost six pounds in seventy-two hours. She realized that she had eaten practically nothing. Not healthy, she thought. I better get some breakfast before I go to the hospital. She put the slacks back on and paired them with a pink, scoop-necked top. She looked in the mirror and saw her exposed breasts. She thought of her boss, took off the top and replaced it with a gray and white crew-neck top. Like her pants, it was snug, but at least it didn't expose any flesh.

She left her apartment at 10:00 a.m. Ten minutes later she pulled into a McDonald's drive-thru, intent on ordering a breakfast sandwich and coffee, but exited without ordering. Instead she stopped at a local diner and ordered scrambled egg whites, toast without butter and orange juice. She ate it without enthusiasm, eyeing the cinnamon rolls in the bakery case. Grudgingly she ordered a coffee to go and left. She was at the hospital at 10:55.

Carrie walked into room 1165, coffee in hand, and stopped dead in her tracks.

There, sitting beside Castro's bed, was an attractive woman, as surprised by Carrie's entrance as Carrie was by her presence. Even more shocking was that the woman was quickly withdrawing her hand from under the covers; that, and the bulge that was left behind in the vicinity of Castro's groin.

"Who…who…who are you?" Carrie stuttered.

"Uh…Holly. Holly Bouquet," the woman said, trying to cover her embarrassment. "I'm Terry's…wife. Who are you?"

You've got to be kidding me, was Carrie's first reaction. Blond, blue-eyed, perfect teeth, a stage name and she's his WIFE?

"I'm Dr. Castro's…um…spiritual guide," she stammered.

"His what?

"Spiritual guide," Carrie said with more confidence. "I'm a medium and I've been hired by friends of Dr. Castro to make contact with him on the other side. To find out what happened to him."

"I didn't know he was into that kind of thing," Holly said, trying to find some unobtrusive place to put her right hand. The lump in the covers subsided.

"I didn't know he had a wife," Carrie replied testily, "and it really doesn't matter if he, or you, are 'into that kind of thing' or not. It's my job to make contact with him. I came this morning for a session with Dr. Castro."

She stood glaring at Holly Bouquet with what she hoped was

her best professional scowl.

"I…I can leave." Holly said hesitantly.

"That would be good." Carrie stepped aside so she wasn't blocking the door. She watched as Holly walked out of the room and down the hall.

Narrow hips and a firm ass to boot: Carrie slumped onto the chair in the corner of the room. Shit. Her faux romance with Castro had aroused her and made her uncomfortable all at the same time, and now to find out he's married. Shit. Shit. Shit! At least she could stop worrying about being a pervert. There was no way she could contact Castro now; not in her state of mind. Did she even want to try anymore? But the 'thank you' was real and so was the feeling that he had not judged her when she messed up their first session. She was certain that she had made contact with Castro. Could she separate herself from her emotions and do this solely on a professional basis?

As she wrestled with herself, a thought struck Carrie that, at least temporarily, solved her dilemma. She shot out of the over-stuffed chair and bolted out the door.

"Did you see where the woman went? The blond woman that came from Dr. Castro's room?" she asked the on-duty nurse.

"I think she may have gone to get a cup of coffee, or some lunch. I'm not sure."

Carrie took an elevator to the cafeteria level and hurried down the corridor toward the smell of food, hoping the nurse was right. She scanned the room without success, then asked a cashier if there was a coffee shop in the hospital.

"There's a Starbucks near the main entrance," was the reply.

As Carrie hustled past the bank of elevators she almost missed Holly who was balancing a vente coffee and a sandwich while punching the elevator button.

"Wait. Miss Bouquet, wait," she said as she turned into the elevator corridor. Holly stopped and turned to face Carrie, nearly dropping the sandwich.

"What?"

"I apologize. I was rude." Carrie held out her hand.

"Apology accepted." Holly turned back to the elevator buttons ignoring Carrie's hand.

"Um…I was thinking that you might be able to help me make contact with Dr. Castro."

"Why would I do that? Besides, I don't believe in *that kind of thing.*"

Carrie was accustomed to disrespect of her psychic ability, so she let Holly's hostile response slide off. "What have you got to lose? He may be stuck in this state for the rest of his life. You're here. I'm here. It may be the only chance to communicate with him. There must be memories that only you and Dr. Castro have. Maybe one of them would trigger a response from him."

Holly hesitated, thinking.

"Listen. If you don't want me to do this, I understand. You're his wife. I'll stop. But you really should talk to Leon and Mahogany Day, his friends who hired me."

For the second time since they'd met Holly looked embarrassed.

"I'm not his wife," she confessed. "I'm his ex-wife."

Relief and anger struck Carrie simultaneously.

"That does change things," she said, trying with only partial success to control her emotions.

"I could still try and help," Holly said. The admission had taken some of the frost out of both her words and her attitude.

* * *

Castro had been depressed since he had slunk away from Carrie, Julie and their sleazy boss. Guilt from coming face-to-face with his attitude and actions toward women was the predominant depressant, and it was intermingled with disappointment when Carrie hadn't returned to the hospital. His disappointment turned to worry and his thoughts drifted toward looking in on Carrie to make sure nothing had happened to her when he sensed a new touch.

He had been hanging out in the hospital coffee shop, hovering above the coffeemakers wishing he had a sense of smell, but even without it old habits died hard. He had always preferred coffee shops to bars when he was feeling down. Then the new sense of touch crept into his consciousness. It had a different quality that he knew was neither the nurses nor Carrie. His curiosity teleported him to his room where the only woman he had ever loved sat next to his bed holding his hand. For the first time since the surgery he wished that he was back in his body and that it was fully functional.

That wish propelled him back into his lifeless, lightless body. Although the sensation of Holly's touch could be felt more intensely, not being able to see Holly was not what he wanted. Castro tried to escape, thinking of her face, sunlight through her golden hair, her soft breathing as she lay sleeping, the swell of her bottom as she lay facedown on the beach. But nothing happened. A moment of panic: *I don't want to be in this body,* and that quickly he was free, floating again above the room.

She was talking to him softly, so softly he could not make out the words. He studied her face: there were new lines around her mouth and eyes since he had seen her last, and a tiny mole below her left eye that he did not remember seeing before, but a few years of maturity had done nothing to detract from her beauty.

How many years has it been, he wondered. Five? Six?

Castro stopped his attempt at mathematical calculation and became transfixed on Holly's right hand. It had let go of his hand and crept under the covers where it was gently caressing his genitals. To his surprise, his penis began to thicken and rise, causing the covers on his bed to do the same. As he contemplated returning to his body to intensify the sensation the hospital room door opened and Carrie stood there, a stricken look on her face.

Oh, shit! He wanted to hide or run or disappear but, of course, he was already invisible...except for his body and the telltale tepee in the covers.

Realization came quickly and his embarrassment passed. For the next few minutes he watched the scene play out between the two women, surprised at Holly's lie about being his wife, impressed by Carrie's resilience, observant of Holly's well-toned, athletic body. But there was one reaction that thoroughly puzzled him: his feeling that he had been caught in the act of betraying Carrie.

Chapter 20

Sleep eluded Urco as he lay under the small lean-to listening to water droplets falling from trees a hundred feet above, plopping on the roof. The nightly rain had saturated the protective green canopy, and now the early gray of dawn was painting the sky. As he rose he paused, gazing at his wife and children sleeping the sleep of innocents. They made him feel strong and proud.

He crept from the lean-to and listened. He heard only sounds of the waking forest: an isolated bird call, the dripping from the leaves, the far-off scream of a howler monkey, the sleepy buzz of insects. The village was still asleep. It pleased him that he was the first to greet the day.

He padded to the gourds that had been set out to catch the rain, chittered softly, then lifted a gourd to his lips to drink. The tiny marmoset was instantly on his shoulder, tail winding its way around Urco's massive bicep.

He took a handful of Chia nuts from a basket and gave one to his companion who chittered its appreciation. He checked the basket for bugs, then popped a few of the black seeds into his mouth, put the cover back on the basket and poured the remaining handful into a small leather bag that he hung around his neck. He picked up his blowpipe and quiver from beside the lean-to, slung them over his shoulder, and left the encampment.

Urco needed to think.

Amaru, his father and great shaman of the mighty Chilco since before any living person was born, had shocked Urco with the revelation that his time as shaman would soon come. Sitting on the snake tree the day before, Amaru had told Urco of the history of the Chilco, and of the promise of the Great Spirit made to the heroic shaman, Hatun Cayo, who had led the Chilco through fire to freedom five hundred years ago. He also talked of the curare and the divine intervention of the Great Spirit that brought the white birds and the seeds that gave long life to all Shaman of the Chilco.

A chittered warning from the marmoset interrupted Urco's thoughts. An emerald boa, perhaps the same one that safeguarded the tree upon which they had sat the day before, was intertwined through the vines growing up the trunk of a kapok tree, eyeing a tree salamander that was clinging to the tree bark several feet above the boa. In a single swift move Urco swung the blowgun off his back, loaded a dart and knocked the salamander off the tree. It quivered once, twice, and then was still.

Urco walked to the base of the tree and pulled the dart out of the salamander.

"Sorry, father snake," he said aloud. "We both need to eat."

He cut the lizard into two pieces, taking the back legs and tail for himself and leaving the remainder, including the most prized part: a mushroom shaped tongue that protruded from the dead salamander's mouth.

"I am in your debt for finding my breakfast," he said to the boa, which had started to unwind itself from the vines. "Now you are in my debt for saving you the hunt."

From a safe distance Urco watched the snake slither to the remains of the salamander and carefully explore it with his darting tongue, then engulf it in its massive jaws. He watched longer to make sure the snake did not follow him, and then resumed his walk, sucking the sweet meat of the tail and hind legs of the salamander. His marmoset, who did not rejoin Urco until he was done eating, was rewarded with another chia seed. The six-inch blossom of a flowering mallow held enough of the night's rain to slake Urco's thirst.

His thoughts turned again to the previous day as he continued his journey. A pond had formed across his path; the damp soil having not yet absorbed the night rain. Urco stopped at the edge of the still water and saw his reflection. He ran his hand lightly over the purple birthmark that covered half his face. It was the totem that had marked him since birth as the next great shaman of the Chilco; the same disfigurement Hatun Cayo had suffered from the fire while leading the Chilco to freedom.

His hunting exploits as a youth, his success as a procreator and father, and his gentle and humble ways had added to the expectations and were often spoken of by the elders at tribal gatherings. Although not tall by Chilco standards at six foot six, his massive body and near-super human strength assured that no one would physically challenge his leadership.

Indeed, the prospect of being the physical leader of his people did not trouble Urco. He was quietly confident of his abilities. What troubled him were his own self-perceived shortcomings: his impatience; his tendency to act first and think later; his lack of knowledge of the ways of the shaman. Was he capable of learning everything he needed to know?

But these things were not the reasons Urco had risen early and left the encampment. At nineteen years he had lived half the life of the average Chilco man, but when he became shaman he might live ten times that long. His great-grandfather had lived to be two hundred. His own father was over one hundred and still strong and virile. That was Urco's dilemma.

He did not want to live so long that he would have to watch his children die.

Chapter 21

"Isn't that a beautiful...ah...mmmm..."

"Spinnaker, dear." Mahogany's worried voice reminded Leon. "And, yes, it's beautiful."

As expected, Vikter had located them on the patio during cocktail hour. His end-of-the-day eavesdropping had become routine, even boring. It produced mostly inconsequential small talk: "Do you want another glass of wine?" "Remember that you have a doctor's appointment tomorrow."

He slid a lemon drop between his lips, then grimaced as sweet-tart saliva aggravated a canker sore in his mouth. He leaned over and laid his iPhone among pages of the Day Pharmaceutical stock prospectus that littered his desk, and tapped the screen to activate the speakerphone.

Today there was mostly silence. Leon must be having a bad day. They had become more frequent. He scanned the other three transmitters. A conversation recorded earlier in the day at the front door caught his attention.

The door chime activated the transmitter. Within seconds Sanjay's feet could be heard padding across the vestibule.

"I have a package for Mr. Leon Day," a muffled voice from outside the doorway said. "It requires a signature."

"Who is the sender?" Sanjay asked in his clipped Indian accent.

"Berrie University."

"I will sign for it."

Then the door closed.

That might be the video from Peru, he speculated. But he hated guessing. I need a camera so I can actually see what, or who, is coming and going, he thought, and another transmitter in the theater.

Vikter switched back to the live feed from the patio, arriving in mid-conversation.

"...ex-wife," Mahogany was saying. "She would like to meet us."

"I don't think I knew he was ever married," Leon said. "What does she want?"

"She said she'd like to thank us for what we've done for Terry."

"What? Send him off to the jungle so he could be in a coma the rest of his life! How'd this woman find us?"

"Apparently she met Carrie at the hospital and got our name from her."

"What's Carrie doing at the hospital? And why is she giving out our name?" Leon's decibel level rose sharply as agitation and paranoia seeped out of his worsening condition. "You sure she isn't just looking for a handout?"

"I don't think Carrie would give our names to anyone who wasn't legitimate," Mahogany said, weariness and resignation in her voice. "We could invite her for a lunch here on the patio, or a glass of wine. Would that be all right with you?"

"I guess so."

"Maybe we should ask Carrie, too, since they've already met. How about lunch Saturday?"

"I guess so."

A wan smile crossed Vikter's pinched face. So, his niece was still visiting Castro in the hospital and now his ex-wife had arrived. If that was, in fact, the Amazon video that had arrived this morning he was sure that, with a little massaging of the situation, he could keep Leon and Mahogany focused on Castro and away from the business for quite some time.

* * *

Saturday morning broke, cloudless with a light breeze, temperatures promising to reach seventy by noon. Mahogany made drop biscuits and chocolate gravy for Leon, a favorite of his since childhood, while the women would be dining on crab and quinoa salad. She hoped the biscuits and gravy would give Leon something positive to talk about. His memory of things from his childhood was still sharp and a happy mood usually followed.

She'd had second thoughts about the lunch, not wanting to expose Leon's failing mental and physical health to a stranger, but, at Sanjay's urging, did not cancel.

"It will be good for him to interact with others on something other than business." Sanjay had reasoned, and Mahogany ultimately agreed.

As was her habit Carrie arrived early for the luncheon, wearing her one good dress. Mahogany greeted her with a big hug, and a "so glad you could come."

Carrie handed her a small box of inexpensive chocolates. "A little hostess gift that I expect Leon will eat," she explained with a conspiratorial grin.

"Come," said the ever-gracious Mahogany guiding Carrie out of the vestibule. "Come out to the patio and talk to Leon while I'm finishing up."

As Carrie passed through the sliding glass wall to the patio, Sanjay handed her a perfectly chilled glass of prosecco. Leon was sitting on a wicker chaise looking out over the bay.

"What a beautiful view," Carrie said as she approached. "Thanks for inviting me to lunch."

Without turning, Leon growled: "Why are you still going to the hospital?"

Both his tone and question caught Carrie by surprise.

"I...I'm still trying to make contact with Dr. Castro."

"Give it up. He's gone. He's never coming back."

Carrie was stunned into silence.

"And why are you giving our name out to strangers?"

"Who? I never...oh, you mean Holly Bouquet?"

"Who the hell is Holly Bouquet?"

"Dr. Castro's ex-wife," Carrie said, defensively. "She just wanted to meet you and say thank you for everything you've done for Dr. Castro." She paused. "I'm sorry. I shouldn't have given her your contact information without asking you."

Leon, still with his back to Carrie, lapsed into silence, ignoring her apology. She stood for what seemed like an eternity. When he said nothing further she warily took a seat on the edge of one of the wicker chairs.

Sanjay fluttered out onto the patio with small plates of caviar canapes and cheese straws. Neither Leon nor Carrie took any. Sanjay placed them on a coffee table and left.

A moment later Mahogany glided out of the house with another guest, partially hidden behind her. "Leon, I'd like you to meet Holly Bouquet," she said. Holly emerged from behind Mahogany, resplendent in a white form-fitting turtleneck and short skirt topped with a loose-knit, calf length sweater in navy blue. Gold hoop earrings and navy pumps completed the ensemble.

Her striking appearance belied her thoughts as she saw Carrie: *What is the witch doing here?*

And for Carrie, it was the second time in ten minutes she was stunned into silence.

Leon turned, leaned on his cane and levered himself off the chaise, his body language and tone of voice doing an instant one-eighty.

"So nice of you to come," he said, offering his hand to the new guest. "May I call you Holly?"

Holly took his hand in both of hers. "Yes. Please do," she said, her radiant smile and silky voice momentarily banishing all other sights and sounds from the patio. "It is so nice to meet you. May I call you Leon?"

Mahogany, pleased to see a spark in her husband even if caused by another woman, seated them around the gas fire ring facing each other.

"Hello, Carrie." Holly's voice had lost its silkiness, replaced by a monotone. "Nice to see you again. Nice dress." She didn't mean either.

Carrie acknowledged her presence with a curt nod.

Mahogany quickly diffused the momentary awkwardness brought on by the chilly exchange by announcing the luncheon menu. She then steered the conversation to Holly and Terry and their time together. No mention was made of Holly and Terry's divorce; the one event about which Carrie really wanted information.

Why would anyone divorce someone like Terry Castro, she wondered? Holly must be a real bitch, sitting there with her white-gold hair like a halo, her expensive clothes and her perfect body. Or really stupid. Maybe she's frigid. Then she remembered the hand under the covers.

When lunch was served Carrie took refuge in her salad and wine, offering monosyllabic answers the few times the conversation included her. When lunch was over she made up an excuse to leave, but Mahogany pleaded with her to stay for one more glass of wine. Carrie gave in, much to the disappointment of Holly who not-so-subtly shifted in her seat so that she was facing Leon with her back to Carrie.

The conversation turned to Terry Castro's work in the Amazon and how he had ended up in a coma in San Francisco.

"We'll probably never know exactly what happened," Leon said to Holly, "but we did get a video the other day, taken at the research site. Would you like to see it?"

"I'd like to see it," Carrie said, a split second before Holly could answer, which caused the former Mrs. Castro to roll her eyes.

Sanjay freshened their wine and they all made their way to the theater room, led by a suddenly energized Leon. He fiddled with the DVR player, but it was Sanjay who eventually took over and brought up the video.

They saw a clearing, just a wide spot in the path, that materialized out of a mass of foliage, vines and tree trunks; then continued, with the jungle as its backdrop, until it began to narrow as it passed out of the camera's view. The picture did not change for several moments until, like apparitions, three naked, white skinned men materialized in the clearing. Long, narrow sticks were strapped across their backs and each wore a scabbard-like pouch against his hip, held in place by a thin cord that encircled his waist. One wore a leather pouch on a similar cord around his neck.

The three men stopped, stood and then faded back into the dense underbrush. Everyone in the room audibly exhaled.

"Wait," Leon said. "There's more." He fast forwarded the DVD.

The warrior with the pouch around his neck reappeared in the clearing. He was thin and sinewy, not fragile. His face was deeply lined and he appeared tall, although that may have been an illusion created by his spare frame. He stood motionless with one end of the narrow stick, now identifiable as a blowgun, held to his lips. He gave an almost imperceptible nod of his head and lowered the blowgun. Then, with quickness almost faster than the human eye could record, he reached forward, snatched something that was below the camera's angle and disappeared back into the jungle. The clearing was devoid of any hint that a human had stood there just seconds earlier.

"Terry certainly found the white-skinned tribe he was looking for," Leon said, breaking the hush that had fallen over the room. "Unfortunately the video doesn't tell us anything that would answer why he's in a coma…or how to get him out of it."

"Could we look at that again?" Carrie's request brought an objection from Holly.

"I don't need to see it again."

"Why don't you take it with you?" Mahogany offered an olive

branch to Carrie. "You can bring it back at your next session with Leon."

Would there be a next session, Carrie wondered.

Chapter 22

Carrie peeled off her dress. It felt neither new nor stylish anymore.

She felt like she had been ambushed: first by Leon and then by the arrival of Holly Bouquet. Mahogany's invitation had simply said, "join us for lunch." It hadn't said anything about other guests, particularly Terry Castro's ex.

And the way Leon had fawned over her…

* * *

The last time Carrie and Holly had seen each other was when they had returned to Castro's hospital room after meeting at the elevator. Carrie had done her best to approach the situation professionally, but it became abundantly clear that Holly believed she was a fraud, a charlatan who was taking advantage of Castro's friends.

After Carrie's attempt to communicate with Castro failed, Holly sneered: "Well, since your *power* seems to have failed you, why don't you give me the Days' phone number so that *I* can contact *them.*" Carrie didn't have the energy or the will to resist. She gave Holly the number and then watched her give Castro a wet kiss and sashay out of the hospital room.

Carrie sat, slumped in the chair beside Castro's bed for several minutes, exhausted from her effort. She reached into her purse and took out a Pixie Stix, tore off one end and poured the contents in her mouth. It was because of Holly's disbelief that the attempt failed, she reasoned. Deep down, though, she knew that it was her jealousy of Holly that caused the failure.

* * *

She changed into sweatpants and a T-shirt, took a bottle of beer from the refrigerator, then replaced it and took out a bottle of water. The entire event had upset her and destroyed her appetite, but she knew a beer would make her sleepy and she had work to do. She had eaten very little at lunch.

She grabbed a bag of pretzels from the cupboard, then walked into her tiny living room and slipped the disc into her old DVD player.

Carrie ran the video several times, toggling between the two scenes where the white men, warriors in Carrie's judgment, appeared. The warrior who had returned to the clearing in the second scene was the tallest of the three and, she thought, the oldest, although it was difficult to judge the age of any of the warriors. She wished the videos had included Castro or some of his students so she could compare their skin color and height with the three warriors.

She paused the video, and forwarded it as slowly as she could in an effort to see what the warrior had snatched. Her best guess is that it was a dart from the blowgun that the warrior carried, but no matter how many times she went through the video she could not see where any of the warriors had shot a dart.

She also paused the second scene at the moment the warrior appeared to nod his head, but when viewed as still frames the movement was lost and the warrior did not change expression. Carrie began to think it was nothing, perhaps a blip in the recording or a figment of her wishful imagination.

She hit rewind so she could study the first scene. She marveled at their over-sized feet and the length of their dangling penises. It made her wonder what the female members of the tribe looked like.

As she fast-forwarded once more to the second scene she detected a slight shudder in the picture shortly after the warriors faded into the jungle, as if the camera had been slightly bumped. Several stops, starts and slow-motion runs produced no clue as to what may have caused the tremble in the filming. Again, perhaps nothing.

Carrie uploaded the video to her laptop and forwarded it to her phone. If she hurried she could get to the hospital before visiting hours were over. She was reasonably sure that Holly, who was into her third glass of wine when Carrie left the luncheon, would not be there.

* * *

While he could teleport himself automatically to other locations, Castro quickly learned that his state of astral suspension did not allow him to go backward or forward in time. He was stuck in the now and he had no comprehension of how long he had been there.

For a time after he had watched the confrontation between his ex-wife and the woman named Carrie he had shadowed both of them. The sight of Holly disrobing in her hotel room left him with an odd reaction. Without his own physical body to be stimulated, Castro found himself looking at his naked ex and wondering what there was about the female form that aroused a man. It was all quite analytical and not in the least sexual.

Watching Carrie in her apartment made him uncomfortable, feeling like a stalker or a peeping tom. He quickly stopped except to check in on her at work from time to time.

He retreated to the haven of the hospital. He had learned that even without a physical body he needed periodic rest and the most efficient way to get it was by reentering his body. When he did so, however, he became aware that his body was gradually losing strength.

"He'll be moved to a nursing home. We can't take up a bed if we can't do anything for him."

That was what Castro heard as he regained awareness after one of his rest periods. He lay in his dark cocoon pondering what it meant; wondering what would happen when his body stopped breathing and his heart stopped beating. Would he continue to float free in this world? Would he enter another dimension? Or would everything just stop?

The door to his room opened.

"Hello, Dr. Castro. How are you today?"

They're going to move me to a nursing home, he would have shouted if he'd had a voice.

He exited his body. Carrie Waters stood just inside the doorway, aglow in a wash of undulating energy, a triumphant smile on her face. He would have hugged her if he could.

Thoughts coursed through his brain a mile a minute: *They've given up on me...I'm getting weaker...I'm going to die...where have you been...can you help me?*

"Slowly, Dr. Castro, slowly," Carrie said as she approached the bed. "I can tell you are trying to communicate with me, but it's all white noise in my head. Let's start with my asking you questions."

The white noise subsided.

"Where are you now?" She asked. His response made her instinctively look up at the ceiling, but, of course, she saw nothing. She smiled at herself, feeling a little foolish.

"Do you know who I am?" She nodded at his answer, and this time her smile was one of satisfaction.

"Why do you think you're going to die?"

The white noise rose again and Carrie shook her head as if trying to clear it.

"Whoa," she said, maintaining a soft tone in her voice. "I can't actually hear what you're saying. I only sense it. I'm not exactly sure why or how it happens, but it only works when everything is calm. If there is a disturbance in the force, so to speak, I lose it. Do you understand?"

"Okay. Now, why do you think you're going to die?"

Carrie listened intently, repeating "slowly" several times.

"Do you remember Leon Day?" she asked. Nodding, she added, "I will talk to him about the nursing home and the doctors."

"Can you tell me what happened to you?" Carrie asked, pulling a chair up to the bed. She held Castro's hand as she listened. Time flew past and dusk started to filter the light coming through the hospital room window. Occasionally she would ask a question. A couple of times she repeated something to make sure she understood correctly.

A nurse barged into the room for a routine check. The interruption broke the connection between Carrie and Terry. Waiting for the nurse to finish her work, Carrie realized she was fatigued to the point of exhaustion. She gently placed Terry's hand back on the bed and leaned back in the chair, waiting for the nurse to complete her duties. When the nurse left Carrie rose, bent over and kissed Castro gently on the cheek, and said, "I'll be back tomorrow."

Thank you. Castro could not feel the kiss but an emotion welled up in him he could not name.

His words formed in her head, and she sighed. A winsome smile lit up her face. Carrie left the room. Had she looked back she would have seen a single tear trickle down the side of Terry Castro's handsome face.

* * *

It was Sunday and she was in love.

Carrie had slept for twelve hours; the most deep, luxurious sleep she could ever remember. Her dreams, which she recalled vividly, had been of sunlit meadows full of flowers and singing birds; an outdoor French cafe with tiny cups of espresso; of satin sheets and feather pillows; and always the two of them: walking, talking, holding hands, making love.

She fairly skipped around her tiny apartment, feeling light

and airy and giddy. She stepped on the scale: one forty-six. She'd lost seventeen pounds without really thinking about it. Wow! Eleven more. That was her target. Then she'd buy herself some new clothes.

Visiting hours started at 1 p.m., giving her time to shower and think about what she wanted to accomplish with Terry today.

At 12:45 she pulled into the hospital parking lot and turned stone cold. Getting out of a car she had just passed was Holly Bouquet. Carrie kept on driving, took the exit lane and left the ramp, lying to the attendant that she had just dropped someone off so she did not have to pay the parking fee.

Now what?

She drove down Masonic Avenue to Haight Street, then over to Market and up toward Union Square. She stopped for coffee but resisted the urge to have an apple fritter. She drove for more than an hour, then pulled off the Embarcadero and called the hospital. Reaching the nurses station just outside Castro's room she asked: "Is Terry Castro still in room 1165?" When she got an affirmative answer, her next question was: "Does he have any visitors?"

"Yes, his wife is with him," was the response.

Fuck! Fuck! Fuck! Why doesn't that lying bitch go back to wherever she came from? That's probably what she was doing to him; fucking him.

Carrie decided to drown her anger in lunch...and a glass—or a bottle—of wine. She drove back to her apartment, stopping at Ernie's Off-Sale on the way to buy a bottle of three-dollar merlot.

She stood in front of her grimy stove making ramen and drinking her cheap wine. In her current state of mind she knew there was no chance of communicating with Terry. She would try again tomorrow.

* * *

Castro was disappointed when the woman who walked through the door was his ex-wife.

Holly turned on the television set, sat down next to the bed, held his hand and watched the 49ers play the Atlanta Falcons.

He hovered above, watching, not wanting to leave in case Carrie showed up. At half time he decided to look for her. He saw her sitting by herself with a bowl of untouched noodles and a nearly empty bottle of wine in front of her. She looked sad. He tried to convey his thoughts to her but she did not respond.

He spent the rest of the day floating above the Presidio, watching families enjoy the fall weather and each other. They were happy. He was not.

* * *

Carrie awoke on Monday with a slight hangover and a new plan. She called in sick, then went directly to the hospital.

"I'm sorry, but visiting hours don't start until 1 p.m.," the nurse at the station informed her.

Carrie explained that she was a therapist, and then played the Leon Day card, dropping the name of hospital administrator Jim Harris in the process. An immediate exception to the visiting hours was made.

She walked into room 1165. "Are you here, Dr. Castro?" she asked. She sensed nothing and tears welled up in her eyes. "Please be here. I'm sorry I didn't come yesterday."

Still nothing. Carrie pulled the chair next to the bed and took Castro's hand. Tears ran down her cheeks. She leaned in, resting her forehead on the sheets covering his thigh, and began to sob.

"Are you all right?" An attendant in scrubs stuck his head in the room.

"Yes. Yes, I'm fine," she said, trying to compose herself, wiping away tears.

"Should I call a nurse?"

"No. Everything is fine."

He quickly checked the monitors. "Okay." The head withdrew.

Carrie exhaled and tried to bring calm back into the room. She waited. I'm trying too hard, she thought. Again, she laid her head on Castro's covered thigh, but this time it was her cheek, not her forehead. She closed her eyes.

Are you all right?

She snapped awake. How long had she been sleeping?

"Dr. Castro?"

Yes.

Oh, thank God, she thought.

Do you think there really is one?

"What?"

God. Is there really a God?

"I don't know." Overwhelmed by emotion, at this point she didn't care. "I am so sorry I didn't come yesterday."

I understand. I came looking for you. You looked sad.

"And a little drunk," Carrie confessed. "How could you see me?"

I am not attached to my body. I just think of someone or something and I'm there instantly. I don't really understand it.

Has he been watching me all the time, Carrie thought, thinking of standing naked on the bathroom scale. "Have you seen me before? Outside the hospital?" she asked.

Yes. There was a long pause. *You look like the women in a Titian painting, Venus of Urbino, but I stopped watching you because I felt like a voyeur.*

The artistic reference was lost on Carrie, but she thought, please don't stop.

"Can you see me now?" she asked.

Yes.

She leaned forward and hugged his torso, tears welling in her eyes. He had actually gone looking for her. After a moment she sat up.

"Are you ready to continue with what we started Saturday?" she asked, gathering her emotions. She waited for a sense of calm to return.

"Tell me more about the white warriors," she said.

Chapter 23

Mahogany was skeptical when Carrie called and said she had made contact with Terry Castro.

After Carrie had left the luncheon on Saturday, Holly had shared with the Days her opinion of Carrie and her "gift," warned them that, in her opinion, Carrie was taking advantage of them. Both Leon and Mahogany had instantly liked Holly. She was intelligent, self-assured, outgoing and left no impression that she wanted anything from them. Her warning about Carrie did not seem to have any ulterior motive. On the other hand, it was clear from her sullen behavior that Carrie disliked Holly.

Holly's opinion, combined with Carrie's demeanor at the luncheon, left both Leon and Mahogany wondering whether it was time to sever relations with her.

Mahogany broached the subject with Vikter, since it was Vikter who had first recommended her and she was his niece, but he counselled against cutting her loose.

"Well, it's obviously up to you," he said, "but it seems to me that her counseling has benefited Leon and it might be tough to start over with someone new."

So Mahogany, despite her misgivings, had scheduled a meeting with Carrie.

They met in the theater room at Carrie's request.

"I'd like to show you something in the video," Carrie said. "Something I learned from Dr. Castro." The lack of enthusiasm from Leon and Mahogany surprised Carrie.

Sanjay loaded the DVD and handed the remote to Carrie.

"Does this have an ultra slow motion function?" she asked. Sanjay showed her how she could forward the video frame by frame.

Carrie fast forwarded to the scene with the three warriors. As they faded back into the jungle she asked, "Did you notice that?"

"What?" Leon responded.

"That little shudder in the video right after the warriors had disappeared back into the jungle. Let me play it for you again."

She ran it twice, once at regular speed and once in slow motion, pointing out the exact moment of the quiver in the recording each time.

"Yes, I see it." Leon said. "So?"

"I saw it too when I started to really study the recording, but I couldn't figure out what made it happen so I just chalked it up to wind, or someone nudging the camera or something like that. But," Carrie continued, "Dr. Castro told me it might have been caused by a dart from a blowgun. Watch this."

Carrie reversed the DVD until the three warriors reappeared. Then she began to roll the video forward one frame at a time. The warriors, moving like robots, backed into the undergrowth.

"Now watch this," Carrie said, walking up to the theater screen.

Two frames later she pointed to a small blur, barely visible against the backdrop of the jungle. In the next frame the blur had moved slightly. She went through several more frames, pointing each time to the blur as it got closer and slightly larger. Then it disappeared. Carrie toggled back and forth between the last frame where the blur was visible, the frame where the blur disappeared and the frame immediately after that. She took the edge of the DVD case and placed it against the screen so that the edge of the case paralleled the trunk of one of the bamboo trees in the background of the video.

"Now watch," she said.

She ran through the three frames again. In the third frame the edge of the bamboo tree could no longer be seen, hidden behind the edge of the DVD case. She rolled to the next frame and the edge was still hidden, but in the next frame the bamboo tree once again was fully visible. She ran through the sequence again.

"That is the shudder," she said. "It was caused by the impact of the dart." She reversed the video and went back to the last frame when the blur was visible, and then forward to the next frame where it disappeared. "That is where the dart went past the camera lens. In the next frame it hits the tree and the shudder occurs."

"So Terry Castro told you all of this," Leon said.

"Not exactly. He told me that the cameras were attached to the front of the observation post and that the tree which the dart hit was part of the back wall. And, of course, he told me about the dart. I figured out the rest when I got one of the techs at my office to show me how to run the DVD on one of our state-of-the-art DVD players."

Leon was still skeptical. "The blur could be a bird, or an insect," he said.

"No," Carrie said, unused to contradicting Leon but confident in her next piece of evidence. "Dr. Castro said that after the dart hit the tree trunk he got the students out of the observation post and back to their Land Rover. Then he went back to get what he thought, at the time, was an arrow. He said when he dug it out of the tree it was too short to be an arrow, and then he realized that the things strapped over the backs of the warriors were blowpipes and not bows. I understood him to say that he turned around after cutting the dart out of the tree and one of the warriors was standing in front of the observation post with a blowgun aimed at him. Terry...err...Dr. Castro said he held the dart out in front of him, thinking that the warrior had come to retrieve the dart, and placed it in a gap in the front wall of the observation post. Now watch this."

She forwarded the DVD to the second scene where the single warrior and his blowpipe appeared. Then she backed it up, reversed it and started forward again.

"See how jumpy the video is in this part," she said. "I think that is where Terry is cutting the dart out of the tree, jostling the camera. We didn't notice it before because we always fast-forwarded to where the warrior was. The jumpy part continues as the warrior comes out of the jungle. Then it stops. That's probably when Terry...Dr. Castro...finished cutting it out of the tree. It's no longer jumpy when the warrior appears to give that little nod. That's when Terry offered the dart back to the warrior."

"Are you telling me that this warrior, as you call him, is thanking Dr. Castro?" Leon asked.

"Maybe he's just acknowledging the offer," Mahogany interjected, speaking up for the first time since Carrie began running the video. It seemed to annoy Leon.

"This is all conjecture, based on a jumpy camera and a blur," he snorted.

"Not entirely," Carrie said, thankful for Mahogany's apparent support.

She turned back to the screen and started to move the video forward on a frame-by-frame basis again. Even at that pace the movements of the warrior were swift. A step forward. A long sinewy arm extended, its hand disappearing at the bottom of the screen. She stopped at the next frame. There, between a thumb and two bony fingers, was a primitive feathered dart with a long narrow head. In the next frame it was gone.

She flipped back to the frame with the dart and turned to face Mahogany and Leon. They both sat staring at the screen. Leon gave a slight shake of his head as if to clear it.

"I'll be damned," he said. "Is that how Terry got poisoned? The dart?"

Carrie nodded, feeling satisfaction in having broken through Leon's hostile veneer.

"But you said the dart hit a tree, not Terry," Mahogany interjected.

"I know," Carrie replied. "I'm still trying to sort that out. The communication from Terry was kind of jumbled at that point. I think he might have gotten a little excited, but as nearly as I could understand he may have cut himself when he cut the dart out of the tree. I plan to revisit that with him when I go back to see him tomorrow."

"Well, it's all very interesting," Leon said, a tinge of exasperation returning to his voice, "but how does any of this help Terry?"

"I'm not sure yet," Carrie responded, "but I'm hoping this is just the beginning. He did ask me to say thank you to both of you and tell you that they are going to move him to a nursing home. He wasn't happy about that."

* * *

Vikter drummed his fingers on his desk. He knew that his niece had been at the Days' home the night before, but they had spent most of the evening out of reach of the transmitters, probably in the theater watching the Amazon video, he thought. But the only thing he knew for sure was that the conversation must have included something about Castro because the front-door transmitter had recorded Mahogany saying that she would call the hospital about Castro being moved to a nursing home.

He picked up the phone and got Carrie's voice mail.

"Carrie. It's Uncle Vikter. Give me a call. Just wanted to see how you're doing and tell you about a call I got from Mahogany Day."

He hung up, then dialed Leon. As usual, Sanjay answered and delivered the phone to Leon. They agreed to expedite their weekly meeting. Vikter would come to the Day home that afternoon. They hung up.

Vikter opened a hanging file drawer, removed the false bottom and took out his last two transmitters. He then opened a small box that had been delivered the day before. The label on the box read: "MAC-SDRRIR Smoke Detector Hidden Camera." He put the transmitters in an inner pocket of his tonal plaid silk

Brioni suit jacket. He put the smoke detector in his briefcase.

He was ready to visit Leon.

Chapter 24

She had mentally asked the question multiple times during her semi-successful effort to concentrate on her work: "Dr. Castro... Terry...are you here?" She had hoped to save herself a trip to the hospital...and that he hadn't stopped watching her...but there was no response.

As she inched her way up California Street in rush hour traffic she asked the question again but got the same silence in return. Disappointed, she checked her messages and picked up one from Uncle Vikter. She hit "call back" and waited. On the third ring Vikter answered.

"How's my favorite niece?"

"You have me on speed dial?"

"Of course I do."

A little ray of self-respect coursed through Carrie. "You called," she said.

"Just wondering how you were. I was concerned because I got a call from Mahogany Day, but I was at their house this afternoon and got it all straightened out."

"Got what all straightened out?"

"Nothing serious. They were just wondering if you still were interested in acting as the intermediary between Leon and his brother. I assured them that you were."

Carrie was silent. Why did they think that, she thought? Are they really that upset with her?

It never occurred to her that Uncle Vikter might be lying.

"I understand that you've come up with some interesting information from the video of Dr. Castro's mishap," Vikter continued after a pause.

"Have you seen it?"

"I saw it this afternoon. They said you had slowed it down so you could actually see the arrow that poisoned Dr. Castro."

"It's a blowgun dart, not an arrow, and I'm still not sure if that is how Terry...Dr. Castro...got poisoned."

"Well, whatever it is," Vikter said, "I encouraged Leon to talk to the university about doing an expedition to track down that white tribe. I thought they might be able to find the antidote for Dr. Castro's poisoning. So, you keep working on it from your end, and together you and Berrie University might solve the problem."

Vikter hung up, pleased with himself. In a few short hours he had managed to plant two more bugs in the Days' home, a camera in the front vestibule, and set in motion a series of events that would keep Leon and Mahogany busy and absent from Day Pharmaceuticals.

Carrie hung up with an idea. Uncle Vikter's mention of an antidote had sent her mind spinning. Forty-five minutes later Carrie walked into room 1165.

"Are you here, Dr. Castro?"

She pulled the chair to his bedside, took his hand and let the room settle until her mind was focused entirely upon him. Then she repeated her question. An affirmative response came immediately.

"You said you can transport yourself just by thinking."

It seems to work that way.

"I want to try something; an experiment. Are you willing to try?

Depends. What do you have in mind?

"I have a copy of the video from your observation post. I'd like you to watch it with me—"

How did you get that? Castro interrupted. *I want to see it.*

"From Leon and Mahogany, to answer your question," Carrie replied. "I want you to watch it and see the warrior that poisoned you—"

Again Castro interrupted: *He didn't poison me. I cut my finger when I was examining the dart. The tip had a dark substance on it that*

I assume was the curare poison. So, to be correct, he didn't poison me. I did it to myself.

"I want you to see the warrior," Carrie patiently continued. "Then I want you to see if you can transport yourself to where the warrior is located. That's the experimental part."

They reconvened at Carrie's office less than an hour later. Carrie popped the DVD into the player and, after confirming Castro's presence, ran it at regular speed, narrating her assumptions about the momentary quiver in the recording after the three warriors had disappeared back into the jungle, and the erratic portion of the video just before the single warrior reappeared. Then she reran it using the ultra-slow speed during the single warrior scene. All the while Castro was silent.

She stopped the recording on a frame in which the tallest warrior was in full view.

"I think he's a chief, or a medicine man, or somehow special because he has the pouch around his neck and the other two don't," Carrie said. "I thought if you could go to where he is you might be able to find the antidote for the poison."

Carrie waited for Castro's response. She could tell he was still there in the video room with her and could sense his brain activity. After a minute of silence she inquired, "Dr. Castro?"

Not sure it will do any good, unless this super power of mine includes understanding languages and pharmacology. What if I can't come back? I really don't know how this teleporting thing really works, or its limits.

Carrie hadn't thought of that possibility.

"Maybe it was a dumb idea," she said, suddenly afraid to lose Castro.

*On the other hand...*the scientist in him coming to the fore... *the doctors have given up on me, so maybe my only chance is to go and observe them. It's worth a try.*

Bittersweet. It was the only word Carrie could think of to describe how she felt. Bittersweet.

I'm worried too, Castro conveyed, reading her thoughts, *but I think we should run a mini experiment right now to see if I can even do it. I'll try to transport myself and then come right back here.*

Carrie held her breath. The Regulator clock on the colorless wall ticked as the skinny second hand made its way around the circuit. Once. Twice. Three times. She tried to force negative thoughts from her mind. Five minutes passed. Ten.

My God, I've lost him.

* * *

Amaru scratched himself, then pushed his scrotum aside to inspect a bite on his inner thigh. He pondered how his end would come, and whether he had enough time to pass on the necessary wisdom to Urco. Surely, the Great Spirit would not take him until he had properly prepared his son. The thought gave him comfort.

He rose from his normal squatting position and ambled toward the place where the shaman of the past instructed him to plant the seeds. At his direction the women of the tribe had built a vine fence around the plot, and he had called upon the Great Spirit to bless the land and the sun that shown upon the space. He then summoned Urco and taught him to plant.

"These," he said, pointing to where they had just planted woorari seeds, "we will replant after they have sprouted and grown to be as long as your finger. They must be replanted next to a tree that is exposed to the sun part of the day."

"And these," Amaru continued, referring to the ashwagandha, "must be replanted in a shady place next to falling water so the mist keeps the plants cool."

"And what of these others," Urco asked after it became apparent that his father was done speaking.

"They will grow where we have planted them."

When the light had ebbed on that day the village gathered

to give thanks. Amaru once again summoned the spirits of the shamans and praised them for their wisdom and guidance, while the men and young boys gyrated in dance, their bodies bone white in the glow of the full moon. The spoils of the hunt from the past few days were consumed and chicha drunk until stomachs were distended and heads bleary. The Chilco had not had such a festival since the last time they had been forced to find a new home. Only Amaru was old enough to remember that time.

Now, as he approached the vine fence, Amaru mentally commended the women for the jumbies they had erected at each corner to scare away the birds. He lifted a rawhide loop from around a post, scooted the gate open and entered the garden. The sun had risen only three times since the festival but already shoots of maca and ashwagandha had broken the surface. He inspected the plot for animal tracks, then conducted his half-dance, half-march around the perimeter while silently chanting a spell to keep predators and pestilence away from the plants. Tomorrow he would show Urco how to spread dried mint and citronella grass to repel insects.

* * *

The rushing sound in her brain, like a freshening wind in the treetops, signaled the end of three of the saddest days Carrie had spent in her twenty-six years.

She was sitting in front of the computer screen at work, the usual cacophony in her brain on mute, when the slow realization she was not alone seeped into her consciousness.

It worked.

She was visibly upset, and Castro did not understand why.

"Where have you been," she blurted. "You were going to come right back."

Julie looked up from across the aisle. Carrie waived her off, mouthed "I'll be right back," and went searching for a private place. Unable to think of any other place, she went to the women's bathroom, entered a stall and sat down.

"Where have you been," she said, barely able to hold back her tears. "I thought I'd lost you forever...because of my stupid idea."

It wasn't stupid. It worked. I saw the white warrior. In fact, I saw the whole tribe.

"But you were coming right back."

I did.

"It's been three days!"

Carrie heard the bathroom door open.

"Are you all right?" Julie asked from outside the stall.

"I'm fine, just some unexpected news."

"Are you sure?"

"I'm fine. I'll tell you about it later."

The bathroom door closed as Julie left.

I'm sorry. I didn't realize how long I was gone. I don't have any concept of time.

Carrie exhaled. "Of course," she whispered. "I forgot." Then, "I missed you," after a long pause.

The last part surprised Castro. The way in which she said it conveyed more than the words. He had had many flirtations before Holly and had always been able to diffuse them with his breezy style and glib conversation, but this was radically different. He was not real, not in a physical sense. He was a wraith. How could someone love him in this state? How could he love someone back? And particularly Carrie. She was not just another woman. She was his link to the visceral world. He decided to change the subject.

The warrior. His name is Amaru. And you were right. He is the head of his tribe. It appears he's also a medicine man and a deity, all rolled into one like the Inca. He looks like he may be the oldest member of the tribe. Maybe that's why they follow him.

Castro told her of the planting of the garden, of the festival and of the strange ritual when Amaru appeared to put himself in a trance and communicate with others. He described the place as being much like the area where he and his students had observed the three warriors: dense plant life, small streams, trees a hundred or two hundred feet tall and sunny patches where there was a break in the leafy canopy. He related his observations of the tribe; only a few hundred in number, all fair skinned and yellow haired, all extremely tall. They had to be a remnant of the tribe the Incas called Chachapoyas, the cloud people.

At Carrie's urging he described the women of the tribe: lighter of skin and hair than the men. Except for the nearly white hair on their heads, virtually hairless. Tall (all well over six feet), slim hipped and small-breasted, he thought it might be difficult for them to have children. Several were obviously pregnant, but he saw very few children. The women did all the physical labor, except for hunting, like most primitive tribes.

"Did you learn anything about the poison or an antidote," Carrie asked.

No. Although I got the feeling that the garden they planted may have something to do with that. I have to go back. Carrie really didn't want to hear those words. "Come back to me," she said.

Chapter 25

His bed was empty.

Carrie spun out the door and confronted a nurse in the hallway. "Where is Dr. Castro, the patient in room 1165?"

"He's been transferred to a rehab facility."

That didn't make any sense. Carrie had told the Days about Terry's fear of being transferred; his dread of being forgotten. They said they were going to take care of it.

"Who ordered the transfer?"

"Dr. Subbiah," the nurse replied. "It was done at the request of Mrs. Castro."

"What?" Carrie shrieked. "She's not his wife!"

The nurse gave a not-my-problem shrug and continued down the hall.

Carrie dialed Mahogany.

"They've moved Terry to a rehab facility," she blurted as soon as Mahogany answered.

"I know."

That was not the answer Carrie expected.

"How? I thought you were going to make sure they didn't move him out of the hospital."

"Leon and I talked it over with Holly," Mahogany said. "We agreed he shouldn't be taken to a nursing home, but at a rehab center he can get physical therapy on a regular basis."

Carrie couldn't argue with the logic, but it stung that they had discussed it with Holly and not with her.

"Oh," was all she could say.

* * *

The rehab center was on the southern edge of San Francisco, more than an hour's drive from the hospital. During rush hour it would be worse. She followed the signs on the large campus to the main building and the admission center.

"Are you related to Mr. Castro?" the elderly admissions volunteer asked, looking at the sign-in sheet.

"No." Carrie shifted uneasily from one foot to the other. "I'm a friend."

"I don't see your name on the list of approved visitors."

"How do I get on the list?"

"The patient would have to add you."

"The patient is in a coma."

The admissions lady hesitated, looking confused. Carrie pressed her momentary advantage.

"I know he's just been transferred here from USFMC. I'm sure Holly just forgot to put me on the list."

The lady looked at the visitor's list again, gave a timid little nod and added Carrie's name. She printed out a visitor's badge and handed it to Carrie.

Castro's room was sunnier and more spacious than his hospital room. There was a couch against one wall and an overstuffed chair in the corner next to it, separated by an end table with a lamp and clock radio. The walls were stark white. A framed poster of a gray kitten hanging from a branch by one paw hung over the head of the bed. The poster and cheap furniture gave the whole room a cheesy feeling. Castro was dressed in a gray sweatsuit and white socks. His hair was wet and, judging by the antiseptic smell, he had just had a bath. His unattended beard was shaggy and uneven with a few strands of gray. The electronic monitors that had been his constant companions at the hospital were nowhere to be seen.

Carrie stood by the bed, holding his hand, watching him breathe. This had to be Holly's choice. The Days would not have moved Terry to a low budget place like this.

She sat on the edge of the narrow bed and thought of trying to contact Castro, then decided against it, knowing his spirit was with the Chilco and not wanting to disrupt him or expend the energy in a fruitless attempt. Besides, angry thoughts of Holly kept interfering with her concentration. She doubted that she could reach the stage of inner peace needed to reach out to Castro.

The press of his covered leg against her bottom was the only bright spot in her visit. She wished that their bare skin could touch. Amid that thought an attendant came in the room. Carrie left.

On her way home she dialed Mahogany again.

"It has an excellent reputation as a rehabilitation center," Mahogany said in defense of the choice of locations. "Holly didn't see any reason to put him in an expensive room since he couldn't enjoy it. If he regains consciousness we can move him to a nicer room."

"But it's so far from you," Carrie said. "It will take you two hours or more to visit him. There must be something closer."

"It was Holly's choice. This is closer to the airport which is more convenient for her."

Carrie hung up and exhaled, blowing hard through her pursed lips to relieve her frustration. The words "selfish bitch" hung like a permanent tattoo in her head.

Her anger, refreshed daily because of the distance to the rehab center and the absence of Castro's spirit, kept Carrie from visiting him the rest of the week. On Saturday she stepped on the scale after her morning shower: one forty. Not too bad, she thought, looking in the mirror. What had Terry called her? "Venus of Urbino". She was surprised that she remembered. She picked up her phone and tapped v-e-n-u-s-o-f-u-r-b-i-n-o in the search engine. A blurb appeared with a tiny picture in the upper right corner. She tapped on the picture to enlarge it.

So that's how he sees me, she thought, looking at the painting of a strikingly beautiful young nude woman reclining on a sumptuous couch, her long hair spilling over the pillows and her left hand tucked between her legs, concealing herself. She had never thought of herself as beautiful, but Castro had compared her to this opulent masterpiece; this virulent, luscious woman. Again, she looked at her naked self in the mirror, this time with new eyes. Tentatively she touched herself, mimicking the painting, and felt an unexpected surge of sexuality course through her. A small gasp shot up through her body, escaping from her lips.

With the effects of the small pleasure still lingering, Carrie picked up a bottle of lavender-scented body lotion from the bathroom counter and squirted a dollop into her hand. She spread it on her arms and legs, then made a leisurely process of getting dressed, slipping on black silk underwear from Victoria's Secret which she had bought as a gift to herself on her last birthday. She chose a seamless cami in burgundy, topped with an ivory semi-sheer blouse. She stepped into a short, burgundy Dirndl skirt she had bought online, then checked herself out in the mirror. She was happy with what she saw.

She decided it would be a good day to visit Terry Castro.

Carrie showed up at his room with a barber kit in hand. He was still lying on his back in gray sweats, but now an intervenous feeding tube was attached to his left arm. The bag hanging from the stanchion beside his bed was filled with a clear fluid. She confirmed with a male attendant passing in the hallway that Castro was not scheduled for rehab until mid-afternoon, and then asked for a chair to set beside the bed, saying she was a barber, there to give the patient a haircut and a shave. He accepted her explanation without question and brought her a folding chair.

Carrie took a towel from the bathroom and wrapped it around Castro, tucking it under his chin, then gently worked the shaving foam into his beard. She had decided not to use the electric shaver in the kit. Shaving him with a razor felt more intimate. She picked up the razor, now suddenly questioning her choice. What if she cut him?

Timidly she began, at first only scraping off the shaving cream and missing the whiskers entirely, but eventually she got the hang of it and inch-by-square-inch the whiskers came off. She wiped the excess shaving cream off with the towel and sat back to admire her handiwork and Castro's handsome face.

She poured a puddle of aftershave into the palm of her hand and then massaged it into his cheeks and neck. Then, as before, she leaned forward and buried her face in his neck, inhaling the combined scent of the aftershave and Terry Castro. She withdrew, kissing him on the cheek, and budged the over-stuffed chair a foot at a time until it was in front of the door. She then went back to the bed and lay down next to Castro, putting her right arm around his waist, careful to avoid the feeding tube. The single bed didn't provide much room for two and that was just fine with Carrie.

She lay beside him, inhaling his essence. She moved her right arm and her hand slid under the waistband of his sweatpants. Yesterday she might have struggled with the guilt of loving a man in a coma. Today she didn't care.

Castro's body responded as she stroked his penis, reaching full erection quickly. Carrie struggled to inch his pants downward, to free it from confinement. She lifted herself so she could use both hands, and, succeeding, took the head of his engorged cock in her mouth. She ran her lips the full length of his shaft, up and down, sucking, until she felt herself become wet. She slid off the bed, stepped out of her panties, and then climbed back on, straddling Castro. She guided his rigid shaft into her wet vagina and gasped as she enveloped him. She allowed herself to be entered by an inch, two, then lifted herself until the head of his cock was about to escape her grasp, then lowered herself again. She repeated the motion once more, then drove herself downward until she had his entire cock inside her, letting out an involuntary, muffled scream as she reached orgasm simultaneously with the culmination of her thrust. She collapsed on top of him and laid there. As her breathing slowly returned to normal Carrie began rhythmically moving her hips, languishing in the feel of his still firm cock in the sheath of her vagina. Her movement gained speed and urgency until she approached climax again, then felt him come inside her. Her moan soared, gaining volume as she exploded in heedless ecstasy. All her muscles and tendons and tissue instantly lost all tension and her body spread over Castro like melted butter. Stars and pinwheels were still going off in her head when she became aware he was there.

Well, hello, Ms. Waters.

She wrapped her arms tightly around him. "You're here," she murmured.

I came when you called.

She felt his humor. He was in her body, and now he was in her head. It was the happiest moment of her life.

"Thank you for coming back," she whispered, again moving her hips, trying to absorb him as deeply as possible. "I know I should have asked first, but you weren't here and..."

My pleasure...really...there is nothing to forgive.

"Did you get pleasure from it?" she asked after a pause. "Is it the same...an orgasm, I mean."

I felt something...but it wasn't the same.

"I'm sorry."

Don't be. It was satisfying, but not in the same way as an orgasm. I can only imagine what it would be like if I—

"Ssh. Someday," she said, burrowing against his body. "Someday."

They lay together for several minutes until words again appeared in her head: *I have a lot to tell you.* That snapped Carrie out of her malaise. She rose up on her elbows so she could look at his face.

"Did you find the antidote?" she said aloud.

No. Not yet. But I think there's a chance that you might.

Carrie rolled off, squeezing Castro one last time with her

thighs, and she settled next to him on the narrow bed. "How," she asked.

I think Amaru may be a medium, too. I've watched him go into a trance and then start talking like he's talking to someone, but there's no one there. At least no one that I could see. I couldn't—

The door of the room banged against the chair. It banged a second time. "Hey." She heard the male attendant's voice.

"Just a minute," she half-shouted as she slid off the bed. She scooped her panties off the floor and stuffed them in the shaving kit bag. She did her best to tug up Castro's sweatpants and straighten her own clothes. The door banged against the chair again.

"Just a minute," she repeated. She threw a blanket over Castro and ran a hand through her hair, then pushed on the chair, moving it away from the door. The instant it cleared the jamb the door swung open, almost hitting her. The male attendant stood in the doorway, along with Holly.

"What's going on?" the attendant wanted to know. Holly skewered Carrie with her eyes.

"I was having a session with my client and I didn't want to be disturbed." Carrie recited the phrase she had rehearsed in case of an interruption. It came out a little too quickly. Holly's expression said bullshit.

"You can't block the door," the attendant said, visibly upset.

"Sorry. I didn't want to be disturbed," Carrie repeated.

"I think you better leave," Holly said. The tone of her voice could have froze water.

On Monday Carrie learned that her name had been removed from the visitors list.

* * *

She reconnected with Castro almost immediately following her return to her apartment. He told her that the white tribe communicated more with subtle actions and body language than with words. Their language was a dialect unfamiliar to him, punctuated with clicking noises and sounds made by fluttering of the tongue. He detected an occasional word or phrase that was similar to Quechua, the native Indian language with which he had become passably conversant during his trips to Peru but, for the most part, he had to guess at what they were communicating.

The tribe called themselves "Chilco" and Amaru was definitely the leader. He spent a great deal of time with a young giant named Urkl or Urco or something like that, and from their interaction it appeared the younger man might be the heir-apparent to Amaru.

He had watched Amaru go through the trance ritual a second time: chewing on some kind of leaves, then apparently passing out and falling on his face, then rising to his knees and conversing with the air in a singsong hypnotic voice. It was during this second trance that Castro considered that Amaru might be a medium, like Carrie.

Have you ever tried to talk to another medium? One who's alive?

"There was a woman who I met at a seminar," Carrie responded. "She lives in Los Angeles. We communicate with each other, but it isn't like we talk. It's more like I sense something about her, like she's sad or stressed, and then I call or text her. Almost without exception my feeling about her is right. It works the other way too. She can sense things about me, but she's the only person I have that connection with."

"I could try to contact this Amaru," she went on, "but I don't know how I'd communicate with him even if we did make contact. I don't speak his language."

The two, Carrie and Castro's spirit, coexisted in silence for several minutes.

What about dead people? When you talk to people who have died do you have to speak the same language?

Carrie thought about that for a moment.

"I don't think so," she said, "because I actually don't hear words. They just sort of appear in my head. Once I contacted an uncle of a Jewish woman. I understood him perfectly. Afterwards the woman said her uncle only spoke Yiddish."

Do you think you could contact the person that he is talking to when he's in his trance?

"I'd have to have a name. If I had a name I could try."

Both times I saw him do that he said a name: Hatun Cayo. That might be who he was talking to.

For the remainder of the day Carrie tried to clear her mind so she could turn inward and find the state of nirvana that was the cornerstone for communicating with those on the other side. Each time she approached the threshold level of inner peace her mind turned to Castro's body and to the quivering that still excited her loins.

Finally, she gave up.

* * *

Despite Carrie's objection, Castro's spirit returned to the Chilco, while she spent an unsuccessful, lonesome week, made more lonesome by her banishment from the rehab center, making futile attempts to contact Hatun Cayo and Amaru. Her week was punctuated with sessions with Leon and two other clients, her boss on a rampage to close out the year-end financial records, and an evening birthday party for one of her friends who tried to hook her up with some guy. In between all of this she did research on the Chilco, Chachapoyas and Hatun Cayo, hoping that by learning more about the culture, or the person, she might be able to find a door that her mind could walk through. She watched the observation post video again, stopping at the frame that showed Amaru's face the best. She tried to meld her mind into the picture; to become Amaru. She attempted to use the frame that showed the dart to guide her mind to a place that might be occupied by Amaru's living spirit.

Nothing she did brought positive results.

On Friday night, home from work with the TV providing background noise, a Marie Callendar's dinner in the microwave, and a just-opened beer providing her only companionship, Carrie relaxed for the first time all week. Relaxation quickly morphed to loneliness. God, how I wish he was here in the flesh she thought, but not even the spirit of Terry Castro made an appearance.

She punched "menu" on the remote and looked for a movie. Finding none, she settled for a network that specialized in old shows. She took her dinner out of the microwave, picked up her half-empty beer and plopped on to the couch to watch *Twilight Zone*.

What else, she thought in resignation when she realized the episode was about a séance and a necromancer who was, or was not, a con man. She was about to switch it off, but something kept her from doing so. She watched as the necromancer conjured a spirit from the other side as a widow in black sat at a tiny round table, gazing at a crystal ball. While the necromancer was communing with the spirit, a second spirit entered his head. He told the woman that a second spirit had appeared. "Oh, no," she said as the two spirits, one her late husband and the other her deceased lover, began to argue.

There it was, right in front of her. She had been going about this all wrong. Carrie clicked off the TV, put the half-finished dinner and beer on the counter, and turned the lights down. She pulled a straight-backed chair to the window and sat, looking out at the lights of the city. Her breathing slowed and peace descended like a silk shroud. Her head slumped into the palms of her upturned hands. Minutes passed. Ten. Thirty. Ninety. Milky thoughts formed in her mind. *Can you hear me, Terry? I need you to come to me now. I know how to contact the white warrior.*

Chapter 26

Boorrrup. Boorrrup.

Drawn by the distinctive croak of the golden frogs, Amaru and Urco crept through a swampy glade, inching toward a pond nestled in a dense growth of ferns and Heliconia. The orange and yellow heliconia blossoms, radiant in the dappled sun, provided natural camouflage for the vividly colored frogs.

Boorrrup. Boorrrup. Boorrrup. The sounds overlapped.

Many frogs, Amaru thought, but if the flowers extended to the waterline it would be difficult, even for his practiced eyes, to detect the tiny creatures. A soft click from Urco's throat drew Amaru's attention. He followed his son's gaze and to the golden spot, no more than an inch in diameter, distinct against the green of a fern. A faint look of satisfaction crinkled his craggy face. They edged closer.

Each warrior carried a curved stick, about eighteen inches long, with a cupped end. Tied through a small hole at the top of the cup was a thin string made of hemp fibers. The other end of the string was tied to a two-pronged dart carved from the root of a walking tree.

In one smooth motion Urco set the end of the dart in the cup, and with his other hand firmly holding the stick, flicked it in the direction of the gold spot. The dart pierced the frog and a simultaneous yank of the cord brought the skewered amphibian back to Urco's feet. He bent, and grasping the shaft, deposited the frog in a leather pouch which hung from a cord around his waist.

The fern had not moved, but the croaking had stopped.

Amaru frowned. His son had much to learn.

* * *

Castro had sensed they were going hunting when Amaru and Urco left the village, but hunting frogs was not what he had expected.

They had passed several ponds where brightly colored frogs and other aquatic creatures made their presence noisily known, but the two hunters had shown no interest until they had heard the distinct croak: *boorrrup, boorrrup*.

Urco's throaty click also drew Castro's attention, and he followed Urco's gaze to the tiny gold frog on the fern. He now understood. They were hunting the most poisonous of all the painted frogs, the golden poison dart frog.

Castro floated above and watched as they speared five more frogs. In each case the frog was speared and retrieved without a quiver of the leaf or reed upon which the frog sat, but the frogs killed by Amaru never touched the ground. He used the string not only to retrieve the frogs but to suspend them in midair before depositing them in his pouch. Urco watched and his third frog went from reed to pouch without sound or contact with the ground.

Amaru's slight nod showed his approval.

They left the pond with six golden frogs, although they could have taken many more. The Chilcos' symbiotic relationship with the rainforest, and the creatures with which they shared it, was not lost on Castro. In all of his studies, only certain tribes of American Indians seemed to have the same copacetic relationship with their environment.

* * *

Upon their return to the village the dead frogs were transferred into a clay vessel half-filled with a mixture of water and fat from a tapir that had been killed in a hunt several days earlier. The vessel was covered and hung from a broken tree branch. That evening, after the cooking fire had burnt itself to coals, the men of the tribe, approximately sixty in number, gathered. Amaru took a metal cooking pot and a gourd from his lean-to. The pot was the only metal object in the village, other than the heads of the blowgun darts.

He summoned Urco to join him in the middle of the ring, then placed the pot on the coals of the dying fire and poured a dark, molasses-like substance from the gourd into the pot. He then asked Urco to fetch the clay pot from the tree. Amaru speared one of the dead frogs on the tip of a dart and dropped it into the pot. The two men squatted, waiting, occasionally uttering a word or a sound in what served as conversation between father and son.

The last light of evening faded as the mixture began to bubble. Amaru stirred it with a flat stick, chanting quietly. The circle of fair-skinned warriors grew quiet. After a few minutes Amaru lifted the stick, touched it with his finger and put his finger in his mouth. Involuntarily he grimaced. He lowered the stick and resumed stirring. Another period of silence passed, the only sound being Amaru's murmured chant and the bubbling of the curare.

Again, he lifted the stick and tasted the curare. His face contorted again, but this time he offered the stick to his son. Urco instinctively reached for the stick, then hesitated and put his hands back at his sides. He shook his head.

Amaru's eyes grew wide. He thrust the flat stick toward his son. Urco did not move. In a loud, animated voice Amaru berated the young man, then tried to reason with him when Urco did not respond to his threats. Only the presence of the other men of the tribe kept Amaru from pleading with his son.

The others quickly injected themselves into the stalemate, most directing their scolding chatter at Urco. Paquin, one of the elders, addressed Amaru directly, pointing at a young warrior across the circle. The young man rose, but Amaru dismissed both him and Paquin with curt words and a wave of the back of his hand. The circle grew quiet.

Through all the cacophony Urco stood, expressionless, saying nothing. When Amaru turned again to him Urco reached out and took the flat stick without it being offered. He held the stick above his head and turned slowly, fixing his gaze on each man in the circle. Then, in a steady voice, he delivered the longest monologue any of them could remember. It lasted three minutes.

When he was done there was mumbling among the men, but Amaru stood, signaling silence. He uttered a few words, then looked at his son and solemnly nodded.

Urco lowered the flat stick and tasted the curare.

* * *

Carrie listened intently as Castro related the story of the golden frog hunt and the curare tasting. She had been watching television in her apartment two days after she had last tried to contact him when he had appeared without warning. She was relieved and didn't mention the time gap. She understood he would have no comprehension of it.

"Why do you think Urco didn't want to taste the curare?" she asked.

At first, I thought he was afraid that he might get poisoned, but when he finally tasted it he didn't look afraid. If anything, he looked a little triumphant, like he'd just won a debate or something. There was another young warrior who, I think, volunteered to taste the curare and he was ready to do it, but Amaru just blew him off. I think it had to be Urco and I think Urco got some kind of concession that he wanted as a condition of tasting it.

"Did you learn anything about an antidote?"

Not yet, but I haven't watched them actually make curare, yet. This batch had already been cooked and I think they were just making it stronger by adding the poison frog. After Urco tasted it all the men lined up and dipped their darts in the pot. I think they'll make a new batch of curare once the garden they've planted is grown. Maybe I'll learn something then.

"Maybe we can shortcut that," Carrie said. "I may I have a way to communicate with your shaman."

Carrie put away the clean dishes sitting on her kitchen counter as she told Castro of the episode of the *Twilight Zone* she had stumbled upon. He was enjoying watching the simple domestic scene, more than listening to the *Twilight Zone* rehash, but Carrie forged ahead with her story.

"A second spirit entered the mind of this medium when he was talking to another spirit," Carrie said.

Okay, how does that help us?

"We, and by 'we' I mean mediums, are most vulnerable when we're communicating with the other side. I think the doors are open to our minds and it's easier for someone to walk in. You've watched the shaman go into some sort of trance and talk with spirits. I think I would have a really good chance of reaching him when he's in one of those trances."

Let's say that works. What are you going to say to him? Remember that guy that you scared shitless who ran away like a baby? That one who tried to steal your dart and poisoned himself in the process? Would you help that fool by telling me the secret antidote for your poison?

Carrie laughed. "Not quite in that way. First, I'll just try to make the medium-to-medium connection. We can work on the rest once we've established that."

This sounds like it's going to take more than one contact with him. He doesn't call on the spirits very often.

"If I can reach him one time it should become easier after that. The first time is always the hardest. After that, it's like we know where the portals are."

So, you don't really need me.

You have no idea how much I need you, Carrie thought, and then blushed, realizing Castro could hear her thoughts.

"I need you to tell me when he's reaching out to the spirits," she interjected, trying to cover her momentary embarrassment. "How long do you think it takes you to go from here to the shaman or from the shaman to here?"

I have no idea. You know about me and time.

"Can we try it? Can you teleport yourself to the shaman, and then think about me and come right back?"

Sure. I think so.

"I can time it on..." Carrie suddenly realized he was gone. She picked up her phone from the kitchen table and set the stopwatch app. She bent over to set it down.

Are you done messing around with your phone?

"Really?" she said. "You're back already."

It was dark and the village was sleeping, so it was easy not to get distracted. How long did I take?

"Less than ten seconds."

* * *

Amaru knelt and carefully studied the transplanted ashwagandha. Clusters of red, maroon and nearly black flowers hung from tiny stems that had thrust their way up through the flat blanket of glossy, deep green leaves. He had already inspected the woorari vines, scraping the bark into his palm, inhaling the pungent scent and rubbing the scrapings between his fingers. It was time.

He returned to the village and counseled with his wife. Within an hour a troupe of village women, bone knives, digging tools and vine baskets in hand, paraded out of the village, singing, following Amaru and his wife. There was an excitement in the air as they began working in the small field. Amaru stood at the edge with Urco, pointing out details of the activities and relaying directions through his wife, as the women cut the taja and uprooted the maca plants. When half the plants were harvested they moved on to cutting woorari vines. The younger women stopped working long enough to entwine the elegant blossoms, the size of a man's hand, in their hair. Urco's wife, a blossom above each ear, rubbed against her husband, bringing a smile to his face for the first time.

Again, the jubilant troupe moved on, leaving half the vines untouched. The singing, dancing caravan came to a halt at the ashwagandha patch. This time Amaru gathered all of them around him in a circle and gave careful instructions in serious tones. The women cut the glossy leaves, careful not to damage the flower clusters, nor to take too many leaves from any plant. When they had finished, the timbre of their voices turned joyous again and singing punctuated their journey back to the village.

Castro, who had watched the festive harvest, came back to Carrie. *They've harvested the curare plants. It's likely that Amaru will summon the spirits soon. Be ready.*

He instantly returned to the village.

The women were stripping the bark from the woorari vines and the stems of the taja and placing them in separate piles. The tough maca root was hacked into pieces the size of a man's fist, and the ashwagandha leaves spread out in the sun to dry. The women left, taking with them the bare woorari vines which they would boil and turn into pliable thongs used to erect lean-tos. Amaru and Urco were alone in the circle that Amaru had chosen to cook the curare. The metal pot and stirring stick, along with an empty harvesting basket, lay on a reed mat next to a fire ring that the wives of the shaman and his son had built days earlier.

"You have tasted the curare," Amaru said to Urco. "That is how you test its strength. Now I will show you in what measures you must combine the makings."

The two men went from pile to pile, Amaru pointing out the various attributes of each ingredient to his son. Occasionally he would discard a piece of bark or a leaf, each time explaining why he did so. At each pile he took a portion of the vegetation and handed it to Urco so that he could feel the volume. Urco then placed each in the basket that he carried.

Amaru stopped the tutorial when their wives reappeared. The shaman's wife carefully carried a piece of wood in which a smoldering coal from the village fire burned, shielding it with her body to prevent the coal from going out. She knelt by the ring and deftly nursed a fire to life. Urco's wife, her belly distended with their fourth child, held the vessel that contained the preserved corpses of the golden dart frogs, her arms extended as far in front of her as possible so that the container did not touch her. Urco took the vessel from her. A young girl, just short of the age of union, carried water in a tall container balanced with one hand on her head. She placed it on the mat beside the fire ring. The two women and the girl left together, and Amaru resumed Urco's cooking lesson.

Amaru poured water in the pot and set it on the fire. As they waited for it to boil he retold the story of how the curare was descended from the Great Spirit, given to the tribe through Hatun Cayo who had led their people from the slaughter to survival. He also proudly told how it was his own idea to add the golden dart frog to give the poison more potency. He had done so because the larger animals, tapirs and jaguars, suffered a slow death from the poison. Adding the frogs caused them to die quickly, making their journey to the great beyond more peaceful. Amaru admitted that he had been wary the first time he added a frog, fearing that it might poison him when he tasted the curare, but he had summoned the past shaman and they had assured him it would not. As always, they were right.

The cooking took three days. Urco and Amaru slept on the ground in the circle, each taking turns stoking the cooking fire and stirring the pot. On the third day Amaru tasted it several times, searching for the correct level of bitterness. Each time he also had Urco taste the poison, which he did without any sign of reluctance.

Late in the afternoon the two men tasted the curare again, then nodded to each other. It was done. Amaru tied a pliable, tightly woven mat on top of an empty gourd. He formed a small indentation in the earth and nestled the gourd into it, testing it to make sure it was stable. He then lifted the pot and slowly poured the sticky liquid. The bones and tattered skin of the frog, now a pale amber, appeared on the mat as the curare slowly oozed through it into the gourd.

He repeated the process four more times. When five gourds had been filled, Urco and Amaru took them to the village and placed them in a neat row in the central clearing.

It was now time to ask the shaman for their blessing.

* * *

Castro had watched the entire process. He had anticipated that Amaru might do his trance-thing as thanks for a bountiful harvest, but when the cooking began it became apparent that it was not going to happen. He watched, hoping he might learn something that would suggest an antidote, but that didn't happen either.

Meanwhile Carrie waited, intellectually understanding Castro's disconnect with time but emotionally often finding herself in a lonesome funk. There was the usual crap at work, plus her last session with Leon had been strained. She was sure that her time with him was coming to an end. But more than anything it was the stress of waiting for her lover to return, the anticipated attempt to connect with the white warrior and her one chance to bring the man she loved back to her in the flesh. It was all taking its toll on her.

Carrie didn't realize how much until the morning of the fourth day since Castro had made his brief appearance to put her on notice. She stepped on the scale. It read 137.

Castro reappeared in her head that evening.

I'm certain Amaru is going to reach out to the other side. I think there must be some sort of blessing ritual for the curare they just made.

"My God, you're back," were the first words that came out of her mouth. "I missed you."

There is no time. He's about to start chewing the stuff that puts him in a trance.

Carrie was surprised by his abrupt response.

"Just go back," she said. "I'll get ready."

As quickly as she said it she knew Castro was gone. She tried her best to stuff her hurt feelings. Carrie turned off the TV and the lights. She pulled a straight-backed chair in front of the window and sat, looking out at the city lights. Her breathing slowed as she focused on the task at hand. Using information previously learned from Castro, Carrie envisioned the village and the clearing, letting all other images and thoughts wash away. She pictured the white warrior sitting on his haunches in the clearing, rocking back and forth on the balls of his feet, chewing. As he chewed, the lines on his face relaxed. His muscles seemed to lose their strength and he fell forward, face first, with no attempt to break his fall.

Voices materialized in Carrie's head. She could identify Amaru's high-pitched singsong cadence. As Castro had guessed, he was asking for a blessing on the new curare. The opaque timbre of the other voices, at least five in number, came from the spirit world. As she listened Carrie realized that Amaru was communicating with tribal shamans of the past.

"It is I, Amaru," he said, "least of all shamans of the mighty Chilco, coming to seek your blessing."

A voice with a nasal intonation responded: *You have prepared the curare well.*

Your hunting shall be successful, said a third voice, and a fourth added, *and the creatures which shall nourish your bodies shall pass peacefully into the great beyond.*

This curare has our blessing, said the fifth voice, one that sounded like the pop and crackle of a blazing fire. *But there is great concern of your son, who is marked as the next shaman. Doubt and disquiet have arisen around his refusal to taste the curare.*

"Oh, greatest of all shaman," Amaru responded to the fifth speaker. "I have taught Urco the history of the Chilco, and the essence of our survival that is the curare. I have taught him how to make the curare, and he assisted me in the cooking of that which you have just blessed. He has tasted the curare many times since he first resisted. I, too, was at first reluctant to taste the curare, but I have now served seventy years as shaman."

But he agreed only after he made a demand that violates the sacred agreement with the Great Spirit, the fiery voice said. *The secrets of the curare are only for the shaman, yet you agreed to that demand.*

"My son is marked with your mark, oh great Hatun Cayo," Amaru responded. "He is the one chosen to lead the Chilco back to our home among the clouds, back to our rightful place at the top of the world. His demand needed to be accepted for that to happen."

You have made a choice of great consequence, Amaru Topac, the burning voice of Hatun Cayo said. *For such a choice The Great Spirit requires appeasement. He will send his messenger for you.*

"I am honored," Amaru said.

The communication between Amaru and the shaman spirits ended but the aura of the meeting remained as the effect of the Devil's Trumpet slowly began to subside. Carrie sensed time was running out. She focused her thoughts.

"Amaru." Her whisper was inaudible to the human ear. "There is another in the spirit world who wishes to speak to you."

Chapter 27

Vikter rose at the executive end of the expansive walnut conference table to signal the end of the meeting. Attorneys, accountants, brokers and administrators, all involved in taking Day Pharmaceuticals from privately owned to publicly traded, gathered their papers and filed out of the room. Vikter motioned to the company's lead securities attorney to stay.

"What's your best estimate?" he asked.

"The prospectus should be ready to go to the securities division next week," the attorney replied. "It will probably take them thirty days to respond. If their changes are minimal, and I think they will be, we should be able to announce the IPO within sixty days."

"Good."

Vikter had been operating Day Pharmaceuticals on the edge for nearly two years: making sure profitability was depressed, laying off people while keeping his allies employed, delaying new drug trials, and most importantly keeping secret the new arthritis drug that he had shelved following successful trials; the new drug that would be announced at the time of the public offering.

Leon's deteriorating health had thrust Vikter into the role of chief operating officer of the company nearly three years ago, and with it came his belief that he was destined to be heir-apparent to Day Pharmaceuticals. When it came to ownership of the business, however, he was looked upon by the Days as just another employee, and that revelation incensed Vikter. By taking the company public he would gain controlling interest of Day Pharmaceuticals.

Vikter had insinuated himself in the Days' personal life, careful to insulate them from the daily operation of the business while, at the same time, regularly expressing his concern over

Leon's health. He regularly followed his weekly business meeting with Leon with a discussion of Leon's health issues with Mahogany. Leon's guilt over the death of his brother had proven to be an unexpected windfall for Vikter's plan. It allowed him to inject his niece into the picture, which gave him another source of information on the Days' daily activities, and also gave him leverage if he ever had to challenge Leon's competence to run the company. The marketplace did not look comfortably upon one of its own regularly consulting with the spirit world.

His access to the Day's home also made it relatively simple for Vikter to add a carefully calculated overdose of vitamin B6 into Leon's already voluminous daily pill regime by replicating a capsule of a different medication. Vikter thought of it as his little assist to Mother Nature for the delayed toll she was collecting from Leon for his years spent as a football player. Abnormal heart rhythm, tingling skin, sporadic gastric distress and a multitude of other symptoms caused by the extra B6 had kept doctors guessing as to the source of his problems, and had kept Leon feeling lousy enough so that business matters were his least concern.

Now the mess in Peru with Terry Castro had given Vikter another tool. With just a suggestion here and a little push there, a campaign to locate the tribe of white Indians in the Amazon could become a reality. It was just the kind of thing that both Leon and Mahogany would get excited about, further removing any attention they might otherwise pay to the company and its impending public stock offering.

And while all of these things evolved, Vikter had been quietly, patiently convincing Mahogany that it would be better to let him take the company public rather than saddle the employees with a "struggling" company whose future was looking bleak.

Not surprisingly, stress had become Vikter's constant companion. After the securities attorney left, Vikter changed into gym gear in the private bathroom attached to his office, then walked down the hallway to the company exercise area. Ignoring other employees who were working out, he climbed on a bike at the end of a row of stationary bicycles and began to pedal. The stress dissipated as the sweat beads formed on his bald head, the pumping of his heart serving to re-energize his thought processes.

He needed to make sure the Days followed through with the Amazon expedition. A meeting with Father Wyman needed to be arranged. Perhaps someone from National Geographic should be invited. The more activity the better, he thought, as he pushed his heart rate toward 150.

Vikter could taste success. Thanks to his personal connections, a Russian investor was poised to take a large position in the company. The IPO should be sold out in twenty-four hours. He would be controlling shareholder of Day Pharmaceuticals, and with the Russian's backing he would have an absolute majority. We'll announce the arthritis drug and I'll take the lid off the company, he thought. The stock price should double...triple. The term "billionaire" popped into his consciousness.

Maybe I should rename it Glass Pharmaceuticals, he mused.

* * *

In row 16, seat C, in an Airbus A380 headed for O'Hare, Holly Bouquet pondered what to do. The weekly flights to San Francisco were taking their toll on her bank account, and her business. Bouquet and Brilliant-Private Detectives, was suffering from lack of attention at the same time that Terry's condition was deteriorating.

She still loved him—the only man she had ever really loved—but she was losing hope that he would recover. The move to the rehab center had not done what they had hoped. He was getting daily exercise. The Days saw to that. But it didn't seem to be doing any good. His body was getting weaker and the medical doctors she had consulted, both in San Francisco and Chicago, had not offered any optimistic prognosis. It was likely, they all agreed, that he would never come out of the coma.

For the second time in her life she faced the prospect that it was time to give up on Terry Castro. This time it was less emotional, but no less painful.

The plane thumped onto the runway and shuddered down to satisfactory ground speed. Holly switched her phone off airplane mode and a text message from Mahogany appeared: "Dinner at our house Friday night. Fr. Wyman from Berrie U will be here to discuss continuing Terry's research. Can you join us?"

Holly sighed. "Sure. What time?" she texted back. Maybe she would make one more trip.

* * *

An invisible warning cloud hung over Amaru.

The blessing of the curare had ended and the village had scattered back into the safety of the rainforest. Amaru, as was so often the fate of the shaman, sat by himself, thinking, his back against the trunk of a bamboo tree, his legs splayed out in front of him. In his one hundred years he had heard many spirits. He had conjured his shaman ancestors, had spoken with the spirits of creatures that inhabited the earth with him, had communicated with his dead sons and, once he believed, had communicated directly with the Great Spirit, but he had never before come in contact with a spirit of this nature. In fact, he had never even given thought to the idea that women had spirits, but this spirit was definitely a woman. How could this happen? Who was the person who wanted to communicate with him who had chosen a woman as an intercessor?

When the voice first appeared it confused him. The spirits of past shamans were fading, and his first thought was that one of them was speaking as they retreated into the netherworld.

But the voice repeated itself after all the shamans were gone. It was then that he realized the voice was female. Amaru had not audibly responded, but he knew that his reaction of surprise had been enough for the spirit to know that he had heard her. He also understood that this would not be the last time the female spirit would reach out to him. If someone in the spirit world wanted to talk to him, they would not give up until they succeeded.

When spirits had reached out to him in the past it had meant change for the Chilco; change that usually meant disruption in their lives and, sometimes, disease, injury and death. He knew his time would end soon. Was this the promised messenger from the Great Spirit coming to take him so soon? It was too early, he fretted. He had not fully prepared Urco. But was one ever fully prepared? If it came from the Great Spirit he could not ignore the summons. But a woman? Could the Great Spirit be a woman? Impossible, he thought. Even a messenger from the Great Spirit in the form of a woman challenged his concept of how the world was ordered.

* * *

I know he heard you. He sort of jerked, like he'd been surprised, and when he came out of the trance he had this puzzled look on his face. I just left him sitting against a tree by himself. The rest of the village is sleeping, I think.

The effort to reach Amaru had exhausted Carrie. She lay on her side on the couch amid the throw pillows, hearing Castro, fighting the urge to close her eyes. She knew that Amaru had heard her.

"I will try again, later, but right now I need to sleep," she said. "Can you lie next to me?"

There was a pause, and then, *I am.* She stuffed a throw pillow between her knees and wrapped her arms around a larger one, hugging it against her. In a moment she was asleep.

* * *

Father Wyman loved the Days' home. Someday, after retirement, he hoped to have one of his own in such a lovely place. He had visited them several times over the past decade in the course of raising funds and they had become friends, brought together by their love for the university, their shared faith and their desire to help those less fortunate. When the opportunity arose to see old friends at a place he loved, Father Wyman jumped at it. A return call to Mahogany from his administrative assistant confirmed that he would be landing in San Francisco at 2:10 p.m. on Friday, Delta Flight number 1347. Mahogany said she would send a car to pick him up.

The dinner would be catered. He should set the table in the main dining room for eight, Mahogany instructed Sanjay, place settings for four food and three wine courses. In addition to Mahogany and Leon the guests would be Father Paul Wyman, Holly Bouquet, Vikter and Anya Glass, and two representatives of The National Geographic Society, Alain Gilbert and Hannah Moncrief. Because some of the people didn't know each other there should be two-sided, printed table tents both to mark the seating and to make sure that everyone, once seated, would know the names of the other guests. Make sure that Father Wyman sat next to Alain Gilbert and that Holly Bouquet did not sit next to Leon. He should confirm that the caterer would provide two servers, properly dressed. The guests would go into the theater after dinner. He should have aperitifs and two dessert wines available. He should also have the video they had received from Berrie University loaded and ready to play.

Mahogany had thought of adding Carrie Waters to the guest list so she could break down the video for them, but discarded the idea after remembering the last time she and Holly had been together. Plus, having a medium present might raise a question in the minds of the people from National Geographic about the seriousness of the proposal to joint venture a "Search for the Lost Tribe," the name she and Leon had settled upon as a shorthand way to describe what they were proposing.

For Leon, it was something to look forward to other than his dwindling health and seemingly moribund business. He relished the chance to bring together the university and National Geographic. Vikter, who had originally come up with the idea of continuing Dr. Castro's research, suggested that Leon personally provide part of the funding ("because the company can't really afford it right now") to assure Leon a spot on the team that would make the trek.

The idea excited Leon: Mahogany and his doctors be damned; he was going.

* * *

Castro drifted among the palm branches a hundred feet above the village, watching the women and children intertwined in activity that combined play, instruction and productive work. He was sure the children saw it only as play.

Triumphant hunters had returned that morning with a large, gutted capybara hanging upside down by its feet from a pole resting on the shoulders of two hunters. They had dumped the kill in the middle of the ceremonial clearing as the entire village gathered. The younger women and the girl children gathered around the capybara, and the older women formed a circle around them, sitting on their haunches, pointing and offering advice. The hunters melded back into the jungle. A handful of elders milled about on the edge of the clearing watching the women and a group of small boys who raced around the clearing, disappearing into the jungle, then reappearing in hot pursuit of imagined enemies.

The women made a game of cutting up the capybara, letting the children do some of the work, stopping them for instruction when needed. When the usable meat and tendons had been cut from the carcass a primitive food fight broke out among the mothers and the children. Bloody bits of skin and tissue were thrown at or smeared upon each other as they laughed and whooped and rolled on the ground. The elderly women made a gap in their circle to allow the young boys to join in the gory melee. When everyone was thoroughly caked with blood and dirt and exhausted, Amaru's wife rose from the outer ring, flicked off a bit of bloody matter that had spattered one breast, and entered the circle. The tumult subsided with, of course, the little boys being the last to settle down. She beckoned Urco's wife, who joined her, and they removed the teeth from the rodent and then made a ceremony of awarding them to the children as trophies for their part in the harvesting and the food fight. They then distributed the meat and tendons among the families.

The combatants, now more bloody brown than white, disappear into the jungle with their spoils, and the older women converged to do the final stripping of the carcass. When they were done there was nothing left. Even the spot where the capybara had lay had been swept and any remnant removed. The clearing was now empty and there was no sign of human, or animal, life.

Castro waited for Amaru to emerge from his lean-to. He marveled at the ingenuity of the tribe and the efficiency of their use of their habitat. The joy with which they went about their day-to-day lives would be a great example for "civilized" societies, he thought.

The huge warrior with the purple birthmark on his face came into the clearing, followed in single file by his very pregnant wife and three children. The wife and children, clean, no longer showed any signs of the riotous food fight. They walked across the clearing toward Amaru's lean-to.

Odd that I always think of this man as a warrior, never a hunter or a shaman or just a native, thought Castro. Odd, too, that I've never seen this kind of social call.

Amaru emerged from the lean-to and greeted the family as if he had been expecting them. The men and children squatted. The woman, prevented from doing so by the baby soon to be born, sat, holding her stomach. Amaru's wife emerged from the lean-to carrying one of the curare-filled gourds that had been blessed a few nights earlier. Amaru took the leather pouch from around his neck and opened it. He took a pinch of its contents and placed it on Urco's tongue. He did the same, in smaller amounts, with his son's wife and each of their children. He took some himself. Amaru did not offer any to his wife.

The group squatted without speaking. One of the children began to rock back and forth on the balls of his feet. Soon all of them, except Amaru's wife, were doing the same. Amaru started to chant.

* * *

Castro's abrupt invasions of Carrie's head were becoming commonplace. This was the fourth time he had appeared to her in the last few days; each time urging her to immediately contact Amaru; thinking that the timing was right. The first time Amaru was conjuring the shaman. She had been successful but had not told Castro everything she had learned from that meeting. She wanted another chance to communicate with Amaru to be sure she hadn't misunderstood. The second time, already skating on thin ice at work, her boss's watchful and wandering eyes had prevented her from leaving to make the attempt. Carrie felt depressed the rest of the day for not having been able to respond to Castro's call. Even worse, the last time she had been unsuccessful, feeling too rushed, never getting into the proper state of tranquility.

This time she was ready.

Carrie could hear the chant. More importantly, she understood it. She was invisibly sitting in on what was, essentially, a business deal. The bargain Urco had made, in exchange for agreeing to taste the curare, was that his wife and children would also be allowed to taste it as often as he so that their lives would also be long, and that he would not have to live many years only to watch them wither and die while he stayed young and virile.

* * *

As Amaru dipped the tip of a flat stick into the curare, he tried to convince himself that the bargain he had made with his son did not violate the sacred teachings of the Great Spirit. Only shaman were allowed to know the secrets of the curare. He wasn't actually telling Urco's wife and children any secrets, he reasoned. He was only allowing them to taste it, and there was nothing in the teachings that specifically forbid that, but in his heart he knew that the taste of the curare was one of its secrets. It was how the shaman measured its potency, and, more importantly, the long life, wisdom and virility that was the curare's secret gift had always been preserved for shamans. He was now about to give it to others.

Amaru explained to the children that this was medicine that they must take to be healthy and live a long life. Despite a growing, foreboding feeling he put a dab of curare on the tongue of the oldest child. The boy grimaced but quickly composed himself so that his father would be proud of him. The two younger children did not fare so well, screwing up their faces in disgust at the taste. Urco's wife declined, gesturing toward her distended stomach to indicate concern for what the curare might do to her unborn child.

His son was marked as the great shaman that would lead the Chilco back to glory and power. Had he, Amaru Topac, stolen his son's legacy by allowing Urco's children to taste the curare? Had he condemned Urco to be the shaman who reigned at the end of the Chilco? Had he condemned his grandchildren to death?

Those thoughts troubled him as the family departed and the effect of the Devil's Trumpet began to wear off. Then Amaru heard the voice: "You have done a wonderful thing, Amaru." It was the woman spirit.

"Who…who are you?" he asked.

"I am like you, one who can talk to the spirits. Because we are the same we can speak to each other. You have done a wonderful thing for your son and for his family."

"I don't understand. Are you a spirit?"

"No, like you I walk in this world. We are different yet we are the same. I am not a spirit, but there is someone from the other side that needs your help."

"I…"

It was at this moment that communication stopped. The only thing that Carrie could think of was that the effect of the drug that Amaru had taken had completely worn off; that the doorway to his brain had slammed shut.

Castro's spirit was suddenly with her. *What happened?*

Carrie related what she had heard and her conversation with Amaru. "We don't have an antidote yet," she transmitted, "but he and I have made contact and he wasn't afraid to talk to me. I think the next time we may have an answer."

I hope soon. The last time I was in my body it didn't feel right, like it was losing its grip. It may not be around much longer.

"You…your spirit will always be here," Carrie said out loud, not feeling nearly as confident as her voice made it sound.

But if my body's gone, what then? There will be no need for the antidote. And we'll never have the chance to do together what you did to me at the rehab center. This was the first time since that day that Castro had acknowledged the sexual encounter.

"Hold on. Please hold on," she pleaded. "We'll find it. We'll be together."

Hope drifted off into silence.

Chapter 28

"This is certainly unusual. Usually I ask you out for lunch." Vikter and Carrie sat across from each other at a small Formica-topped table in a cheap buffet-style restaurant. Vikter had sniffed liked there was a bad odor, and tried not to touch anything when he sat down, but he didn't make a scene, for which Carrie was grateful.

"Thanks for meeting me on such short notice," she said. "I know this isn't where you'd choose to have lunch, but it's close to where I work and I only have about twenty minutes." Tuna salad sandwiches in red plastic baskets, chips tumbling over the side, sat on their tiny table. There was barely enough room for two well-worn plastic glasses filled with ice water.

"You said you had something I might be interested in," Vikter said.

"I've made contact with Dr. Castro and also with the native in the video. He's the shaman of a tribe somewhere in the Amazon."

Vikter picked up his sandwich between his thumb and forefinger like it might be diseased, took a tiny bite and dropped it back in the basket.

Carrie took a big bite of hers and kept talking out of the side of her mouth while she chewed.

"I've learned that every tribe has its own version of curare, but this tribe's version is really unique."

"So? What is it? What's the big secret?" Vikter interrupted, making no effort to disguise his disinterest.

"This curare extends the life of anyone who tastes it."

"Curare is poison, isn't it? How do you taste it without getting poisoned?" he asked.

"Curare is only poisonous if it gets in your bloodstream. Tasting it doesn't poison you," Carrie said, around another bite of her sandwich. "If my sandwich was laced with curare it wouldn't hurt me. That's why the natives use it for hunting. They can shoot an animal and eat the meat right away because the poison that killed the animal doesn't get into the human bloodstream; only in the animal's. But that's not the important part. It's the life-extending part of this particular curare that I thought might interest you."

Vikter leaned forward over the table. "How confident of this life-extending quality are you?" he asked.

"I've listened to several conversations where this came up. I'm pretty sure it's real. I think the shaman I'm communicating with is a lot older than the other people in the tribe."

Vikter sat back in his chair. "A primitive tribe in the Amazon; normal life expectancy has to be, what? Thirty? Forty? How old do you think this guy is?" He picked up a potato chip from the basket without thinking and took a bite, then winced as the salt hit a canker sore.

"I don't know, but the guy who is supposed to be the next shaman wouldn't agree to taste the curare unless his wife and children could too. He didn't want to outlive them. I think that's what happened to this shaman. His wife looks to be about half his age, and she looks old enough to be the next shaman's mother. If I were to guess I'd guess the shaman is probably about seventy or eighty."

"Have you told anyone about this?" Vikter asked nonchalantly as his tongue tried to irrigate the salt out of the open sore in his mouth.

"No. I would have told Mr. and Mrs. Day but I'm kind of on the outs with them."

Vikter pursed his lips and thought for a moment. "Let's just keep this to ourselves," he said. "No need to get them excited until we know if there's actually any truth...uh...benefit that might come from this."

"Uncle Vikter?"

"Mmm?"

"If you could get of some of this curare do you think the people at Day Pharmaceuticals could find an antidote for its poison?"

"I think that might be possible. If we ever get some, I'll do it just for you as my little gift for this lunch."

* * *

The dinner was an elegant affair.

Mahogany deftly kept the food, the wine and the conversation flowing. Leon, invigorated by anticipation of an adventure and the return of Holly Bouquet, had been equally adept at nurturing the discussion between the National Geographic representatives and Father Wyman until their own enthusiasm for the hunt-for-the-lost-tribe project gathered sufficient momentum to carry itself.

Evening was beginning its soft purple flow over the Tiburon peninsula as the dinner party made an unscheduled detour onto the patio to watch the city lights come to life. Vikter, who had been uncharacteristically quiet during dinner, took the opportunity to pull Father Wyman aside and lobby for Leon's inclusion in the proposed expedition.

"He needs something to look forward to," Vikter said. "The business runs itself and he's just sitting around here wasting away."

"What about his health?"

"Look at him tonight, when he has something that excites him," Vikter answered. "Does he look healthy enough to you?"

Father Wyman nodded.

"Besides, without Leon the lost tribe would never have been discovered in the first place," Vikter said. "Of all people, he should help carry on Castro's work. And he *is* the university's biggest benefactor." Vikter had saved his best shot for last.

A few minutes later they assembled in the Days' theater room and settled into lush leather chairs. Holly and Anya Glass had excused themselves to the powder room. Sanjay was circulating with a silver tray of snifters and cognac while the others chattered about the beauty of San Francisco Bay in the evening and the idyllic setting of Leon and Mahogany's home. The two women returned and Sanjay made sure everyone had a full glass. Then the lights were dimmed and the video of the lost tribe flashed onto the one-hundred-inch screen.

Vikter looked with renewed interest at the three light-skinned men that emerged from the undergrowth. When he first viewed the video it had been with mild curiosity. Now he studied the three in detail, particularly the one with a pouch around his neck. He does appear to be older, Vikter thought, but even after four re-runs, two in slow motion, he still had no real idea of the age of the natives, so he asked.

Hannah Moncrief was a veteran of multiple treks into the jungles of the world. She was a tall woman with leathery, wind-burned skin, shaggy hair and piercing gray eyes. "Clearly the taller one is older than the other two," she said. "His skin had less elasticity and his pubic hair had striations of white. There was also cloudiness in his right eye, suggesting cataracts."

"You saw all that?" Holly asked, incredulous.

"I'm trained to look for those kinds of details," Moncrief said. "We don't often get a chance to see a video and rerun it like this. Usually we only get a few seconds and we have to identify the important aspects quickly. Otherwise they're lost."

"I thought I was pretty good at picking out details," Holly continued, "but I'm an amateur compared to you. Where did you get your training?"

Before Moncrief could respond, Vikter interrupted. "How old do you think they are? The natives."

"Based on my experience, I'd say the two younger ones are probably between sixteen and twenty. The older one, maybe forty. That's really quite old for this type of culture. It's remarkable that someone that old would be in a hunting party.

"And I got my formal training at Oxford," Moncrief continued, turning back to Holly, "and my powers of observation in the jungles of Africa and Indonesia."

"If you ever decide to change occupations look me up," Holly said, handing Moncrief her business card.

Moncrief smiled a "kind-of-you-but-no-thanks" smile and turned to join an ongoing conversation about the logistics of a jungle trek.

Vikter smiled, too.

My sister's brat may have come up with something after all, he thought. He had sicced her on the Days to make Leon look like he was crazy, and now she may have discovered the fountain of youth. Let them find the lost tribe. I'll take the drug…right after I take the company.

Part III

Chapter 29

Adam Starling sat, his prominent chin in hand, staring at snow that had piled up against the retaining wall that kept the forest from overtaking his backyard. His memory drifted to the Peruvian jungle and the village of San Roque. The assistant professor he had taken with him on the trip had gotten excited about finding some footprints, and Starling had passed it off as nothing, misguided optimism by a young anthropologist too eager to make a name for himself. He had seen it before.

But if the video he had just watched wasn't a hoax Terry Castro had been correct, and Starling was on the threshold of one of the greatest anthropological discoveries in recent history: a tribe of giant white-skinned natives from the highest elevations of the Andes Mountains that had migrated to the rainforest to escape Pizarro's destruction of the Incan empire, and had survived for six hundred years.

He had received the video from Father Wyman, along with a note explaining how the video had come about and of the events that had put Terry Castro in a coma. More important, Father Wyman had asked him to consider leading an expedition to the Amazon to locate the lost tribe. "We are planning an expedition to find the Lost Tribe of the Incas," Father Wyman had written. "You started those trips almost twenty years ago while you were at Berrie so I can think of no better person than you to lead that expedition."

Starling couldn't have agreed more, even as he mentally corrected Father Wyman. This was not a lost tribe of Incas. This was the Chachapoyas, the cloud people whom the Incans had conquered seven centuries ago.

As the world's preeminent authority on Incan culture he *should* be the first to find this tribe, Starling thought. He would, of course, acknowledge Castro's contribution; a footnote in the annals of anthropological literature, which, he supposed, Castro deserved for stumbling upon them. Meanwhile he would cap his own career with speaking engagements, television appearances, and a book that would be both a fixture in academia and a bestseller, outshining and outlasting Hiram Bingham's book about finding Machu Picchu.

A smile crept across his craggy face. That National Geographic was co-sponsoring the expedition was an added bonus. Alain Gilbert was handling logistics, and Gilbert had produced a film of one of Starling's early summer program trips. He had found Gilbert competent, affable and, most important, willing to take direction. The film had highlighted the discovery of several new sites that had produced significant Incan artifacts and had contributed to Starling's professional reputation.

Starling was not acquainted with Hannah Moncrief, the person who would be the lead National Geographic representative on the trip, but her presence would be a minor nuisance he could put up with considering what she brought with her: Gilbert, expert photographers, a feature spread in the magazine and another film.

The only potential problem that he could see was that he might have to share credit with her, but he would cross that bridge later.

When he left Berrie a decade earlier, Starling had tried to catch on with another university. He'd had several offers, but even with his reputation and expertise he'd found it difficult to convince university presidents and boards of regents that they should pay him to spend most of his time in South America. Finally he accepted a teaching position at a university in Boston, but it lasted only one year. He had, he was convinced, outgrown the confining halls of academia, the annual budget battles, and the skimpy salary. He spent the next three years writing a book about three light-skinned tribes, the Chachapoyas, the Nemadi and the Nuristan, that had each survived in environments that were socially hostile because of their skin color. While the book had been given significant accolades in archaeological and anthropological circles, it was a financial bust. Out of fiscal necessity he accepted an offer from the Peruvian government to oversee exploration of areas surrounding Machu Picchu, but he had failed to take into consideration the political situation. Two months after starting, a new Peruvian president was sworn in, and the new regime decided assets could be better used elsewhere. Two weeks later he was back in the United States and out of work.

When the call came from Father Wyman, Starling was relieved. Not only would it pay him well, and allow him to stop eating into his dwindling retirement funds, but the expedition would put him back in the center of Incan anthropology. It was his pathway to celebrity status.

* * *

On the other end of the country a different conversation was taking place.

Vikter sat in a wooden booth in a dimly lit bar across from a man built like a boulder, with no neck and a bullet-shaped head. Dmitri Petrov loomed over a hot beef sandwich like a solar eclipse, blocking the meager light from the single bulb hanging from the ceiling. He was oblivious to the gravy on his chin.

"So, what is it you want?" he asked.

"I thought Mr. Vasiliev told you," Vikter said, unawed by the man twice his size.

"So, you tell me again," Petrov said between bites.

"I need a tactical team of five men to fly into the Amazon jungle to recover something from a native tribe," Vikter said. "They will need to be military trained and well-armed."

"What is it you want them to get?"

"That's on a need-to-know basis," Vikter answered. "Mr.

Vasiliev said you could arrange the team. That's all you need to know for now."

Bogdan Vasiliev was the head of a St. Petersburg-based venture capital firm poised to buy a major stake in Day Pharmaceuticals. His provenance, like most Russian capitalists, included stints in the military and the KGB. That had given him connections, a twisted moral code that embraced violence, and the opportunity to hire people like Dmitri Petrov.

Dmitri concentrated on devouring his mashed potatoes and roast beef as Vikter waited for a response, worrying that the gravy might splash across the table onto his perfectly tailored sharkskin suit.

"How much you willing to pay?" Dmitri finally said. As he chewed the meat a spritz of au jus landed on the table, just short of Vikter's hand, causing him to jerk it away and reposition it in his lap.

"Again, that has been worked out with Mr. Vasiliev."

"How soon you want?"

"I would like them ready and on standby two weeks from today."

"Fast. A little extra would help speed up."

Vikter had expected this.

"I will personally give you five thousand dollars if you have them armed and ready to go in two weeks."

"Ten."

"Five," Vikter repeated, glaring at the hulk.

Dmitri wiped his chin and stared back.

"Seven."

"Perhaps I should call Mr. Vasiliev to have someone else arrange this."

"Five. Okay," Dmitri agreed. "How I reach you?"

"You just tell Mr. Vasiliev when they're ready, and he'll contact me." Vikter got up to leave.

"Half now."

Vikter slowly shook his head, as though in disbelief at the audacity of the hulk. He fixed him with a condescending look, turned and walked out the door. He knew he would have his team.

* * *

A half hour later Vikter was drinking espresso in a Sausalito coffee shop. The apparition across from him was a vast improvement from his earlier table companion. Mahogany Day, even when dressed down in simple white blouse and jeans, turned heads.

"Leon is really set on going on this Peruvian expedition," Vikter said, broaching the subject.

"I know," was the resigned reply. "I'm just so worried about him. That he'll get hurt or become so disoriented they'll have to hospitalize him over there."

"I assume you are sending a medical person with him." Vikter took a sip of espresso, carefully nursing the conversation toward its intended destination. He reveled in these cat-and-mouse word games as long as he was the cat.

"National Geographic is taking care of all that. Leon says they always have a medical team on treks like this. They even have medi-vac helicopters on standby in case someone has to be airlifted out of the jungle, but it still doesn't stop me from worrying."

"Why don't you go with him?"

Mahogany cocked an eyebrow at the suggestion. Her quizzical look turned into a frown. "I think one of us needs to be here in case of an emergency."

"The most likely emergency would relate to Leon's health," Vikter said. "And nobody knows Leon's health better than you. If you go, you could keep an eye on him, make sure he doesn't overdo it. I can handle any situations that come up at Day Pharm. I really think you should go."

Mahogany swirled the last of her skim latte, mulling over the suggestion. "I'd have to reschedule a bunch of things, and I'd miss the Bay Area Soundwaves fundraiser," she said, sorting through obstacles.

"Anya and I could attend if you think it's important for someone from the company to be there."

She shifted in her chair, trying to get comfortable with the idea. "Do you think it would be all right with Father Wyman and the National Geographic people?"

"I think they'd welcome it. I can call them for you if you'd like."

Mahogany nodded in agreement. "Let me know what they say."

I can tell you right now what they're going to say, Vikter thought, because I'm not going to give them an option. With both of you thousands of miles away, there will be no one to interfere with the public offering.

Vikter allowed himself a mini dose of malicious satisfaction, camouflaged by polite conversation, mostly about Leon's health. He finished his espresso and rose to leave.

"Oh," he said, making it sound like an afterthought. "I'll have legal send over powers of attorney for you and Leon to sign just in case there is anything that needs to be taken care of while you're gone."

* * *

Vikter pointed his Bentley north on 101, keeping one eye on the road and the other scrolling through his contacts to find a number for Father Wyman. Now that the mouse was nibbling at the bait he needed to make sure the trap snapped shut. He tapped the number with his thumb and waited while Father Wyman's secretary tracked him down.

"Mr. Glass. To what do I owe the pleasure?"

"Hello, Father. I just wanted to call and let you know that Mahogany is going to go on the Peruvian expedition too, more to keep an eye on Leon's health than to search for a lost tribe, I suspect."

"I think that's wonderful. Have you contacted National Geographic?"

"Not yet."

"I'm scheduled to talk to Alain this afternoon. I'll tell him. He's handling all the logistics for the trip. And I'll call Dr. Starling and let him know."

"Who's Dr. Starling?"

Father Wyman related the history between Adam Starling, Berrie University and the summer program trips to Peru. Starling, he assured Vikter, was the preeminent authority on Incan culture. While his personality might be a little prickly, if anyone could find the lost tribe, Dr. Starling could.

Vikter asked for Starling's contact information.

Vikter logged off the call, swearing under his breath, wanting to strangle something or someone. Another fucking ego to deal with, he raged, but, as he as so adept at doing, his thought process evolved the obstacle into an opportunity.

He dialed Starling at ninety miles per hour. Dispensing with ordinary pleasantries, he informed the surprised archaeologist that Leon and Mahogany Day were sponsoring the expedition, that they were going on the trip, and he, Vikter Glass, was their representative through whom all communication must be funneled.

"They won't be a problem," Vikter added. "They're excited about making the trip but they're coming as observers. They tend to be behind-the-scenes people."

"They're going on the trip?" Starling's voice came out in a squeak. Annoyed by the person on the other end of the phone giving orders, and in his own less-than-robust response, he cleared his throat loudly. "I suppose I'll have to arrange for extra vehicles and lodging, probably need an extra porter or two," he grumbled.

Knowing that National Geographic was handling the logistics, Vikter responded to the whining by curtly reminding Starling that without the Days there would be no trip.

"If their presence is inconvenient for you, we can find someone else to lead the expedition," he said.

"No. No. No. It'll be just fine," Starling said, back-pedaling.

"One more thing," Vikter said. "One of the requirements of the Days funding this expedition is that you send me daily reports once the expedition reaches Peru. The report must include the exact area covered in that day's search, any findings or events of interest, and the status of Leon's health. The report must be filed immediately after you've finished each day's exploration, before you eat dinner. Of course, if you find the tribe I will want a report immediately. I'll equip you with the necessary satellite link and electronics."

Starling agreed, realizing that although he might be leading the expedition, he was no longer in charge.

Vikter's next call was to his lawyer.

"Heard anything from the SEC?" he asked.

"Got their response this morning. There are some things we need to clean up in the prospectus, but we can have it back to them next week."

"Then what?"

"Then we get their approval, we print and we're ready to go."

"I'd like to announce the IPO in early February. Is that doable?"

"I'd say the timing will be perfect."

Vikter's last call was made from the Day Pharmaceuticals' parking lot.

"Bogdan, I have good news," he said, marveling at how easy it was to call Russia from a parking lot in California. "We will be announcing the IPO in early February. And I need six people and a second helicopter for that little mission to the Amazon. We don't want to go in without enough firepower to do the job."

Chapter 30

Carrie looked up from the computer screen in her cubicle and her jaw dropped. Walking down the aisle was the last person in the world she expected, or wanted, to see, Holly Bouquet. She closed her mouth and locked her gaze on to the approaching woman as the hair on the back of her neck bristled and her stomach muscles tightened.

"Hello, Carrie."

"Hello, Holly." The chill in Carrie's voice caused Julie to look up from her cubicle across the aisle.

"Can we go someplace and talk?" Holly asked.

"Anything you have to say to me you can say right here."

"I'd like to…uh, hire you."

"What? Why?"

"Um…to contact someone for me…on the other side."

Carrie's eyebrows rose. "I thought you didn't believe in 'that sort of thing'."

"I'd like to try."

Carrie should have been enjoying Holly's discomfort, but the humble way she had asked took the edge off Carrie's hostility. She asked Julie to cover for her.

"You've lost weight," Holly said as the two women rode down the elevator. "It looks good."

"Thanks."

The rest of the trip to the corner coffee shop was in silence as Carrie tried to glean the motivation behind Holly's sudden turnabout. Carrie settled on: she's trying to set me up, make me look like a fraud.

"What do you really want?" Carrie asked when they were seated in the coffee shop, the animosity returning to her voice.

"I think Terry is dying," Holly said. "His body is wasting despite the physical therapy. I've been told that you have talked with Terry on...ah, on...the other side."

Carrie sat and stared at her adversary, not acknowledging the statement. She wasn't going to make this easy for Holly.

"Do you think you could contact him for me?"

"Why would I do that?" Carrie responded.

"I would pay you."

"You don't have enough money."

Holly flushed, felt her face grow hot. "I didn't think you'd help." She started to rise.

"I'll do it on one condition." Carrie's words stopped Holly's exit.

"What is it?"

"Put me back on the visitor's list, and I'll try to reach Terry for you. And you won't have to pay me."

"Seeing him is that important to you?"

"It must be for you," Carrie shot back. "You fly out here from Chicago every weekend."

"But I'm..." Holly stopped. She had almost said that she was his wife.

Castro's infidelity had crushed Holly, sending her into a spiral that resulted in a payback romance and ill-conceived second marriage. From the moment she said "I do" she knew it was a mistake, and the marriage lasted less than two years. She had dated a few men since, but they only served to confirm what she knew deep in her injured heart—the love she and Terry Castro had known was something very special.

She thought about Carrie's request for a moment, then took her phone out of her purse and speed-dialed a number.

"You're back on the list," she said when the call ended.

"I can meet you at the rehab center tonight at seven," Carrie said, "but I need to warn you that we don't always connect. He spends most of his time now with a tribe in the Amazon trying to find the antidote for his poison."

"I know about the Lost Inca Tribe," Holly said. "I was there when you broke down the video, remember?"

Carrie nodded. "Oh, yeah."

"Did you know that the Days are funding a trip to find the lost tribe and the antidote?" Holly asked.

"Whatever," she said, "I'm just telling you that I'm not successful every time I try to reach him." She tried to hide the hurt that the news of the trip had inflicted. Once again, she had been excluded.

* * *

They met in the lobby of the rehab center, Holly visibly uncomfortable.

"I understand this is outside your comfort zone. Many of my clients are skeptical the first time." Carrie gave her usual speech to a first-time client as they walked to Castro's room.

"Will I be able to talk to Terry directly?"

"No. I'm the conduit. I relay communication back and forth between the two of you."

"How do I know that what you tell me isn't just something you're making up?"

Six hours earlier that statement would have made Carrie go off like a car bomb, but the anticipation of seeing Castro again had changed her. This time she kept her anger under control, maintaining a professional demeanor.

"There's that skepticism," she said. "If you go into this feeling that way it will make this harder than it should be, maybe impossible. How about if you think of something that only you and Terry would know. Tell me what question you want me to ask him and I'll tell you what he says. Will that satisfy you?"

Holly nodded. "If the answer is the right one."

They entered Castro's room.

"Oh!" escaped involuntarily from Carrie's lips when she saw him. He was laying on his side in a fetal position. He looked as if he had shrunk. His skin had a gray cast and had lost its tone. He looked twenty years older. Did I do this to him? She wondered. A tear coursed a path from the corner of her right eye down to her cheekbone.

Holly noticed. After a moment she whispered, "I'm afraid he's dying."

Carrie nodded, afraid to speak. "This is going to be hard," she finally said, "I-I need to be calm. I don't know if I can get there."

The two stood in silence looking at Castro's body, curled in the narrow bed, covered by a thin sheet. Carrie tried to maintain control, sniffing back tears.

"You really care about him, don't you?" Holly said.

The question unleashed a cascade of tears. She nodded.

"Go." Holly gently put her hand on Carrie's back and guided her toward the bed.

Carrie collapsed onto the bed, wrapping both arms around the frail body as sobbing convulsed her body.

Holly watched the man she loved being held by another woman. But her love was of a different sort; older, tested. She wanted this man that she loved to survive for his sake, so that he could be back in the world doing the amazing things that he was so capable of. So that if he chose to, he could love her again, or love Carrie, or someone else.

Tears now trickled down Holly's face. She was willing to let him go.

"Let's try another time," she said after Carrie had cried herself out.

"Thank you."

The two women embraced, both spent from the emotional firestorm.

* * *

Carrie called Holly on her way to work the next morning.

"I tried to reach Terry last night after I got home," she said. "I'm sorry, but I needed to talk to him so much. I shouldn't have done it without you. I'm sorry. But it didn't matter because he didn't respond. I know he's still with the Chilco and Amaru. I'll try again tonight, after work. If I reach him I can call you and we can meet someplace and talk to him."

"If you can't reach him, do you want to meet some place for dinner?" she asked.

They met at a delicatessen in Lower Haight.

* * *

Leon seemed distracted, not particularly interested in communicating with his late brother, so Carrie changed the subject, thinking it might help him refocus.

"Holly told me that you're sponsoring a trip to the Amazon," she said.

"Hmm," he grunted, acknowledging the statement.

"She said you were going to try and find the tribe in the video and the antidote for Dr. Castro's poison."

Leon nodded. "National Geographic and Berrie University are jointly doing the trip. An old friend of Castro's, Adam Starling, is leading it. Mahogany and I are both going."

"That's great. When do you leave?"

"I think the first week in February."

"I might be able to help," Carrie said meekly.

Leon scowled.

"Dr. Castro's spirit has been following the white tribe," Carrie continued in spite of his dismissive look. "I've been able to make contact with the shaman of the tribe. His name is Amaru. He is the tallest of the three warriors in the video."

"Why haven't you told me this before?" Leon barked.

She looked down at the floor. "I had no idea you were still

interested in Dr. Castro until Holly told me about this trip a couple of days ago."

"So you just went behind my back and kept on without my permission?"

"Sorry. I didn't mean to upset you. I didn't know I needed permission."

The answer infuriated Leon even though he realized that Carrie was right.

"Do you, or rather does Dr. Castro, know where this tribe is located?" he asked, still with an edge to his voice.

"I don't know, but the next time I communicate with him I can ask him."

"You do that and let me know what you find out," he ordered. Leon had intended to terminate Carrie's services, but this changed his mind for the moment.

"I will, but could you do me a favor?"

"What?"

"Would you have your doctor check on Dr. Castro? He looks terrible, like he's deteriorating. I'm afraid that his body is giving out, and if something isn't done soon there may not be any reason to find an antidote."

* * *

It had been more than a week since Carrie had communicated with Castro. Holly had gone back to Chicago, her boss was piling on more work, and the wet winter gray of San Francisco was doing its best to depress her. Then her phone buzzed. It was Uncle Vikter.

"Got time for lunch tomorrow?" he asked. "I'm going to be in the city. We could go to Scoma's and eat abalone."

They met a few minutes after noon, sitting inside, watching the wind whip the rain across Al Scoma Way. Carrie's mood matched the dismal weather. She ordered broiled cod. Vikter ordered the abalone.

"You've lost more weight," he said. "Trying to be a runway model?"

"No," she said, shaking her head. "Just haven't had much appetite lately."

"You aren't sick, are you?" Vikter asked, trying to sound concerned.

"No. Just busy."

His feigned concern for Carrie disappeared. "I wanted to follow up on our last conversation. We're sponsoring an expedition to find the tribe in the video, and I thought you might be able to give me more information about them."

"I know about the expedition. I told Mr. Day that I might be able to help."

"What did you tell him?" Vikter asked, alarmed.

"That Dr. Castro was with the tribe and that I had made contact with the tribe's shaman."

"Anything else?"

"Just that I thought I might be able to help him locate the tribe."

"Have you been able to do that?"

"I haven't had contact with Dr. Castro for over a week, so I don't know if it's possible or not. The next time I talk to him I'll find out if he knows, or can figure out, where the tribe is."

"So what did Leon tell you about the reason for the expedition?"

"That it was to find the tribe and the antidote for Dr. Castro's poison."

"Did curare ever come up in your conversation with Leon?"

"No."

"I ask because I have someone doing research on curare and we have found no evidence that any version of it, including the artificially made pharmaceutical versions, has any life-extending effects. You know that Leon's health is not good, and I don't want to fill him with any false hope, so please don't say anything to him about what you told me until we can actually do tests on this particular curare.

"Oh," Vikter continued, "After the expedition is launched next week, funnel any information through me. I'll be in daily contact with the Days. If your Dr. Castro comes up with any information about the location of the tribe please let me know right away."

Chapter 31

I missed you entered Carrie's head without warning.

"Where have you been?" Her frustration at being unable to reach him on multiple occasions reflected in the sharpness of her words.

His simple explanation, *with the Chilco,* did little to reduce her irritation.

"There are things happening here and sometimes it's important that I get in contact with you. Didn't you feel or hear anything when I tried to reach you?" He had not. He could return to her just by thinking of her, but she, apparently, was unable to summon him in the same way.

"We have to figure some way for me to reach you. It's going to become more and more important."

I'll listen more carefully, and I'll check in on a more regular basis.

That mollified Carrie for the moment. She told him of the expedition and offering their help in locating the tribe. Castro was not enamored with the idea.

These people are special, not just because they're biologically unusual or because they've survived for centuries, but in the way they respect the world they live in. They never take more than they need. They share everything, even with the creatures that inhabit the rainforest with them. They treat each other with such respect, and there is an uninhibited joy in the way they live their lives. The more I watch them, the more I'm in awe of their culture. I'd hate to see an expedition like this disrupt or destabilize them, as well intentioned as it may be.

"But weren't you trying to find them when you got poisoned?"

There was silence.

That was before I knew them. The words in Carrie's head sounded meek.

"I don't think they're trying to take anything from the Chilco, just learn the antidote." She conveniently omitted her conversation with Uncle Vikter.

Terry and Carrie discussed the pros and cons of the expedition: Leon's health; the cost of such a large undertaking; the likelihood that they could actually locate the Chilco. That was when Terry raised the subject of who was leading the expedition.

"A woman from National Geographic and a friend of yours from Berrie, can't think of his name."

Castro riffled through his memory, thinking of everyone in the natural sciences that was teaching at Berrie.

"He has a bird name," Carrie said. "Like crow, or blackbird. No, starling. That's it."

Oh, god. Not Adam Starling.

"Why? Is that bad?"

It couldn't be worse. He's only interested in his own fame. The man is all ego and no discretion. He'll put the Chilco on display like they're so many artifacts without a second thought about the culture he might be destroying.

"I thought he was a friend of yours."

He's no friend. He started the trips to Peru when he was at Berrie ten, fifteen years ago. I went along a couple of times. It was on my second trip with him that we found the footprints, but he never would acknowledge that the footprints were an important find. I always thought it was because he couldn't take credit for finding them. Now that we have proof that the Chilco exist, he's going to take credit for everything. I will say that the likelihood of them finding the Chilco is much higher with him leading the expedition. He has a lot of experience in the Amazon and he's very good.

"I'm sorry. But if he can find the antidote..." Carrie's voice trailed off.

Grudgingly Castro agreed that Starling's presence made that more likely, but it didn't make him any happier. *You need to get back in contact with Amaru. We need to warn him about the expedition.*

Realizing that the expedition was not going to get any help from Castro as long as Starling was involved Carrie changed the subject, telling Castro of her budding friendship with Holly, and how she had tried to reach him on Holly's behalf.

"Do you want to talk to her?"

Sure. What does she want to talk to me about?

"I think she's worried because your body is getting weaker."

Sure, I'll talk to her. But there's a question I've been wondering about, and she'll probably ask me. What happens if my body dies? Do we lose contact? Does my spirit disappear? Do you know?

It was a prospect that Carrie couldn't face. "Don't think like that," she said. "We will find the antidote."

* * *

Four days before expedition launch they gathered in Tiburon: Leon and Mahogany, Starling, Moncrief and Gilbert. Father Wyman had come for the meeting. The Days had also invited Vikter and Carrie to sit in.

"I have printed copies of this itinerary for all of you," Gilbert was saying, "including our three guests. Attached to the itinerary is a map of the area we will be exploring. Let's take a few minutes to go through this."

The group listened as Gilbert explained that in addition to those present the expedition would include another cameraman; two medical personnel, one of whom was an expert in tropical diseases and curare poisoning; and two helicopter pilots. The group of ten would fly to Houston and from there to Tarapoto, Peru, with an overnight stopover in Lima. In Tarapoto they would be joined by the rest of their party: a guide, a cook, a camp coordinator, four porters and an interpreter. The party, except for the two helicopter pilots, would depart Tarapoto the next day, flying one hundred fifty miles to the village of San Roque on the Ucayali River. The pilots would fly a leased helicopter to Contamana, about thirty miles up-river from San Roque where there was an airstrip. They would operate from Contamana while the rest of the party split into two groups, one headed by Hannah Moncrief and the other by Dr. Starling.

At this point Moncrief took over.

"Each group will have one medic, one cameraman and one porter who will also serve as the boat pilot. Each boat can hold up to six people so, Mr. and Mrs. Day, you can split up or alternate between the two groups, or stay at the base camp, whatever's your pleasure. The base camp is a floating string of barges that will follow the two scout boats and establish camp each day at a point near the end of the day's exploration. The kitchen, supply storage, and dining hall, which will also serve as working space when meals aren't being served, are located in the two largest barges. The smaller barges are living quarters: accommodations for two complete with showers, air-conditioning and Wi-Fi. We will eat breakfast each morning at 6:00 a.m. and plan to be on the water by 7:00. Lunches will be packed and taken with us. Boats will be back at base camp by 6:30 p.m. Debriefing will take place at 7:00 p.m. And dinner will be served at 7:30.

"Dr. Starling, would you like to explain how the exploration will roll out?"

Although Gilbert and Moncrief had been seated during their presentation, Starling chose to stand.

"It's our theory," he began, "that the tribe's village will be located adjacent to or in proximity to a water supply. That is why we will be exploring by boat. We will be traveling north on the Ucayali River into an area that is virtually unpopulated except for the occasional small village, exploring both sides of the river as well as its tributaries. Each boat will be equipped with two drones that have thermal imaging capabilities. This will allow us to search several miles inland from the waterway. From the thermal imaging we will know if there is a village or encampment that we should explore more thoroughly. We will coordinate with the helicopter crew from Contamana. The helicopter also has thermal imaging equipment. It will allow us to more thoroughly investigate any site of interest identified by the drones. Primarily, however, the helicopter will be used to explore areas between our location and the Brazilian border seventy-five miles to our east. We have set up a grid to enable them to thoroughly cover areas that we are unable to reach by boat or by drone.

"The initial site where my earlier expedition discovered the footprints is on the first tributary north of San Roque thirty clicks northeast of the village. The site where the video of the hunting party was taken is another fifteen clicks east. We will initially concentrate our exploration in that general area. From there, assuming we are not successful, we will move north along the Ucayali. We will have approximately four weeks of exploration, which should take us as far north as La Paz. We are confident that we will find the Lost Tribe of the Incas somewhere in this area."

* * *

That was interesting.

"I knew you were there," Carrie said. "I felt you."

I told you that asshole would take credit for finding the footprints.

Carrie changed the subject, not wanting to disparage the person most likely to find the antidote. "Do you think the Chilco are still in the area where you saw them?" she asked.

Judging by their minimal possessions they're very mobile, and I don't think they've survived for centuries by being stationary. My guess is that they moved after our confrontation at the observation post. When I go back I'll try to figure out where they are, although I'm not sure how. One part of the Montana looks pretty much like the next.

"If we looked at a map do you think it might help? I could stop at a travel store tomorrow and get one."

You trying to keep me around?

Carrie could feel humor in his words and a warm feeling

infused her body. "Will you spend the night with me?" she asked.

No place I'd rather be.

"Not even with the Chilco?"

Not even with the Chilco.

* * *

Within minutes of the end of the meeting Vikter was speeding north on Highway 101, on the phone with Bogdan Vasiliev. "Is the hunting party ready?" Vikter asked.

"Yes. When do you want to meet with them?"

"Next Tuesday."

"They will be staying at the Hyatt Embarcadero. Do you want to meet them there?"

"That will be fine. Shall we say six o'clock? We can order room service."

"I'll tell Dmitri."

"Dmitri. Why?"

"He's leading the team."

Vikter started to object but caught himself. Just was well, he thought. Dmitri's motivated by greed, and he won't have any qualms about doing whatever it takes to get the curare.

* * *

The session with Holly and Castro had gone nicely. Carrie had been her best professional self, and Castro had responded to her summons. The communication between Castro and Holly had been warm and loving, like two old friends who cared deeply for each other. When it was over Holly was quiet, a wistful look on her face. "It's good to know he isn't feeling any pain," she finally said.

Carrie allowed Holly to process the experience before asking the question that had been in her mind from the beginning of the séance: "You really got a tattoo on your inner thigh?"

It was the answer to the personal question Holly had chosen to prove the veracity of Carrie's communication with Castro: "What is the tattoo that I got in the Bahamas and where is it located?" Of course, Castro knew the answer instantly.

"Yeah, we did some pretty crazy things when we first got married," Holly answered.

"Didn't it hurt? That's really tender skin."

"I'd had enough rum so I wasn't feeling much of anything."

They laughed.

"Are you going to the airport tomorrow to see Mahogany and Leon off?" Holly asked.

"Yeah."

"I'll see you there." The two women hugged, and Holly opened the door to leave. "Thanks. I know you didn't have to do that."

"Anytime you want to talk with him again, let me know."

Two minutes later Carrie was sitting on her couch, exhausted, opening a Pixie Stix, when Castro said: *That was really quite a magnanimous thing you just did.*

"She loves you too."

That makes it even more impressive.

"She's a good person. I've learned a lot from her. One thing she made me realize is that I have this ability that I believe God has given me. I could have you all to myself right now, but if I refused to share my ability with someone who loves you, what kind of a person would that make me?"

I wish I could hug you right now.

"Me too," Carrie said, thinking: someday, and then you'll have to make a choice between us.

After a long, quiet time, Castro said, *I need to go back to the Chilco.*

"I thought you'd gone."

Not yet, but I need to go. We need you to talk to Amaru.

"I love you."

It was the first time she had said it out loud, even as a whisper. There was no response. Had he heard her? Had she said too much too soon? Was it even possible? She didn't know the answers, but she did know this: He was gone.

Chapter 32

Amaru was the jaguar, crawling on all fours with a skin draped over his back, stalking the mighty hunters. Suddenly they descended upon him, shrieks filling the air. He roared and tried to rise to fend them off, but they were upon him, their combined weight forcing him to the ground where the whole pile rolled and seethed among giggles and Amaru's booming laughter. The hunters, none of them more than five years old, had won. The great jaguar had been vanquished.

He hugged each of them and bade them on their way, noisily off on another quest.

Two hunting parties had left the village that morning, one led by Urco. Amaru had declined to lead the other, bestowing that honor instead on Maita, another of the young men, knowing that the natural competition between the two would result in a successful hunt.

Now that the Chilco had settled after their long trek, Amaru found more pleasure in playing with the children, and tending the gardens with the women, than in the hunt. He sat in the dappled sunlight with his back against a tree, smelling the smoke of the cooking fires, content in the sounds and activities of his tribe. It would be time for the midday meal soon. His wife, or one of the young girls, would bring it to him. He dozed.

Above the village, Castro waited. He was certain that the Chilco had relocated after his confrontation with Amaru. The fire pits had been recently dug, and the gardens were giving up their first harvest. The occasional slash in a tree trunk, where a lean-to was attached, was only mildly weathered. What he hadn't been able to determine was how far they had moved or where they were located. His memory of Carrie's map was of little use. He could not will himself to an elevation where he could view the rainforest panoramically. He felt tethered to

Amaru by a long, invisible cord, for it was always the thought of Amaru that brought him back to the Chilco.

He watched the shaman: Amaru's long legs splayed out in front of him; his head tilted forward; and his chin, sparsely covered with graying whiskers, rested on his chest, as he snored quietly. The whole village was quiet. Castro had promised to check in with Carrie more frequently and decided this would be a good time.

With no sense of transition he was suddenly suspended above her in her office. She was bent over, banging away at the numeric pad on the keyboard in her cubicle, her eyes alternating between a ledger on her desk and the monitor. After a few minutes she sat back and flexed her shoulders, wincing as she tried to loosen the muscles of her neck and back.

Hi.

Carrie jumped.

"I should be used to this by now," she said, laughing, then stopped talking when Julie looked up from across the aisle.

"I'm going to the bathroom," Carrie said to Julie, trying to cover her momentary faux pas.

She opened each stall to make sure no one else was in the bathroom, then took her place in one.

"Hi, yourself."

Checking in like I promised. Anything going on?

"You were only gone a few hours."

Really?

"Yes. But it's really nice to have you back in my head again."

Castro didn't respond. Had she overstepped again?

"Nothing new here," Carrie said, trying to keep the conversation alive. "Have you learned anything?"

They've moved recently, I'm guessing after Amaru and I crossed paths, but I can't tell where they are or how far they traveled.

"If I could talk to Amaru it might help."

I know, but he hasn't gone into one of those trances lately. He seems peaceful. The whole village seems that way; just happy and content. I left him snoozing under a tree.

Carrie's eyes widened. "Snoozing, like in taking a nap?"

Yes.

"Let me concentrate. I'm going to try something."

What.

"Shhh." Carrie closed her eyes and exhaled. Without intention she started to slightly rock back and forth. When the rocking stopped she opened her eyes.

"Let's go to my place," she announced to Castro.

Carrie told her boss that she was not feeling well, fatigued to the point of exhaustion, and that she was going home to get some rest, hopefully to ward off any germ or virus that might keep her out of work for a lengthy period of time. He grumbled, as always, but nodded consent. As she walked to her car she tore off the top of a Pixie Stix and swallowed its sugary contents.

What just happened?

"I hope I got into Amaru's consciousness while he was napping. He didn't say anything, but I felt something."

How does that work?

"Most people, when they nap, are not in a deep sleep. They float somewhere between consciousness and REM sleep. It's kind of like being in a trance. When someone is in that state sometimes you can make contact, although, if you wake them it causes disorientation. I learned that at a seminar I took.

"I told him I was back and needed to talk to him about the future of the Chilco. I said I would contact him tonight after the sun went down and asked him to be ready."

* * *

The dream had troubled Amaru. The woman spirit had appeared again, upsetting his contentment, saying that she had information about the future of the Chilco.

She must be a messenger from the Great Spirit, Amaru thought. If she has information about the future of the tribe, then she might have information about me; about how long I have left before the Great Spirit takes me. He wished Urco was back from the hunt. There was still much to teach him.

Amaru ambled down a seldom-used footpath, pondering, until he saw a cluster of large, trumpet-shaped flowers, white with a fuchsia throat, stretching up from a blanket of shiny green leaves. He cut off several leaves and carefully removed the stamen from two of the flowers. He stuffed his harvest in an empty pouch hanging around his neck. The Devil's Trumpet would help him talk to the woman spirit tonight.

* * *

Vikter eased the Bentley into the passenger drop-off lane in front of the Hyatt Embarcadero and pulled to the curb. He handed the attendant a hundred-dollar bill and told him to "keep it at the curb." He didn't like parking ramps and the door dings they created, and he didn't like to wait for someone to get his car. The attendant got a hundred dollars, and the hotel got a quarter of a million-dollar convertible parked by its front door for an hour. Everyone was happy.

He had just come from waving goodbye to the Days at the San Francisco airport, and, although he had been assured that the Wi-Fi on the barge was adequate for regular communication, Vikter had equipped both Leon and Mahogany with the newest satellite technology. He had also provided the same technology to Adam Starling. He was not going to leave communication with them to chance.

On the fourteenth floor of the hotel waited Dmitri Petrov and his five henchmen. He knew Dmitri would try to shake him down for more money, but Vikter was prepared. He had ten thousand in hundred dollar bills in an envelope in his vest pocket and a plan that would keep the Russian thugs focused on their task. It would cost him, or, rather, it would cost Day Pharmaceuticals, up to a quarter million dollars but that was small change compared to the payoff.

As he ascended in the elevator Vikter thought of his conversation with his niece at the airport. She had seemed sad. He had asked about the location of the tribe. She was "still working on it." He asked for information about the curare. "It looks like motor oil and they keep it in gourds." Did she have any more information about its life-lengthening effects? "No."

* * *

He knocked on the hotel room door.

A man whose chest and arms were bursting from his sleeveless muscle shirt, looking like they had been inflated with an air pump, opened the door.

"Da?"

"I'm here to see Dmitri." Vikter stepped into the suite, but his way was barred by the human steroid.

"Stop. Spread." it said.

After a thorough pat-down he ushered Vikter into the living room of the hotel suite. Dmitri sat on the swivel desk chair with his back to the desk, his bulk completely hiding the chair except for the chrome post and the five coastered feet attached to it, giving the impression that he was balancing on a post stuck up his ass. Two others sat on a couch in front of the television. The other three stood.

"Have a seat, Vikter. Good to see you again. Did you bring my money?"

Subtlety and patience were not Dmitri's long suit.

"I did, but we will get to that later. First…"

"Get to now or we all go home."

Unruffled, Vikter walked across the room to the one

unoccupied chair, sat and said, "You'll get your money." He took the envelope out of his vest pocket and riffled the bills to show them that he had the cash. "But we will do this my way, or we won't do it at all. Do you understand?"

"How about we just kill you and take money?"

"Bogdan would be most disappointed. He would lose out on several billion rubles. I'm thinking that none of you would make it back to Mother Russia alive."

He let that sink in, then said to the stone-faced Dmitri, "Let's get started." He handed them each a folder that included itinerary, airline tickets and lodging confirmation.

"You'll leave Wednesday morning on American Flight 7255. Twenty hours later you'll be in Iquitos, Peru. You're staying at a small inn, La Casa Chacruna. We've booked all seven rooms for the next forty-five days so there won't be anyone around to ask questions. The day after you land in Iquitos you will take a charter flight to Buncuyo.

"Which of the two of you are pilots?"

One of the standing Russians nodded, another lifted a hand in acknowledgment.

"At the Buncuyo airstrip there will be two Mi-24V helicopters."

The two pilots smiled. "Flying Tank," one of them said.

"They are each armed with six S-8 rockets, a 23-millimeter gun pod and a light machine gun on each side."

"I don't think we having a war," Dmitri interjected. "That will cost more."

Vikter fixed Dmitri with a withering look. "We have no reason to believe that there will be any situation that will necessitate you using this weaponry, but better to have it and not use it than to need it and not have it."

It was a nice speech, but everyone in the room knew that "going to war" was exactly why this team had been assembled. Slowly Vikter let his gaze drift from Dmitri.

"The helicopters are also outfitted with the most sophisticated heat-sensing equipment available," Vikter went on. "Which of you are familiar with using heat-sensing equipment?"

Again two of the Russians responded, one of them a pilot.

"You," Vikter said, pointing toward the pilot, "will have to train one of your crew to monitor the heat-sensing equipment, preferably your mechanic. Can you do that?"

"Da."

"You will be trying to locate a very unique tribe of natives," Vikter continued. He showed them the video taken from Castro's lookout post. The Russians sniggered at the hanging genitalia of the naked warriors.

"Immediately contact me when you've located their village," Vikter said, ignoring their behavior. "Your objective is to take possession of a viscous black liquid called curare. They keep it in hollowed out gourds that will look something like this."

He showed them a picture of a calabash gourd on his smartphone.

"They store many things in gourds similar to this so you will have to check the contents of each gourd that you find. The stuff we are looking for looks and feels a lot like motor oil. It also tastes bitter. Confiscate all the gourds you can find that have curare in them. If you're not sure if it's the right stuff, take it.

"This stuff has some religious significance for them, so it's likely you will have to take it by force, but you must be careful not to damage or destroy any gourds until you've checked the contents. Do not leave the village without at least one gourd filled with curare in your possession. This tribe is small and does not have firearms, so it should not be difficult to scare them off long enough for you to do what you need to do.

"Once you have the curare in your possession fly the helicopters directly to Iquitos, stopping only for refueling, if necessary. I will meet you at La Casa Chacruna. When you hand the curare over to me, I will pay you each one million rubles, except for you, Dmitri. I will pay you one million five hundred thousand rubles as the leader of the team."

"We want U.S. dollars," Dmitri said. "Rubles are worthless."

Vikter paused for effect, stroking his chin with his right hand. "All right," he said. "I will give you one hundred thousand dollars and you can decide how to divide it among you."

"Hundred thousand for me. Fifty for each of them," Dmitri countered.

They haggled, finally settling on two hundred thousand dollars, fifty thousand less than what Vikter had been prepared to pay. When they had agreed Vikter resumed his briefing.

"These Mi-24Vs are outfitted to travel at two hundred miles per hour with a crew of three and all the equipment and armament. If one of the choppers malfunctions, the other is large enough to carry you all." He spread a map on the desk and pointed out the river valleys that they would be covering in search of the Chilco: Rio Buncuyo, Rio Guanache, Rio Blanco and Rio Tapiche south of Clemente. "With two teams and the speed of these helicopters you should be able to thoroughly cover those valleys in four weeks, but"—Vikter leaned over and put his hands on his knees, continuing in a conspiratorial tone—"there is another team also looking for this tribe. They will not be exploring the same territory that you are." Vikter indicated on the map where the Starling expedition would be searching. "I have a source inside that expedition that will let me know what they are doing and where they're doing it. In the event they find the tribe first, I will be able to let you know within minutes. You should be no more than an hour's flight time from their location.

"And just so there is no misunderstanding, if you engage this other team while taking the curare, take all necessary steps to assure that there are no witnesses and that all evidence is disposed of before you leave."

Chapter 33

She had not wanted to tell Leon and Mahogany that there was no reason to search for the antidote.

Amaru had been perplexed when she had asked. It took several moments of searching for a word that he could understand before she came upon "remedy."

"None," was his answer.

"There must be something," Carrie pleaded. "What happens if one of your tribe gets cut and the curare enters his body?"

"He dies."

That response left Carrie incredulous until she learned that the last Chilco to die from curare poisoning happened during the lifetime of the fourth shaman, over three hundred years ago.

"Chilco not get cut," was Amaru's explanation.

She tried to explain Terry Castro's situation. Amaru remembered the confrontation with Castro but could not comprehend that a person could have been poisoned by the curare and not be dead, nor how he could be in the spirit world without being dead.

"Your man. He dead," Amaru had said. "Sorry."

She asked whether any of his shaman ancestors might know of a remedy.

"You are not from the Great Spirit." he said, surprised. "The Great Spirit would know answers to these questions."

"I am from this world, like you." Carrie explained. "We have both been given a gift by the Great Spirit. By that gift we can talk to those in the spirit world, and we also talk to each other."

"But you said you had a warning for Chilco."

"I do, but it did not come from the Great Spirit. There are people from the world I live in who are coming to look for you. They will be in boats, and in vessels that fly above the trees. They will find you. They come as friends and do not want to hurt you or your tribe, but they seek the curare. We have great men who will be able to make people live longer because of your curare. And they may find a remedy for Dr. Castro."

"I cannot give them the curare," Amaru said matter-of-factly. "It is a gift to the Chilco from the Great Spirit, and if I give it to anyone other than my son, the Chilco will be no more."

Carrie tried to think of something that would convince Amaru to give up some of his curare, but when the perceived alternative was death to his entire tribe, words were unpersuasive. She wanted to hate Amaru but could not. Even if his fear of extermination was absurd, he obviously believed it, and who was she, a person talking to someone halfway around the world through some sort of mental telepathy she didn't understand, to question what was truth and what was fiction.

"You must stop these people," Amaru finally said.

"I will try."

But she knew she wouldn't.

* * *

The gate where the Days and the National Geographic team gathered was noisy and fraught with anticipation. Carrie stayed on the fringes of the group until the voice on the intercom called for boarding to begin, then squeezed herself into the throng and wished Leon and Mahogany good luck. Uncle Vikter, who had not previously acknowledged her, approached when the flight had departed and asked about the curare. She gave him answers but received no encouragement about finding an antidote in return.

Now, driving home, she faced the real possibility that Castro was going to die. An unseen fist tightened around her heart, squeezing tears from her eyes and breath from her lungs. At a red light on Market Street she leaned forward, and, as her forehead bumped against the steering wheel, she began to sob. She stayed that way through two light changes until the car behind her honked angrily. With blurred vision and snot running down her upper lip, she zoomed away from the stoplight, nearly hitting a woman in the crosswalk.

* * *

If Castro's astral spirit had skin, Uncle Vikter would have made it crawl.

He had watched the smarmy little dandy prance and preen his way around the departure gate, ingratiating himself to those he saw as important and ignoring those he didn't, including Carrie. He made sure he was the last to wish Leon goodbye and to hug Mahogany, watching her well-tailored pants a little too long as they disappeared down the jetway.

As the last of the people left the gate, Castro found himself with a decision to make: should he return to the Chilco in a further attempt to determine their location, and to see how Amaru had responded to Carrie's warning? Should he follow Starling, the Days and the National Geographic crew? Should he do what he really wanted, go with Carrie? She looked and felt like she needed support. Or should he follow his instincts and track the little bald-headed creep who had such an extraordinary interest in the curare?

His instincts won and it got him a ride in a plush convertible that smelled like expensive leather and Creed Aventus cologne. It also made him the proverbial fly on the wall in crowded suite 1430 of the Hyatt Embarcadero where he listened as Vikter rolled out his plan.

What in hell, Castro wondered, is so valuable about this curare that would make someone send an armed force to South America with instructions to kill if that was necessary to get the stuff? He knew it wasn't to save him.

Having heard enough from Vikter, Castro's thoughts turned

to Carrie and their earlier conversation about Amaru's revelation that there was no antidote for his poison. He had felt useless, unable to console her with thoughts and physically powerless to touch her; able only to watch her grieve. It had not come as a surprise to Castro that there was no antidote. He had long ago shelved as unrealistic any hope of coming back from his current state. He was more concerned about what would become of his spirit when his physical body finally expired.

He found her driving south toward the rehab center. His spirit glided into her car and waited, trying to gauge her state of mind.

"I know you're here," she said, surprising him.

How?

"Don't know. I just know it."

Sorry I didn't leave the airport with you. I had another thing I had to do.

Carrie seemed happy to have him back with her as she maneuvered the old Honda south on I-280, but, at the risk of putting her back into a funk, he had to ask the question. *What is there about this curare that I don't know? Is there something you haven't told me?*

"What? I don't know. What do you mean?"

Why would someone send mercenaries to Peru to find the curare, with directions to kill anyone who got in their way?

"WHAT! Who...?"

That's exactly what your Uncle Vikter is doing. I followed him from the airport. He's hired a half dozen Russians, ex-military, armed to the teeth, including helicopter gunships, to search for the Chilco, with instructions to take the curare and leave no witnesses or evidence.

"Oh my god, no!"

So, I repeat, what is there about this curare that is so important that someone would kill for it?

Carrie pulled the car to the shoulder. "Oh, my god, what have I done?" She looked pitiful, with nothing or no one to hold on to, as the car rolled to a stop.

Just tell me. He repeated. Finally, as her grief subsided, he said it again. *Just tell me. Maybe we can do something about it before someone gets killed.*

Between gasps and sniffles she told him: how her communication with Amaru, and analysis of the observation post video had led her to the conclusion that Amaru was much older than the rest of the tribe. How, when Urco made the bargain to have his wife and children taste the curare, until then a ritual reserved only for shaman, she became convinced that it was because Urco did not want to outlive his wife and children. This, along with several of her communications with Amaru, led her to the theory that there were only a handful of shamans who led the Chilco from the time of Pizarro's defeat of the Incas in 1532 up to the present, and the reason was that the curare made the shaman live longer.

In their last communication, the one in which she learned there was no remedy for the curare, Amaru had confirmed it all. He was over one hundred years old, sixth in the line of shaman since the great Hatun Cayo had led the Chilco to safety. The curare gave the shaman long life and virility. His own father had lived two hundred years but that he, Amaru, would die soon and his son, with the mark of Hatun Cayo on his face, would lead the Chilco back to greatness as a nation and to their mountain homeland.

Holy shit! So this curare that poisoned me is the fountain of youth?

Carrie nodded.

But it only extends life if you eat it. If it gets in your bloodstream it kills you. Do I have that right?

Carrie nodded.

Just my luck. Castro tried to make a joke, but when it didn't bring the hoped-for reaction from Carrie, he asked: *How did Vikter find out about this?*

Carrie looked down at her hands in her lap for a long time.

Barely audible, "I told him," she said. "I thought he'd like to know about it if they found some on the expedition. Maybe they could make a medicine out of it. It would be good if people lived longer, right? I also thought it might help Mr. Day."

So Leon and Mahogany know about this too?

"I don't think so. Uncle Vikter said not to mention it to them until we found out if it was real. He said he didn't want to get them all worked up about it only to find out it was nothing."

And now he's willing to have them killed if they get in his way?

Before Carrie could respond, blue lights flashed in her rearview mirror. A California Highway Patrolman got out of his car. As he approached Carrie rolled down her window.

"Can I see your driver's license and insurance card, please?" he said. As she dug through her purse and glove compartment he asked. "Are you all right?"

"Yes. Why?" She handed him both cards.

"Looks...uh, like you've been crying."

"I've been doing a lot of that lately."

He handed her back her driver's license and insurance card. "Next time you need a good cry, find a safer place to do it, ma'am."

The patrol car's lights were still flashing blue behind her as she eased into the traffic lane. No longer feeling the need to visit Castro's body at the rehab center, she made a U-turn at the first exit and headed north, toward her apartment.

You couldn't have known that your uncle would do something like that? Don't beat yourself up over it. The important thing is to warn Amaru.

Castro's thoughts didn't diminish the guilt she felt. She reached out to him, searching for solace. "Can you stay for a little while before you go back?"

I can, but we should give Amaru as much warning as possible. How about if I go see what's happening, see if there is any opportunity for you to contact him. Either way I'll come right back.

Carrie, unsure whether she could actually bring herself to warn the shaman if it meant the end of any chance for Castro's recovery, reluctantly agreed.

She had gone less than half a mile. *There's something wrong. When I think of Amaru nothing happens.*

A cold chill gripped Carrie. "Has something happened to you?"

I don't think so.

A minute ticked by. Two. She could sense Castro was gone again. She did another U-turn and headed back in the direction of the rehab center.

Doesn't seem like anything's wrong. They're doing physical rehab manipulations. I entered my body and everything seemed the same.

"You went back and forth to the rehab center?" Carrie said, relieved. "Try Amaru again."

The word formed in her head a moment later: *Nothing.*

"Try someone else," she urged. A moment later: *Your Uncle Vikter is getting ready to play golf at Stone Tree in Novato.*

"Maybe it's not you. Maybe something happened to Amaru."

Chapter 34

Only in the last few weeks had Amaru shed the specter of death that had dogged him since the day his hunting party had met the whiter-than-clouds- people. His people had cheered his bravery and told stories of his prowess that caused the intruders to run like scared chickens, but his instincts told him that the confrontation had stirred things in the world. He had hoped the forced march to this new home would delay the threat, perhaps past the end of his days, and the peaceful, joyful existence they had found in this small patch of jungle had buoyed his spirits and given him peace.

But the woman spirit had shattered all of that. Their communication had resurrected his worst fear, and, despite her assurances, he did not think she could stop them from coming.

Amaru called together Urco and the elders.

"A spirit has warned of the coming of the whiter-than-clouds people," he announced when they had gathered in the meeting area. The statement set off a cacophony of questions and blustering around the circle. When the din subsided Amaru again spoke. "I do not know when they will come, or how many there will be. The woman spirit said they would come as friends, but the spirits of the past shaman have warned against them."

"What have we to worry," said Obed. "They are frightened children who run when we go 'boo'."

Amaru let the laughter die down. "This time they may not run. They come seeking the secret of the curare."

"We will give them the secret on the tips of our darts," Obed chortled amidst another round of laughter.

"History has taught us that our darts are no match for their thundersticks," Amaru said, gravely, trying to convey the seriousness he felt. "Weigh it in your hearts. Speak to your young men. We will gather again in two days to discuss it further and to consult with the spirits of the shaman." Amaru raised his right hand, palm out, to dismiss the gathering. With a nod of his head he motioned Urco to stay.

"We will speak to the shaman together," Amaru said after the rest had left. "It is time for you to speak with the spirits of the shaman. Then you will have learned all I can teach you."

* * *

The moon lit the treeless glade like an opaque spotlight, hinting at the brilliance of the flowers that made it a magical garden by day. An occasional breeze moved the silver-green foliage, and a steady, discordant chorus of frogs and insects added to the haunted air.

Three marsh deer picked their way toward the standing water at the center, the moon allowing them to see the hummocks that provided solid footing. It also gave a pair of ocelots a clear view of the deer as the spotted predators positioned themselves for an ambush.

Gliding in a smooth serpentine around the hummocks, through the standing water, was the thick body of a bushmaster. When its slithering body was at the perfect angle moonlight would reflect sharply off the dragonlike gold scales that connected the black diamonds on its back. The eight-foot-long pit viper made its way on a course that would lead it back to the tangled jungle and its nest, a layer of dead leaves, offal and fur shreds tucked between the roots of a walking bamboo tree.

The bushmaster stopped, sensing the approaching deer, then adjusted its course to avoid them. It had fed for the night, a tree rat having provided its supper, victim of the two-inch-long, hollow fangs that unfolded from the bushmaster's mouth when its jaws opened; the delivery system of the world's most poisonous venom.

* * *

Amaru took the pouch from around his neck and emptied the contents into one hand. His slender fingers picked out two leaves and one stamen of the Devil's Trumpet. He handed them to Urco.

"Spit," he said. "Mix."

Urco spit into the palm of his hand and used the forefinger of his other hand to mash the ingredients together.

"You swallow now," Amaru said, even as he was putting out his arm to stop him. "I want you to see the world tonight through the eyes of the Devil's Trumpet, so tomorrow you can concentrate to summon the great shaman of the past."

Amaru dropped his hand from Urco's shoulder and the young man lifted his own hand and ate the Devil's Trumpet.

"Sit," Amaru ordered. He began a singsong chant: "oom-layo-lau, oom-layo-lau, bahn nota clk huayna, oom-layo-lau."

In a few minutes Urco's massive shoulders began to sway. He put both hands flat on the ground to steady himself but the effects of the drug toppled him sideways. He lay there as Amaru's chant burned into his brain, and brilliant lights danced on the inside of his eyelids. Visions swirled among the lights. He was inside the womb, warm and safe, and then sudden pain. Involuntarily his hand reached for his face, touching the birthmark that had ordained his destiny. He experienced his birth, the pain and the relief and the terror of a new environment where learning to breathe was a thin thread to life. The visions changed, arising and receding in waves: a woman mourning over a disfigured body; smoke, or perhaps clouds, angrily colliding with the side of a mountain; people falling, falling, falling; a giant bird soaring as tufts of feathers were torn from its wings; his wife's face, too big, too close, her tongue lolling out of the side of her mouth; now sounds of violence, terror; his father fighting with a huge serpent, his hands around the serpent's throat, holding its dripping fangs at bay.

The brilliance of the lights began to subside, growing dimmer, less vivid. The visions faded. Urco lay on the ground, his sides heaving as if he had run to the water hole and back. Slowly his ordinary senses returned and his breathing became normal. Still he lay there, trying to absorb all that had happened.

Eventually he sat up. There, watching him, was his father, sitting on his haunches.

"How long?" Urco asked. Amaru shrugged as if it did not matter.

"Tomorrow you will talk to the shaman and you can ask them about your visions."

Urco nodded and took his father's offered hand to rise from the sitting position. "Go home to your family," Amaru said, and watched as his beautiful son walked away. Knowing the magnitude of the burden that he was about to pass on to Urco, the shaman turned and walked out of the meeting circle with heavy strides and heavier heart, down a path that led away from the village.

He hummed quietly as his long strides took him farther and farther away from his sleeping tribe until he came to a split in the path. Coiled in the middle of the split was the bushmaster, waiting.

"I am sorry to have kept you waiting, great king of all serpents," Amaru said, stopping just two feet short of the snake. "But now I am here. I am honored that you are the one to take me to the great beyond. I offer myself to you."

Amaru extended his foot toward the snake. With lightning quickness the wedge-shaped head of the bushmaster buried its fangs into the heel of Amaru's foot and as quickly withdrew, returning to its coil.

"I felt almost no pain," Amaru said, sinking to the ground. "May you live a thousand years."

He died on the footpath, a look of peace on his face and tears of joy streaming down his cheeks.

Urco found him the next day, and in the privacy of the glade he wept for the loss of his father, and for himself, and for his tribe. As evening drew near, and the initial ache of mourning started to wane, Urco hoisted the lifeless body over his shoulder, careful to balance it so that neither fingertips nor toes touched the ground. With each step back toward the village Urco felt his burden grow, even as the weight of Amaru seemed to grow lighter as if through the touching of their skin his essence was being transferred to his son.

With great sadness the village built a funeral pyre that evening in the middle of the clearing and, as the moon reached its zenith, the spirit of Amaru Topac was released into the heavens as his bones and tissue turned to ash. For three days there was fasting, great wailing and ululating in the village as they mourned the loss of their shaman, until, on the fourth day, Urco said: "Enough."

Chapter 35

The two men warily circled each other. Neither wanted to be there, but family pride and honored tradition had put knives in their hands and lives on the line. Sixty-one warriors, every Chilco male over twelve, stood in a loose circle around the two.

Maita, sinewy and strong like a lianas vine, knew his survival depended on being aggressive and quick. Urco, his friend and rival, would not attack, but he would defend himself, and if he succeeded in getting Maita locked in a contest of strength Maita knew that he had no chance.

Urco circled to his right, away from Maita's knife hand. Maita feinted with his knife and swung at Urco with his other hand. The bigger man leaned back and easily avoided the punch. Shouts and cackles from the older men rose from the circle. In no one's memory had two Chilco warriors fought, but neither in their lifetime had the leadership of the Chilco been at stake.

Maita slid to the ground and kicked at the bigger man's legs, the blow landing on the right calf. As quick as lightning Maita was on his feet and out of Urco's reach. Obed, Maita's father, cheered his son's success. It was Obed that had challenged Urco's right to lead the tribe, who had caused this combat between friends.

Again, Maita attacked with his feet, spinning and aiming a kick at Urco's head that might have ended the battle if it had landed, but it stopped inches short of its target in the grip of Urco's right hand. He held his adversary's leg in the air while Maita's arms pinwheeled in an effort to keep his balance. Urco shoved the foot away from him, sending Maita sprawling into the dirt, as shouts rose from the onlookers. Maita leaped to his feet. The two eyed each other at a distance.

Obed screamed at his son to attack. Again, Maita dove, feet first, at Urco's legs, aiming his kick at the same vulnerable spot on Urco's calf. As he jumped back to avoid the kick Urco's upper body bent forward. Maita slashed with his knife and a tiny ribbon of blood appeared across Urco's chest. As Maita scrabbled away on all fours, Urco put his hand on his chest and looked at the blood on its palm. Maita leapt to his feet, pressing his advantage by lunging at the bigger man with knifepoint extended. As anticipated, Urco circled away from the thrust and Maita flung a handful of dirt into his face.

Momentarily blinded, Urco spun sideways to make himself a smaller target and swung his arm to defend himself. The instinctive maneuver caught Maita's wrist, blocking his thrust and sending the knife spinning from his hand. As Maita scrambled after the knife, Urco blinked and wiped the tears and dirt from his face.

Knife retrieved, Maita turned. Blood was trickling down Urco's chest and from his wrist where Maita's knife had nicked it before being knocked away. Urco wiped away another tear, then cocked his head and looked at his friend. Disappointment was in his eyes.

Emboldened by his success and by shouts of encouragement, Maita aggressively began to circle Urco, feinting with his knife, dancing forward and back, relying on his quickness. Stolid and unruffled, the bigger man crouched in a defensive stance, his knife hand in front of him, turning only enough to face Maita.

Maita sprung forward, feinting with his knife. Urco's knife dropped from his hand, drawing Maita's attention for a split second. It was enough.

Urco stepped forward and his hand shot out, grabbing the wrist of Maita's knife hand. He jerked it toward him, causing Maita to lose his balance. His other, now knifeless, hand shot upward and closed around Maita's throat. He held his adversary in that pose as he slowly tightened his grip on Maita's wrist until the pain forced him to drop his knife.

With his adversary completely immobilized, Urco turned to face Obed.

"I understand why you challenged me," Urco said. "And I understand that Maita fought me for the honor of your family, but now, upon the life of your son, do you acknowledge me as your chieftain?"

Obed rose from the circle and knelt in front of Urco, head down. "I am your loyal subject," he said.

Urco released his grip on Maita, holding him up by placing his arm around him.

"You are no subject," he said to Obed. "We are both men of the Chilco nation. We are not so many that we can make artificial classes or hold grudges. We are all equals. Rise."

He turned Maita so they faced each other.

"You are my friend and a great warrior. I will always want you on my right whether we are at council, in the hunt, or go into battle." He enveloped Maita in a bear hug. Maita, stained with the blood of his chieftain, returned the embrace.

* * *

The next evening the council of elders, together with Urco and, at his insistence, Maita, gathered to discuss what Amaru had said on the night of his death. Should the tribe move to another location? Should they be like the oil bird when a predator comes, creating a diversion to draw them away from its nest? Should they stay in place? Should they be prepared to fight the whiter-than-clouds people or should they treat them as friends? And what of the curare?

As the fire died and the nighttime sounds of the rainforest grew, the council disbanded, agreeing on only one thing: Urco should try to summon the spirits of the shaman and ask for their guidance.

* * *

Castro found himself on the edge of the Embarcadero looking out over San Francisco Bay. He had drifted away from Carrie without realizing it, immersed in thought about all that had happened since he first discovered the footprints. It's like I tipped over the first domino when I found those footprints, he thought. Now the tribe was facing extinction because of him, and he was helpless to do anything about it.

Deep in his own funk, he felt Carrie trying to reach him. He hesitated, thinking how distraught she was and how his efforts to lift her spirits had failed, but he relented and went to her.

"Maybe if you just think about the tribe's location you could get back to them," Carrie suggested as they resumed their conversation about trying to warn Amaru. Her lone effort to reach him had met with the same results. Nothing. She needed Castro to go back to the tribe so he could tell her when Amaru was susceptible to her calling.

I've tried that but it didn't work, probably because I don't really know where they're located.

"What about thinking about someone else in the tribe, maybe Amaru's son?

Castro pictured the young hulk, and his pregnant wife, and their three children. And he was suddenly in the rainforest looking down at the Chilco camp. It was midday with the usual comings and goings of the women and children. There was no sign of Amaru or Urco.

It worked. There was excitement in the communication in Carrie's head. *I thought about Urco and his family and it took me back to the Amazon.*

"Did you see Amaru?"

No. Didn't see Urco either. I'm going back. I'll let you know as soon as I know something.

He was gone, leaving Carrie torn between a glimmer of hope and an empty feeling whenever Castro's spirit was not with her.

He came back that evening.

Amaru must be dead. Urco is in charge now, and it looks like he's been in a fight. He's got a cut across his chest that can't be more than a day or two old. Maybe he killed Amaru. Whatever happened, he's in charge now and it looks like he's getting ready to summon the spirits.

Castro's rapid-fire communication had shocked Carrie, leaving her emotionally unprepared to exercise her "gift." As Castro bounced back and forth between the Amazon and her apartment, Carrie tried unsuccessfully to get in contact with Urco.

Chapter 36

The two twenty-four-foot flat-bottomed boats glided out of the main channel of the Ucayali River into a hairpin channel that formed the entryway to an unnamed tributary. The narrow passage opened into a wide waterway, allowing the two boats to pull alongside each other.

"About ten miles upstream was where we first found the footprints," Starling shouted over the idling outboard motors. "I'll take the right side. Hannah, you take the left."

Hannah Moncrief, already accustomed to Starling giving orders, nodded. Three days into the trip and she had already grown tired of the little prick, but she had dealt with super egos on previous trips and had learned to pick her battles. Besides the boat pilot, the other passengers in Moncrief's boat were a photographer turned drone operator, and the team's interpreter. The drone operator signaled the boatman toward the left shoreline. The drone soared off the deck and hovered at two hundred feet above the trees on the shore, while he checked the heat sensors and camera mounted on the drone.

As the boatman steered steadily upstream, Hannah made radio contact with the helicopter crew. They had left Contamana, twelve miles north of San Roque, a half hour earlier.

"Where are you, Crocko?" she asked.

"We're south of you, working the grid east of the Ucayali," Ned Dial, the helicopter's veteran pilot, answered. "Good thing we've got the heat sensors. Until this morning mist burns off visual observation is impossible."

"We just entered the first tributary running east off the Ucayali north of San Roque," Hannah said. "If the maps are right, this is about forty miles long. It should take us about two and a half hours to cover it. Make sure you contact us before you come into our airspace so we can bring the drones down."

"A drone in the rotors is a pain in the ass," the man, affectionately nicknamed "Crocko" by his colleagues, joked. "Don't worry. I'll stay at least five miles south of you and work my way up the west side of the Ucayali until I have to go back to Contamana for fuel."

When the conversation ended, Hannah nodded at the drone pilot. The tiny aircraft zipped out of sight as the pilot watched its progress on a twenty-inch monitor mounted on the gunwale of the boat.

On the right side of the waterway, Leon and Mahogany sat in Starling's boat, much to his chagrin. Having amateurs along, even if they were the trip's sponsors, was not, in his opinion, how to conduct a scientific expedition. As he stared into the fog that hung among the trees he mentally sorted through ways to shift them to Moncrief's boat.

On the other hand, Alain Gilbert, whom Starling insisted upon having as his photographer and drone pilot, kept up a steady conversation with the Days as he maneuvered his drone inland, telling them of other trips he had been on, warning Mahogany to keep her hands inside the boat, identifying creatures that inhabited the water that might like fingers or hands for a meal, and naming the trees and plants when they came close enough to the shoreline so that they could see through the mist.

"Use your binoculars and look for footprints on the shoreline," he said after the fog had lifted. "You might see some local inhabitants, but they'll be the four-legged reptile kind, not members of a lost tribe. When we're doing a visual search like this we're pretty much looking for clues that someone has been here. If we do see any of the locals, we'll try to talk to them. If they're willing, we might learn something about the *criollos* from them."

"*Criollos?*" Leon asked.

"White people."

* * *

"Are we going to stop at the place where you first saw the footprints?" Mahogany asked Starling an hour after the boats had entered the tributary. She had become bored staring through her binoculars at the dirty sand and reeds on the shoreline or watching the coffee-colored water swirl, forming little whirlpools around the boat. She would relish an opportunity to get out of the boat and stretch her legs.

"Uh…no…we won't be stopping," Starling responded. "The place we…I…found the footprints was not right on the riverbank. From the river it's hard to tell the exact spot…where it is. We were on foot, not on the river, when we found them."

Mahogany thought it strange that they would not be returning to the place where it all started, and Starling's fumbling response added to her budding concern about his competence. Leon, meanwhile, was riveted to the monitor and took no notice of the exchange.

As Gilbert maneuvered the drone and manipulated the gimbal-mounted camera Leon watched and spouted a steady stream of questions about both the technology and what they were seeing. Most of the time the monitor showed only the treetops that formed the canopy of the rainforest, but the heat sensors provided indications of life forms that lived below. It was like watching a constantly shifting hologram.

"How would you know if any of those could be humans?" Leon asked, pointing at ever-changing bright spots on the monitor.

"Size and shape," Gilbert responded. "Those spots on the monitor are from small animals. At two hundred fifty feet these sensors can pick up something as small as a mouse. If we pick up something larger, like a human, it will not only be a much brighter light, but you will actually be able to make out the shape of a human."

By noon they were back at the mouth of the tributary. The search, that had extended two and a half miles on each side of the tributary thanks to the drones, had turned up no sign of human life. The two boats tied up to the barge train, anchored in shallow water just outside the mouth of the tributary, and the explorers took the time to stretch, relieve themselves, eat lunch and compare notes from the morning. Like the river-bound explorers, the helicopter crew had not turned up anything.

"Not surprising," Starling announced, primarily for the benefit of the Days. "This kind of search is tedious work, looking for a needle in the proverbial haystack. It's likely we'll be at it for many days, even weeks. It's going to get hot this afternoon. You might want to rest and relax here. Don't wear yourself out the first day."

Leon didn't bite. He was excited to be part of the hunt. Mahogany, who had watched Leon's health improve virtually since the time they had decided to join the trip, elected to stay.

* * *

As the twin turbines of the Mi-24V whined to life, Sergei Kuznetsov gave a thumbs-up to his counterpart in the other helicopter. He got the "good to go" return signal and slowly moved the throttle forward, feeling a surge of adrenalin as forty-four hundred horsepower began to spew out rpms. This is why he hired himself out to any private security company or black ops group that would pay him: the adrenalin rush that came from being in control of a precision flying machine that could outmaneuver, outrun and outgun any helicopter in the sky.

The rotors of the two behemoths stirred up clouds of dust and debris, leaving a thick blanket of dirt on the three small aircraft and one rusty DC-3 that sat on the Buncuyo airstrip, tucked between two weather-beaten hangars made of corrugated metal. Kuznetsov turned his head, gave his two passengers a nod, and the airship lifted off and banked eastward, doing a one-eighty until it was headed south, following the Buncuyo River. The plan was to search east of the area the National Geographic helicopter had covered the day before.

* * *

Vikter received his first daily field report from Starling on Friday evening. Unsatisfied with the information he received, he insisted that Starling put him in contact with the expedition's helicopter pilot. Reluctantly Starling admitted that Moncrief, not he, was the person in charge of the aerial search. He did not have the contact information.

"Take the phone and walk it to Hannah Moncrief," Vikter ordered. "I'm going to stay on the line. If I get disconnected and Ms. Moncrief doesn't call me within five minutes, I'm going to call Leon and have you fired."

He could hear Starling sharply inhale, then footsteps and then, as if far away: "Here."

Hannah Moncrief came on the line.

Vikter reminded her of who he was, and of their meeting at the Days' home at the initial planning session.

"Of course, Mr. Glass. What can I do for you," she said.

"I had made arrangements with Dr. Starling to get daily reports," Vikter said. "You know, if anything was discovered, the status of Leon and Mahogany's health, what areas were covered, things like that, but now I find out that you are really the person in charge, the only one with knowledge of the aerial search results."

Moncrief cheerfully gave him a rundown of that day's activities and agreed to provide him with daily reports.

"The Days are doing just fine," she said. "Leon is enthralled by the whole experience, I think. Mrs. Day, less so. She took the afternoon off and stayed on the barge, but her health is fine."

"One more thing, Hannah, if you'd be so kind. I gave Dr. Starling a map. I have one exactly like it here with me. For my own interest, I'd like to track the expedition: where you've been and what you've covered and where you're going the next day. Would you be so kind as to get the map from Dr. Starling so I can follow along?"

Moncrief agreed, getting more than a little satisfaction from the opportunity to stick a pin in the bloated balloon of Starling's ego. Later in the evening Moncrief called back, describing in detail the area that had been covered that day, and telling Vikter of the next day's plans.

Vikter hung up, did a quick calculation on his map, and called Dmitri. He could hear clinking glasses in the background as the Russian answered: "Da?"

"Have Sergei and Ivan get out their maps, and then get them on the line with you," he said without introduction. Dmitri switched to speakerphone, and Vikter confirmed that both pilots and the other navigator were there.

"The other group searched in the San Roque area today," Vikter said. "They didn't find the tribe. Tomorrow they will be on the west side of the Ucayali River in the Rio Pisqui. That gives you a clear shot at everything east of the Ucayali to the Brazilian border. Make sure you don't cross over into Brazil. You are not authorized to go into Brazilian airspace, and we do not want an international incident. Your presence is to be known by as few people as possible. For that reason, steer clear of any other aircraft you might come across."

He gave them coordinates for the search, which included much of the area covered by the National Geographic team that day. With two helicopters, both faster by half than the National Geographic chopper, Vikter had the luxury of duplicating the other team's search in case the white Indians had eluded them. As he hung up he could again hear clinking glasses.

He hoped that vodka would not be the undoing of his plan.

* * *

Sergei kept the lead helicopter at three hundred feet, electing to skim over the treetops rather than follow the Rio Buncuyo channel where a fisherman might see them and start asking questions. During the half hour it took to reach the beginning point for the day's search Dmitri tested the heat-sensing equipment, grunting once when the monitor showed a cluster of people close to the Buncuyo riverbank. Sergei dropped the chopper low over the river and buzzed the area. There were a half-dozen thatched huts and several brown-skinned natives looking up with wide eyes and mouths agape as the helicopter roared past.

"If heat images show people in the jungle how are we going to see them?" Sergei asked as they resumed their flightpath over the thick tree cover. "We won't be able to buzz them."

"Camera." Dmitri said, pointing at a contraption attached to a large spool of thin wire. "We lower through canopy and scan. If that doesn't work, one chopper land to check them out on foot." Dmitri said. "Other chopper hover to locate them with heat sensor."

"What if there's not a big enough area to land."

"Maybe we blow hole in trees to make place to land."

Chapter 37

"Where is Amaru?"

The thought came from somewhere inside Urco's drug-addled brain as brilliant colors and images of humanlike forms danced in his head.

He had carefully placed the talismans in the configuration taught to him by his father, had chewed the Devil's Trumpet, and had begun the chant, "um, um, um," as it took effect. Amid the undulating lights and hallucinations Urco fought to maintain a thread of control. He was aware the shamans had come, but the lucid thread allowed him to be surprised at his success in summoning them, and also be disappointed that his father was not among them. It had caused him to ask the question.

Who dares walk in the company of the shaman of the Chilco? a voice boomed, seeming to come from every direction.

"Oh wise fathers, it is I, Urco Amaru, shaman of the mighty Chilco, survivors of the great scourge, who seeks your counsel," Urco said, trying to correct his mistake by reciting the litany taught to him by his father. "Please look kindly upon the remnant of your progeny and your humble servant."

When no answer immediately came forth, Urco added: "And please forgive your humble servant for his mistakes which are, and will be, many, as he learns the ways of a shaman. These mistakes are made without guile but with the hope of learning from you."

We see you, Urco Amaru, the disembodied voice said. *For what do you seek our counsel?*

Carefully Urco explained Amaru's warning about the coming of the whiter-than-clouds people seeking the curare and of the debate among the tribe's elders.

Flames in the loose form of a man emerged, black holes formed eyes and mouth. The mouth spoke: *If you fight many will die, including some of your own family.* The black holes were engulfed by flames that faded until they were an indistinguishable part of the dancing colors on the inside of Urco's eyelids.

You cannot give them the curare, said another of the shaman, emerging. Only his pockmarked face, encircled by a shimmering silver shroud, was visible to Urco. *The Great Spirit has decreed that the Chilco will pass from this earth if the sanctity of the curare and its shamanic passage is not honored.*

"I have already violated that sanctity," Urco said. His declaration brought great wailing and sounds of anguish as the colors whipped violently.

"I refused to become shaman unless my wife and children also tasted the curare," he shouted above the din. "I do not want to live so long that I watch them die, and watch their children's children die. We are now few and our numbers are not growing. I believe the Great Spirit wants all Chilco to have the curare, not just the shaman."

The cacophony of the shamans was suddenly stilled as the largest of the spirit shaman, with diaphanous, smooth skin and robes the color of a rainbow, emerged from the miasma.

The sanctity of the curare has already been broken, he intoned. *When Amaru Topac added the golden frogs he changed the formula given to the Chilco by the Great Spirit. Yet the Chilco nation still survived.*

The colors danced, as though deep in thought. A large head, covered with burn scars, thrust forward on a scrawny neck until it was only inches from Urco's face. It studied the young shaman.

You are my legacy, marked to be the greatest of all the shamans, it finally said, referring to the birthmark that covered two-thirds of Urco's face. *It is different now than when the Great Spirit spoke to me and allowed me to lead our people from the mountains. Your counsel about giving the curare to all Chilco is well received. I will speak to the Great Spirit on this matter and you and I will talk again. Until then lead our people with the wisdom and humility that befits a shaman and a chieftain. You have been born into that right and you have fought for that right. Your leadership will be soon tested. You must lead our people back to the clouds. As in my time, there will be great tragedy and great personal loss, but it is time. You must go.*

Hatun Cayo faded, as did the colors in Urco's mind.

"But how am I to know where to go?" he shouted at the fading spirits.

Amaru Topac will guide you," the omnipresent voice said. *"His spirit will not rest until you are back on the mountaintop, in the clouds.*

And the visions were gone.

* * *

Tears streamed down Carrie's cheeks.

"I failed," she sobbed. "I messed up our one chance to warn them."

Castro realized that no matter what he said, she was not going to be consoled. *We'll get another chance*, he communicated, while at the same time wondering how things could have gotten so fucked up. He started to drift away, lost in his own thoughts, when Carrie's voice interrupted.

"I've got to stop them. I'm going to tell Uncle Vikter he's got to stop."

I wouldn't do that. Castro had been jerked back into Carrie's thought stream. *From what I've seen he's ruthless. He's willing to kill the Days to get the curare. He probably won't hesitate to kill you.*

"I'm family," she said. "He wouldn't hurt me. Remember, I was the one that gave him the information to begin with."

Castro wasn't convinced. *Maybe you should just call the cops.*

"And tell them what? My uncle, the chief operating officer of one of the country's biggest drug companies, has hired a bunch of Russians to kill some people on an expedition in Peru? They won't believe me, and they'll probably have me committed."

Okay. Bad idea. How about the press. You could go to... Castro didn't finish the thought because it wasn't any better than the previous one.

"I have an idea," Carrie said out loud. "I haven't watched all those cop shows for nothing."

* * *

At exactly 11:08 the next morning Carrie walked into the executive offices at Day Pharmaceuticals and announced to the receptionist that she was there to see her uncle. No, she didn't have an appointment, but she was sure he would want to see her because it had to do with the expedition in Peru. At 11:21 she was ushered into Vikter's office by his administrative assistant.

"How nice to see you," Vikter said as the assistant was leaving. Carrie suddenly wanted to leave too. Face-to-face with her uncle her resolve suffered a meltdown, but the office door closed and flight was no longer an option. All that was left was fight.

"I know you hired a bunch of Russians to go find the curare, and that you told them to kill anyone who got in their way and get rid of the evidence," she blurted, wanting to have it all said at once. Her face was bright red, and she was afraid she was going to hyperventilate. The shocked look on Vikter's face gave her no comfort.

"Where on earth did you get such a crazy idea," he said.

"From an unimpeachable source that was in the hotel room at the Hyatt Embarcadero when you met with the Russians."

"I'm afraid you are mistaken, young lady." Vikter's voice turned to ice. "I don't know who is giving you this information, but it's a lie."

"You've got to stop them, Uncle Vikter," she said with a shaky voice without acknowledging his denial. "You can't hurt people just to get that stuff. You can't destroy that tribe just to get it."

"Why would I want to hurt anyone or destroy anyone?"

Vikter responded. "The Days and National Geographic and Berrie University are out there looking for the tribe and for the curare. I work for the Days. If they find the curare we'll all benefit, including all of mankind if the life-extending qualities you claim are true. Why on earth would I want to do anything so heinous?"

"I don't know, but some Russian guy is going to make millions of rubles because of it."

"How did…" Vikter stopped himself. "That's enough of this. There is absolutely no truth in anything you've said. I think you better go back and talk to whoever gave you that information and find out what their motives are. They are dangerous."

Don't let up, Castro urged Carrie, floating above them. *"You've got him on the run. He almost admitted it.*

Despite everything inside her screaming "run," she sat in the chair, her hands overlapped demurely on her knees, and calmly delivered the ultimatum.

"If you don't call off your expedition, I will call Father Wyman at Berrie University and tell him about this. I will also send the information I have to the Marin County Sheriff's Department, the county district attorney, the *Chronicle,* all the local television stations and I'll post it on Facebook and YouTube."

She was shaking inside, and she might have wet her pants, but she had said it. A feeling of calm washed over her.

"This is blackmail, young lady. After all I've done for you and this is how I'm thanked. You should leave my office right now."

Vikter buzzed his administrative assistant. "Call building security. Ms. Waters needs to be escorted off the premises."

She didn't move from the chair. "For your information, Uncle Vikter," she said. "If I don't show up at work this afternoon, packages of this information will be sent out to all the news media and law enforcement offices before the last mail pickup today, and they'll be posted on social media by tonight."

As soon as Carrie left, Vikter called Vasiliev.

"One of Dmitri's people must have talked, probably too much vodka. I've got my niece on my ass because she knows all about the expedition. She's threatening to go to the press and the police."

"Tell me about your niece."

* * *

Carrie got into her car and locked the doors. She grasped the steering wheel hard with both hands as she started to shake, and then to cry.

After a minute she pulled herself together long enough to exit the parking lot, turning left on to Old Redwood Highway. My god, what have I done, she thought and began to shake again. She forced herself to steer the car onto the shoulder.

Castro was suddenly with her. *You were great, strong. As soon as you left his office he called Vasiliev.*

"What did they say?" Carrie asked, her voice shaky.

Vikter told Vasiliev about you and the meeting. Other than that he mostly listened.

"Did they say what they were going to do?"

I didn't hear anything about that. Vasiliev was doing most of the talking.

"Do you think they'll call it off?"

You had him pretty shook up and the telephone call didn't seem to calm him down any. They might.

Carrie got back to her office and checked her messages. There were none. She checked with Julie.

"No. Nothing." Julie said. "Do you want this envelope back?"

She held up a large manila envelope. Carrie hesitated, then took it from Julie and put it in her bottom desk drawer.

An hour and a half later her phone buzzed with an intra-office call. She picked up.

"Can you please come into my office." It was her sleazy boss.

Carrie stood and checked herself to make sure nothing she was wearing could be considered suggestive. She wished her skirt was a little longer, but skirt length was the least of her problems. Two uniformed police officers turned toward Carrie as she walked into the room.

"Sit down," her boss ordered from behind his desk.

One of the police officers stepped closer to her as she sat.

"I am Officer Orlov and this is my partner, Officer Patterson," he said. "We have here a court order for civil commitment."

He showed her a legal looking paper.

"You must come with us. This is not an arrest, but this order requires us to take you into custody, and deliver you to the Bellevue Psychiatric Hospital for evaluation."

Carrie's head was spinning, able to comprehend only part of what was said.

"What? Who?" she babbled, looking at her boss for an explanation. He leered at her.

"Get your stuff and get out," he snarled.

The two officers escorted Carrie back to her desk to get her purse. Coworkers gawked at the processional, or buried their heads in their work to avoid watching the embarrassing scene.

"What's going on?" Julie directed her question at Carrie who could only stand with her mouth open, in shock.

"It's a personal matter," Officer Orlov responded.

Carrie picked up her purse from the kneehole in her desk. She turned to Julie.

"Call..." but she couldn't think of anyone to have Julie call.

"You'll get a chance to make a call when we get to Bellevue," the officer said to Carrie.

"Bellevue!" Julie stood with a stunned look on her face.

Chapter 38

They scattered the contents of her purse on a table, picking through it for anything that was, or could be, sharp: nail file, mirror, fingernail clippers, pen. They dumped the rest back into her purse and handed it to her. Carrie stood in the antiseptic hallway, bare feet on terrazzo floor, wearing only her underwear and a hospital gown, holding her purse.

She had been allowed one phone call. She had called her mother.

"Mom, I've been put in Bellevue Psychiatric Hospital by Uncle Vikter. I need your to help. Call a lawyer, or something."

"You got money for a lawyer? I ain't got money for a lawyer," her mother replied.

"You've got to help me," Carrie pleaded. "Uncle Vikter said I threatened him. He lied, and now they say I'm a safety threat."

"I'd do more than threaten the sonofabitch if I had the chance. Did you threaten him?"

"No...yes...but not with physical harm. He sent some Russian thugs to Peru to find a drug and to kill anyone who got in their way."

"You're not making any sense," Katrina said. "You hearin' those voices again?"

"Mom, this is serious. I'm not crazy and I'm not dangerous, but I've got to get out of here. Some people need my help, and I'll lose my job."

"How long they goin' to keep you?" Katrina asked.

"They told me they could hold me up to seventy-two hours. Something called a 5150 hold. They're going to give me a bunch of psychological tests."

"See what I can do." Katrina's tone wasn't convincing.

"Mom, there has to be some kind of legal organization that looks out for people who are wrongly accused. Can you find out who they are? Can you do that for me?"

"Sure."

"Please."

"I said I would, didn't I?"

"Yes…Mom? I love you."

"Yeah. Me too."

* * *

They led Carrie down a corridor past doors with single tiny windows, some of them reinforced with bars, to her own single-windowed door which opened to a square white room with a twin bed made up with white sheets, a white table, a straight-back chair of the same absence of color, and a cheap wall clock, white. There were two white plastic hooks on the wall, and a large window that wouldn't open that looked out on a dingy courtyard. An attendant in scrubs sat on a bench with a person wearing a hospital gown identical to Carrie's. Carrie couldn't tell if the person was a man or a woman, but she could see the shackles around their ankles.

At least the courtyard wasn't white.

Someone brought Carrie a tray occupied by a slab of some kind of opaque meat; lumpy mashed potatoes with watery, tasteless gravy; and a mound of rubbery vegetables—corn and carrots and beans, she thought. Carrie couldn't touch it. She drank the apple juice that came with pills that had been given to her "to help you sleep," but she didn't take the pills.

It was dark outside when an attendant came to pick up the tray.

"Could I get something to read?" Carrie asked, although the room, dimly lit with a single overhead light, was hardly conducive to reading.

"Lights out in ten minutes," he said. "You see the doctor in the morning. Better get your sleep."

She crawled onto the hard mattress, pulled the thin blanket up around her neck and waited for the lights to go out.

She thought of Castro: Terry, are you out there? Can you hear me? I need you to come to me. I need you to tell me what to do.

The lights went out. Carrie cried herself to sleep.

Three thousand miles away Terry Castro's spirit agonized over his inability to help the small band of people strung out in a single file below him.

* * *

Fifteen small horses, tethered together, woven baskets hung over their backs, splashed single file across the shallow river. A woman waded knee-deep in front of them holding a rope attached to the lead horse, eyes scanning the river for potential predators.

Already half of the tribe, bundles across their backs, had crossed. They journeyed westward into the sunset along a path they had carved out of the rainforest little more than a month ago when they had come to this place believing it would be their home for the rest of their lives. Urco and other young men, bodies glistening with sweat in the fading light, led the exodus, hacking away at the foliage that had grown over the path since their earlier pilgrimage.

Within an hour the camp that had been home to two hundred was empty, only small notches in tree trunks where lean-tos had been anchored gave countenance to the fact that the Chilco had once lived there. In a month that, too, would be erased by the relentless advance of the rainforest.

Through the night they pushed on until Urco halted the column as the first shafts of daylight leaked through the trees. A party of four materialized out of the jungle toting baskets similar to those carried by the horses. They dumped the contents, piles of silvery flopping fish, on the ground. Immediately a group of women began gutting the fish while others distributed the cleaned fish to the quarter-mile-long human convoy. Baskets of acai berries, picked during the evening's march, were circulated. When everyone was fed two fishermen gathered the fish carcasses and entrails in a basket and returned them to the river. Fishing nets were stretched over vines to dry, and the horses were led off the path and tethered. Several women cut palm fronds and swept the path, removing all signs of human use.

The remnant of the once-mighty Chilco nation faded into the rainforest to wait out the day.

* * *

Castro had traveled with them since they broke camp, marveling at their efficiency and the minimal impact they made on the environment. That two hundred people and fifteen horses could literally become invisible in minutes, leaving no trace that they had ever been there, left him in awe. But his awe was tempered. They could deceive the human eye but heat sensors could see what eyes could not. Castro wondered if either expedition was close.

One hundred thirty miles to the southwest Moncrief, Starling and crew were starting the third day of their search on the Rio Pisqui, a meandering river that stretched one hundred fifty miles to the highlands at the base of the Andes Mountains. Stops at the villages of Vencedor and Nuevo Egipto failed to turn up any sightings of, or information about, the *Criollos,* and thus far the highlight of the trip had been Gilbert teaching Leon how to fly a drone. The expedition's helicopter, which had been biting off three hundred square mile chunks of the rainforest daily, was no more successful.

"We've always thought that it was unlikely." Starling was shouting over the sound of the outboard motor as Castro's spirit materialized over the boat in which Starling, Leon, Gilbert, and the driver were sitting. "But we have to eliminate it as a possibility."

"Why do you think it's unlikely they would be in this area?" Leon, whose growing friendship with Gilbert had kept him in Starling's boat, asked.

"Two reasons," Starling said, still trying to reestablish his authority following the embarrassing episode with Vikter Glass and Moncrief. "Since we didn't find them around San Roque, I believe they have moved. There's more population as you move south from San Roque, and the ancestral home of these people is north and west. It is my judgment that they will stay away from populated areas, either moving east toward Brazil, an area literally devoid of population which would take months, maybe years, to explore, or they will move northwest toward the Andes Mountains and their ancestral home. That is what I am betting on."

Grudgingly Castro had to agree. Starling might be a narcissistic ass, but he knew his stuff.

"Tomorrow, when we're done here, we'll start north on the Ucayali," Starling continued. "I believe they are somewhere north of Contamana. Except for the villages along the river there are about seven thousand square miles of uninhabited jungle that would be an easy place for a small tribe to live without being discovered."

Castro was not exactly sure where the Chilco were, but he was satisfied that the expedition was not close at the moment. He feared that Starling's intuition, born of experience, might change that.

* * *

One hundred fifty miles east of Starling's position the two Russian Mi-24Vs whistled through Peruvian airspace at nearly two hundred miles an hour, intent upon completing their scan south of San Roque from the Ucayali to the Brazilian border, thirty-six hundred square miles of treetops, streams and marshland. During the three days they had devoted to the area they had buzzed two more river villages. Both Dmitri and Sergei took pleasure in the wide-eyed amazement of villagers as the powerful gunships swooped down upon them. They had also seen the glowing images of large animals, and had flown over one area that triggered more than a hundred electronic reactions on the sensor monitor. It created excitement in the chopper, believing they had found the tribe, but after several passes the source of the multiple heat reflections was identified—a herd of cows.

Castro heard the familiar *whup, whup, whup* of the rotors, taking him back to his medical evacuation from the rainforest. He had remembered Vikter calling the man with the bullet-shaped head "Dmitri," and that was enough to teleport him to the helicopter with Dmitri, Sergei and a third Russian. He couldn't understand their conversations, and the navigator's flight maps were unintelligible. He left the Russians, frustrated, not knowing their location or their proximity to the Chilco.

He decided to check in with Carrie.

* * *

Where are we?

"Thank God you're back." Carrie had never been so happy to hear a voice in her head. "I tried to reach you. We're in Bellevue Psychiatric Hospital. They brought me here yesterday."

She told Castro about Uncle Vikter having her committed and all that had happened since.

"They are supposed to be giving me psychological tests to evaluate me, but I haven't seen anyone yet," she said. "I don't know what to do. If I tell them I talk to dead people, they'll never let me out of here. If they ask me for my source of information about what I said to Uncle Vikter, what am I going to tell them?"

Castro could literally see the panic in her. He knew that words were not going to calm her.

Lay down on the bed. I'm going to lie down with you. Take the pillow and wrap your arms around it. Hold it against you as tight as you can… That's me you're holding…slow down…shhhh…relax…I'm right here next to you. We're like two spoons…relax…

They lay that way for several minutes, the young woman in a fetal position, for all outward appearances looking like she might belong in a mental ward, and the invisible man, wishing he could feel her warmth and that she could feel his.

Now, let's think this thing through.

She lay still, quiet, trying to hold on to the fantasy that she was actually holding him.

How long have you been here?

"Since yesterday. Late afternoon. They took me right from work. I was so embarrassed."

What time is it now?

"Nearly noon. They should be bringing lunch soon."

And you haven't seen a doctor…or a psychiatrist?

"No."

When you do you need to tell them you're a medium, a spiritual consultant. They'll already know about it from Uncle Vikter. If you try to cover it up it will just make you look guilty, like you're ashamed of it. Face it head on. Tell them as many stories as you can. Tell them about Leon and his brother.

"I'd…I'd feel uncomfortable doing that. It would be breaking a confidence."

Ordinarily I'd agree with you, but you need to get out of here and the best way to do that is to look honest, make them believe in your ability and show them you're not dangerous to yourself or to anyone else.

"They are going to ask me about threatening Uncle Vikter.

What do I tell them?

Tell them the truth. Tell them about me. About the poison. About the Chilco. Have them confirm the expedition by contacting Father Wyman at Berrie. Have them call the rehab center to confirm I'm there. Tell them everything.

"Should I tell them I got the information about Uncle Vikter from you?"

Castro thought for a moment.

Tell them you got it from one of the Russians. When they ask who, tell them you can't tell them because he'd get killed if anyone found out.

There was a knock on the door and the same attendant from the prior evening entered with a lunch tray in one hand and a magazine in the other.

"I brought you this," he said, handing the magazine to Carrie. "You should eat something." He was staring at the untouched breakfast tray on the desk.

"When am I going to see the doctor?" Carrie asked.

"Haven't you seen one yet?"

"No."

"That's unusual," he said. "I'll check and let you know."

The attendant left. He didn't come back.

Chapter 39

Forty-eight hours into her 5150 hold Carrie had a visitor.

"How did you know I was here?" she asked.

"I couldn't reach you by phone and you weren't home last night, so I went to your office this morning. They told me you don't work there anymore." Holly said. "Your friend, Julie, told me. She also gave me this. Said it was yours."

Holly held up a manila envelope for Carrie to see through the thick glass that separated the two women.

"Oh my god, I forgot about that."

"What is going on?" Holly asked.

Carrie related the nightmare of the last four days: her confrontation with Vikter, the threat to the Days and the Berrie University expedition, the police coming to her office and bringing her to Bellevue.

"Everything is explained in that envelope," she said. "I gave it to Julie before I went to see Uncle Vikter just in case something happened. The envelope was Terry's idea. When I went back to work after the meeting Julie gave it back to me and I tossed it in a drawer. Did she really say I wasn't working there anymore?"

Holly nodded. "What's happened since they put you in here?" she asked.

"Nothing. I haven't had any tests, haven't seen a doctor, haven't been outside my room except to go to the bathroom, and now to come and see you. The cops told me that they could hold me for seventy-two hours to do a psychiatric evaluation, but I haven't seen anyone. Yesterday an orderly said he'd look into it and I haven't seen him since."

"Something isn't right," Holly said. "I'm going to talk to whoever's in charge and get you out of here."

Minutes later Holly was sitting on the opposite side of a metal desk, facing a large woman with a florid face and a hostile attitude.

"Our medical staff will be evaluating Ms. Waters in the next twenty-four hours," the woman, "Annetta Fielding" according to the nameplate on her desk, said. "You are not family so that is all I can tell you."

"Can I speak to the psychiatrist who will..."

"No. All communications go through me."

"I don't suppose the evaluation report will be made available."

"That is correct," Mrs. Fielding said. "Now, if you'll excuse me, I have a meeting."

Holly, simmering over her failure to learn anything, got closer to the boiling point when a nurse informed her that "Ms. Waters is no longer allowed visitors" because she would be going through intense evaluation over the next twenty-four hours.

That is so much bullshit, Holly thought to herself as she left the hospital. She punched in the speed dial number of her favorite criminal attorney in Chicago.

"I need a lawyer in San Francisco that knows about civil commitments from the defense side," she said.

* * *

Less than an hour after her meeting with Holly a nurse came into Carrie's room pushing a cart filled with vials and syringes.

"You'll be seeing Dr. Karalov shortly," the nurse said. "He asked me to give you this to relax you."

She took a syringe off the cart, pushing the plunger to squirt a little of the clear liquid from the end of the needle.

"What is it?" Carrie asked.

"Just a mild sedative."

Carrie offered her arm, palm up. Holly really made something happen, she thought.

* * *

In the first hour of the seventy-two-hour institutional confinement allowed by section 5150 of California's code, the video of the Chilco hunting party went viral on YouTube. A voice-over explained that it was a fraternity hazing prank gone wrong at an unnamed Midwestern university. A few hours later a story, with screenshots from the video, was circulated through social media, and to every site on the web related to spiritual advisors, mediums, séances and the spiritual world. It claimed that Carrie Waters, a medium located in San Francisco, had used the photos to try and blackmail unnamed persons and had been arrested.

The broadcast brought an avalanche of negative response, mostly on the theme that no bona fide spiritual adviser would use their gift for such base activity, but also speculation, stated as fact, that she was possessed by one evil spirit or another. A post twenty-four hours into the social media tsunami let it be known that Carrie had been committed to a mental institution, confirming in the minds of the more extreme the accuracy of their evil-spirit theory. For the less conspiratorially minded it was the final straw. Carrie was no longer welcome in the realm of necromancers and spiritualists.

* * *

Vikter was impressed by Vasiliev's ability to mount a campaign of such magnitude and thoroughness, and by his connections in the San Francisco police department. His own relationship with the Bellevue administration had been the cement that welded all the pieces together.

His sister's brat wouldn't be able to hold her head up when she finally got out of Bellevue, and no cop or prosecutor would take her seriously if she did try to level charges against him. Plus, he thought, there was an added benefit. The YouTube thing would undermine any scientific claims of the Berrie University/

National Geographic expedition and cast doubt on Leon and Mahogany's credibility. It was a win-win for Vikter.

* * *

"It's been more than seventy-two hours and she hasn't been released," Holly said, her decibel level rising.

She had hoped for someone a little more dynamic than the phlegmatic sixty-year-old lawyer with thinning, sandy-colored hair and a tweed jacket with leather elbow patches sitting across from her, but her attorney friend in Chicago had assured her that Nigel Davies was the best civil commitment lawyer in San Francisco.

"If they determine that they need more time for evaluation, section 5250 of the California Code allows institutions like Bellevue to hold a patient for an additional fourteen days," Davies said.

"Fourteen days!" Holly shrieked the words. "She is no more crazy or dangerous than I am. Her uncle is orchestrating this to cover up his own dirty dealing."

Davies raised his hand to calm Holly.

"We can file a habeas corpus and ask for an adverse psychiatric examination," he said. "We can probably get a hearing in less than a week. How soon we can get the adverse will depend on schedules."

"And after that you've got to schedule another hearing where the psychiatrists will play he-said, she-said and the judge will take sixty days to guess who is right. Correct?" Holly said.

"I would not use the word guess, but essentially that is correct, assuming, of course, that the adverse determines that your friend is sane and not a danger to herself or the community."

Holly slumped in her chair.

"There may be another way," the mild-mannered lawyer said.

Holly looked up, hopeful.

"Please remember that I said 'may' because it depends upon what Bellevue has, or has not, done with respect to Ms. Waters. I could file the habeas corpus tomorrow and subpoena all medical and psychiatric records from Bellevue. If they have done everything by the book, then they will comply with the subpoena and we will have to go through the process we just talked about. However, if, as you suspect, this has somehow been orchestrated by the victim's uncle, then they will probably not have done everything by the book, in which case they will have something to hide. They could try to quash the subpoena or, as I will suggest is a better alternative, to avoid the bad publicity and the legal costs they could simply release her, in which case we will call off the dogs and their ethical indiscretions will disappear without scrutiny."

Holly's hunch, and Davies's persuasiveness, paid off. Bellevue's administrator quickly decided that the favor he was doing for Vikter Glass didn't include malpractice claims, bad publicity and getting fired from his job. He informed Vikter that he had to release Carrie Waters. To his surprise, Vikter was not upset. "You've done everything you could," Glass had said, apparently satisfied that four days in the hospital were sufficient to cure his niece's problems.

Within twenty-four hours of Nigel Davies's ultimatum Carrie was released. Holly, back in Chicago, had called Sanjay to send a car to pick up Carrie at the hospital.

"Miss Holly." Sanjay said three hours later, cradling the phone between his shoulder and his cheek as he attended to Carrie, "Miss Carrie was drugged when we picked her up at the hospital. We brought her back to the Days' home where we can watch her. When she's ready I'll have her taken back to her apartment."

"Keep me posted on her condition," Holly said. "And, Sanjay, thank you."

* * *

Carrie drifted in the fog. She could hear a singsong voice but could not make sense of the words. Other voices were in her head. Voices she didn't recognize. Her body had no substance. There was sunlight. She wondered if she was in heaven. The name Terry Castro passed through and she tried to catch it. Who was Terry Castro? She felt dampness on her face. No, just her forehead. The singsong voice again. Who are you, she wondered?

Amaru.

The name was familiar.

Chapter 40

"Hannah. Pick up if you're there."

"I'm here, Crocko. What's up?

"Heading back to Contamana for refueling and just picked up something on radar. Judging by the speed looks like a couple of helicopters. Want me to check them out?"

"Probably one of those fishing junkets, but I'll have our people check with the Peruvian government to see if they're running any kind of military exercise in the area, just in case?"

"I'll keep an eye on them, but you're probably right, somebody out chasing peacock bass. I'll let you know if anything changes."

The National Geographic pilot watched as the two blips on the radar screen moved north, eventually dropping off the screen. I'd like to do that someday, he thought, just take a trip for pleasure once. Maybe fish peacock bass, or tarpon, or marlin.

The two Mi-24Vs sped north toward Buncuyo having completed the day's search grid. Sergei and Ivan bantered back and forth over the radio as they drove the choppers onward at two hundred miles per hour, talking about a woman they had seen the night before in a Buncuyo bar, needling each other about how many shots of vodka it would take before either of them had the courage to approach her.

Approaching the Buncuyo airfield from the southwest they passed over the tiny village of Tabalosos, eighty-five kilometers out on the banks of the Rio Tapiche. Ten clicks farther, scarcely two minutes of flight time, there was a large cluster of heat marks on the monitor. Dmitri brought it to Sergei's attention.

"We come back tomorrow and check it out," Dmitri said, too thirsty to take the time for a second pass. "I have coordinates. If it's tribe they still be there tomorrow."

The next morning the Russian helicopters retraced their flightpath over Tabalosos but the monitor didn't light up as it had the night before.

"Probably just herd of cows, like before," Dmitri said.

The Mi-24Vs banked east, toward the Brazilian border and the grid that Vikter had designated for the day. Fifteen minutes later they flew over a river, unnamed on their charts, which, six days earlier, had been the home of the Chilco.

Urco had heard the terrible sounds of the monster beetles that flew without wings as they passed overhead. He listened as the *wump, wump, wump* sound faded and was confident that they had not been seen, but that night he pushed the tribe harder to put as much distance between themselves and the strange flying insects as possible.

They covered six miles before stopping, drinking from the natural water reservoirs of the bromeliads that grew abundantly in the rainforest, and eating the meat of the white ibis. They had seen a flock of the flamingo-like birds the night before, wading in the shallows of the Rio Tapiche. The hunting party that Urco had sent out as the Chilco began their nightly pilgrimage waited at the river's edge until the birds settled for the night, then took them without sound, butchering them in the water where they were captured so that river-born predators would devour the remains by morning. Only the thick bodies of the tall birds were carried off by the hunting party which caught up with the column at dawn as it stopped for the day. The meat of the ibis was stripped from the carcasses and soaked in the juice of camu camu fruit, picked during the night's journey. The acidic juice cured the meat, giving it a piquant taste.

As full daylight approached the tribe again disappeared into the dense cover to wait out the day. Urco, with his wife and children under the leaves of a low-growing palmito tree, his little marmoset perched on his shoulder, meditated, blocking out the sounds of the rainforest so he could listen for the silent voice of his guide. There was no need to quiet his children. They were already sleeping, tired from the night's journey. His wife, whose time was soon, also dozed, dreaming that this child would forever be remembered as the one born on the great trek back to their home in the clouds.

Urco knew that Amaru was his guide. He had been told so by the spirits of the shaman, and subtle signs confirmed it—the flightpath of a butterfly, the distant growl of an ocelot, a tree forked in a peculiar way—were like beacons, leading him to a path, or to food or safety, but inevitably westward toward the mountains. Urco's own skills were not insignificant, but alone they would not have been enough. The Chilco might have wandered for years, never finding their way home, but Urco was being led by an unerring scout providing signs that were as clear as points on a compass.

Seventy-five miles to the southeast the Berrie University expedition joined the helicopter crew in Contamana for the evening, a week of unsuccessful exploration behind them. Mahogany was happy to be back on solid ground. She had asked one of the crew to ferry her to the city earlier so she could stroll in the open market. Children followed her like she was the pied piper, and before long she purchased candy at the market and was passing it out to the youngsters who clustered around her. By evening, when she returned to the river to join the rest of the team, she was the talk of Contamana, and, as far as the children were concerned, a candidate for sainthood.

When the crew walked from the river to one of the city's restaurants word spread quickly among the fifteen thousand inhabitants of Contamana. White people were seldom seen, but the presence of a black couple, whose six-foot-two-inch heights dwarfed the locals, was unprecedented, and the people lined the dirt streets, hoping to get a glimpse of the Days on their return trip to the barge.

Next morning the boats headed north on the Ucayali, Leon now a permanent fixture in the boat with Gilbert and Starling, Mahogany joining Moncrief in the other boat. A day on dry land with the Contamana children had refreshed her. The team would spend the day investigating the Rio Ipacta tributary while the helicopter crew continued its sweep east of the Ucayali as far as the Pampas del Sacramento highlands.

Mahogany sat in the bow, relaxed. The trip had not been easy for her, but it had been worth it. Leon, without all the medications he had been taking for the past few years and with a new challenge in his life, was his old self. She had her husband back.

* * *

"What am I going to do?" Carrie wailed. "I don't have a job, and I'm all over the internet. They've trashed me. Uncle Vikter has trashed me."

It was her second day back in her apartment after recovering from the overdose of drugs she had been given at Bellevue. It was confirmed that she no longer had a job when she picked up the mail after being dropped off by the Days' driver. Her paycheck was in the mail, stamped "final," as well as a check for her accumulated vacation. That, and the few dollars she had in her checking account, was what she had to live on until she found another job. By that evening she knew it was not going to be easy.

What about your spiritual adviser clients?

"I doubt that I have any left. I was gone for over a week and missed both my appointments, and I've been dissed on every blog and billboard on the web. People aren't going to want to come within ten miles of me."

Castro was quiet. He didn't have any ideas, and he knew she wasn't in a fix-it mood. She wanted to be angry, and she wanted to vent, and she had every right to. She had been royally screwed.

As the intensity of her anger wore itself out Castro maneuvered the conversation away from Carrie's plight hoping to distract her. He described how the Chilco had left their village leaving no trace behind. How they traveled by night and fed themselves on their march by using things that their environment provided. He was particularly effusive about how quickly and completely they could disappear into the rainforest.

His thought train was interrupted by a phone call. Holly was calling to see how she was doing. It gave Carrie another opportunity to unload her frustrations and her angst.

"Look at it as an opportunity," Holly said. "I would imagine that mediums are always being threatened by those who don't understand your gift. Call your existing clients and tell them that a relative who doesn't understand the spiritual world, and is jealous of your psychic powers, had you involuntarily committed. Tell them that while you were fighting to get released you had great revelations, revelations about the spiritual world that made you more insightful and will enable you to become a better practitioner of your craft. I'll bet if you approach it that way you won't lose a client. Then use the same approach on the internet. See if you can get a couple testimonials from existing clients that you can put on your website or post on Facebook. You're in one of the few areas that might benefit from this kind of publicity."

A few minutes later the conversation ended.

I could give you a testimonial.

It made Carrie laugh. "Did you hear all of that conversation?" she asked.

Most of it. Actually, I think Holly had a good idea…did you really have a revelation?

"I didn't have any spiritual connection the first couple of days. I was too upset. When they drugged me, though, I was kind of in a euphoric state. I remember seeing your name, although I don't remember talking to you. Everything else was swirling stuff, like fog or smoke."

She thought for a moment.

"I remember seeing some heads, not clear, black and silver and orange, disfigured, and I remember a singsong voice. I heard it twice, but I don't remember anything it said. Then I remember seeing the name Amaru, just like I saw yours."

Maybe he was trying to reach out to you.

Carrie sat quietly, lost in thought. "He's on the other side now," she finally said. "I shouldn't need him to be asleep or in some drug-induced trance to reach him now."

It might be a way to warn Urco of the Russians.

Carrie nodded. This time there was no hesitation. She would not let Uncle Vikter exploit these people for his own greed.

Chapter 41

For two days Carrie tried to reach Amaru, interspersing her attempts with phone calls to her spiritual consulting clients, all the while fearing that Uncle Vikter was not yet done ruining her life. Holly's straightforward approach in explaining what had happened proved to be appealing to three of her five clients, even evoking sympathy from one. One, however, had clearly been poisoned by the negative media campaign, telling Carrie that she didn't want to be involved with "a crook and a charlatan." The fifth client, Leon Day, of course, knew nothing of what had transpired.

She was venting on the phone with Holly and answering the door for the pizza delivery boy, when she sensed that Castro had returned. She put the pizza box on the kitchen table and said goodbye to Holly.

"Hi," she said.

Hi yourself. Did you get that pizza for us?

"I wish."

Funny, I hadn't thought at all about food until I watched the Chilco on the trail. It's amazing how they do it. Bad news is that now pizza looks good to me. I'll bet it smells great.

"Pepperoni, mushrooms, green peppers. I shouldn't have, but I splurged. If I'm going to go broke and be out on the street I might as well do it with a full stomach."

Good for you. You need to pamper yourself once in a while. It shows optimism. Besides, you're getting too skinny.

"No such thing," Carrie said. Then: "Do you feel hungry? You know, like growling stomach hunger pangs?"

No, but it looks good. Have a piece.

"It seems weird eating when you're here, like I'm being rude."

Then eat two, one for you and one for me.

"Hmm. At least that way I won't be accused of being too

skinny."

Like two sweethearts they continued the lighthearted banter until it inevitably turned to events in Peru. Carrie pushed the pizza box to the edge of the kitchen table and spread out her map.

The tribe crossed the Rio Tapiche, two days ago. They seem to be heading west, toward the Andes. I think Urco is leading them back to their ancestral home. Otherwise I think he'd be leading them in the opposite direction, deeper into the rainforest. Have you been able to reach Amaru?

"No. I've tried a couple of times. Is there any sign of either the Days or the Russians?"

I've visited both. I can't understand the Russians or read their maps so I don't really know where they are. They're doing an aerial search with two helicopters using heat sensors and are covering a lot of territory, but so far they haven't found them. The Days and their crew are on the Ucayali River just north of Contamana. They will intersect with the Chilco if they both stay on the same route.

"That's good, isn't it?"

If Starling wasn't leading the trip I'd say yes, but I can't believe that his finding them won't result in a disaster.

"But we need them to get the curare." Carrie was about to say, that's your only hope, but caught herself.

I know.

Castro had read her thoughts.

"I'm sorry. I didn't mean to think that way."

Don't be sorry. I've reconciled myself to the fact that there is no antidote. This is me. At least until my body gives up.

Carrie tried to lighten the mood, even as a tear leaked out of the corner of her eye. "This is hard," she said. "I can't even lie to you because you can read my mind."

* * *

Vikter saved cigars for special occasions and this definitely qualified.

The IPO had been a success. He and Vasiliev had bought in at the opening price of $24.25 per share. News of the successful trial and FDA approval of a new asthma drug, released just before the IPO launch, drove the price to $36.00 per share by the time the offering sold out later in the day. Vikter had made a profit of over eighty million dollars in less than eight hours.

Smoke spiraled upward from his Cohiba Behike 52, mingling its aroma with the other hundred-dollar cigars of the people who had made it possible for him to become controlling shareholder of the company.

After suppressing the value of the company during the past two years Vikter could now change tactics and, with millions in the coffers from the stock offering, drive the company to new heights. If the poison from Peru proved to be a real fountain of youth drug, Day Pharmaceuticals would become the biggest pharmaceutical company in the world, making him, Vikter Glass, one of the wealthiest men in the world! Perhaps for a long, long time, while lesser men without access to the life-extending drug, watched their health and their fortunes dwindle.

The Days did all right, he reasoned. They kept five percent of the company and got nearly one hundred million in cash from the offering. With any luck, in five years their five percent would be worth more than the entire company right now. And if they raised a stink over the clandestine IPO, he had Vasiliev's support, which gave him an absolute majority to vote them down. If they tried to take legal action, he held their power of attorney to run the company as he saw fit.

He doubted he would need to use it. Vasiliev's internet campaign would make any claims about the lost tribe look like a hoax. It would be one more piece of evidence that Leon was crazy. The likelihood that a judge could find Leon legally incompetent would keep them from challenging his takeover. Of that he was confident.

The only gloom in Vikter's otherwise sunny day was the failure of either expedition to find the lost tribe. He could tell his Russian crew was losing interest, evident from their daily phone conversations. The failure of Starling's expedition was equally concerning. Reports came in from Starling and the National Geographic woman but they were like a broken record: no sign of the tribe had been found.

The prospect of wasting several million dollars on an unsuccessful attempt to find the curare left him unable to enjoy the fruits of the successful day. It was the money. The money spent without return. More important, the money that he would not make if the expedition failed.

In the back of his mind he also knew it was about his age and losing a chance at near-immortality.

* * *

Only the prospect of U.S. dollars kept Dmitri going. Amid grumbling and mild threats of mutiny, he used his formidable size and nasty temperament to drive his crew back into the air each day, zigzagging over the tree canopy and the hundreds of rivers of the rainforest.

"No one said would be easy," he bellowed. "You have nice bed. You have vodka and food. You being paid. You not being shot at. Get your asses in the helicopters. We make big money at the end. You see."

Their search continued to take them east and north of Buncuyo, into thousands of square miles of the Peruvian Amazon, as the Chilco column stealthily crept just fifteen miles south of the Russian's base city, crossing the Rio Buncuyo in the wee hours of the morning on the tenth day of their journey.

* * *

Castro's body no longer looked like him. Skin and muscle hung loose. His hair had grayed. He now breathed with a ventilator. Only his heart seemed to function properly, pumping a steady fifty-eight beats a minute, pushing blood through his withering frame.

Carrie stayed for an hour, holding his flaccid hand. She called Holly on her way back to her apartment.

"We're losing him," she said. "They put him on a ventilator. His body's wasting away."

"I'll fly out this weekend," Holly said. "Could you get me at the airport Friday night?"

"Let me check my social calendar. Oh, yeah, I forgot. I don't have one. Of course I'll pick you up. Just text me the flight details."

"Could you do a session for me so I can talk to Terry? I'll pay you."

"We can do a session, but you can't pay me. I already owe you more than I'll ever be able to repay for getting me out of Bellevue."

On Friday they stopped at the rehab center on the way from the airport. The state of Castro's physical condition squeezed the normal effervescence from Holly.

"I talked to Terry a few days ago," Carrie said as they motored north on 101 past Candlestick Park. "He said he's known for some time there wasn't a cure. He seems okay with that."

"Are you okay with that?" Holly asked.

"Not really. I cry a lot, but I have to be. With the way this is coming down, with Uncle Vikter and everything, I don't think there's a chance he would even try to find an antidote. Even if he did, it's not likely it would come in time to save Terry."

The two sat in quiet the rest of the way to Carrie's apartment. Over cheap beer and baloney sandwiches they commiserated, trying to avoid saying anything that would bring tears.

"What happens when his body dies?" Holly asked.

"I'm not sure. I've tried to do some research but this is a pretty odd situation. There's not much out there to learn from."

"I'm going to miss him," Holly said, and that was all it took. The dam broke and Carrie's tears flowed, giving Holly's tears permission to do the same. The two women reached out and embraced in their mutual sorrow over the man they both loved.

* * *

Saturday morning's fog burned off. They sat in a coffee shop, Holly swirling her biscotti in her latte. "What are you going to do when this is all over?" she asked.

"When what is all over?"

"When this expedition is over, and the Days come back. When Terry's body finally gives out?"

"I don't know. Keep trying to get a job, I guess, and keep on with my spiritual counseling."

"Why don't you come to Chicago? Work with me."

The offer caught Carrie by surprise. "What would I do? I'm no private investigator."

"You have nothing to keep you in San Francisco, and you have talents—abilities—that could be useful in my business."

Carrie thought of her last conversation with her mother. Holly was right. She had nothing keeping her here.

"I'll think about it," she said.

That afternoon they talked with Castro. Carrie morphed into professional mode, acting only as a communications conduit without emotion or nuance. The ex-spouses, now two old friends still in love but on a different level, communicated freely, happily for nearly an hour until Carrie had to call a halt. She had reached the end of her stamina. She needed sugar and sleep.

Before I leave, Castro communicated to Carrie, *can you and I talk later this evening? I've some thoughts about how we might reach Amaru.*

"Yeah, sure." Two Pixie Stix later Carrie was sound asleep, sprawled on her bed.

Holly ordered in Chinese for dinner.

"I'm really sorry I had to end your session," Carrie said between bites of moo goo gai pan. "You guys were enjoying yourselves so much."

"I didn't realize there was so much stress involved for you."

"I go along just fine and then suddenly hit a wall, like someone pulled a plug and all my energy runs out. You two can talk more when I get back in touch with him tonight."

When they did reconnect, Castro reminded Carrie of *Twilight Zone* and how she had first made contact with him.

I think we should set it up like one of your regular sessions. We each sit in a chair with a table between us. Turn the lights down. I ask you to contact an old friend, Amaru, who has passed away. You treat it just like any other session and reach out to Amaru. It sounds contrived, but it worked with me.

What's to lose, Carrie thought. She arranged chairs around the table, explaining to Holly what she was about to do.

The séance began.

Chapter 42

Starling and Moncrief stood knee-deep in a river grass bank on the west branch of the Rio Maquia, their bodies positioned to reflect their peaceable intentions: arms extended, elbows bent, palms out. Maria Garrido, the expedition's interpreter, standing with them, had repeated the phrase: "We come in peace to speak with the leader of the Chilco" no less than a hundred times in each of the many dialects of Quechua and Aymara, the two most common native languages spoken in Peru.

A quarter mile away Gilbert controlled a drone from one of the boats, flying it over the forest that grew within twenty yards of the river. Leon and Mahogany sat on each side of him, looking at thermal images dotting the monitor.

The three emissaries had remained at the same spot on the grassy bank for more than an hour, not moving because the thermal images hadn't moved.

They were in the third week of their expedition, searching the backwaters of the Ucayali River north of the city of Orellana, when Gilbert's drone flew over a separate, nearby waterway and picked up a sprinkling of hot spots.

"That would be the Rio Maquia," Starling had said. "There's less than a half mile between the two rivers at this point. The spots on the monitor are probably a flock of flamingos."

Gilbert, with Leon eagerly looking on, spun the drone and flew it back over the same area.

"The hot spots aren't in the water," Gilbert said. "They're about a hundred yards back in the jungle. Maybe we should call in the chopper and have them take a closer look."

Moncrief's boat, cruising on the opposite side of the backwater, overheard the radio call to the helicopter and joined them. They beached both boats on the muddy shoreline to allow everyone to stretch their legs. Twenty minutes later Dial positioned the

National Geographic helicopter a half mile upstream, and Gilbert explained what the drone had picked up. The chopper pulled away, gaining altitude, and headed east, the *wop, wop* of the rotor fading but audible as it methodically crisscrossed the area.

"We've got something hot here," Dial said after a few minutes. "Heat images, a hundred or more, in an area about the size of three or four football fields. Some of them are clearly people. But I don't see any signs of a village or encampment."

He continued to circle the area. "I think there are more than I thought. Maybe two hundred," he said.

"Getting low on fuel," he radioed a few minutes later, disappointment evident in his voice. "I'm heading back to Contamana. Be back in about an hour."

"We'll keep an eye on them with the drones," Gilbert said.

"We've got them. We've got them." Like a kid on Christmas morning, Starling bounced up and down with glee. There were hugs and congratulations all around even as Moncrief warned against jumping to conclusions. They radioed the barge train to join them. The next hour was spent portaging one of the boats the half mile to the Rio Maquia. The rest of the evening they discussed how to approach the people concealed in the jungle. They were all mindful of Castro's slow-motion video of the flying dart.

* * *

He had expected them.

For three days the apparition had appeared to Urco in a dream: a woman spirit who foretold of whiter-than-clouds people who would come in peace seeking the curare, but the dream always dissolved into a vision of a black-skinned god and goddess, with shimmering smiles and arms extended in welcome, as he and his people floated towards them. The words of Hatun Cayo then blotted out the serene image, warning of violence that would befall the Chilco and his own family, the last of the words drowned out by a sharp, rattling sound as huge flying beetles appeared, spitting fire from their eyes; and then his own face, purple birthmark turning blood red and flowing from his face, staining the rainforest until its only color was red. And always, at the end the apparition, standing on a mountaintop among the clouds, beckoning him with one hand while pouring curare from a gourd with the other.

When he awoke from the dreams he felt the presence of his father. He prayed to him for clarification but none came; only the same dream the following day, and the next. The fourth day there was no dream, but a strange, loud voice wakened him. Other tribe members were already awake, eyes wide in fear. With hand gestures he calmed them.

Urco edged in the direction of the voice. Through the wall of the rainforest he could see three whiter-than-clouds people standing on the riverbank; the river the Chilco were intending to cross that night. The voice that had awakened him, a woman's voice, continued to say words he could not understand.

He slipped back into the jungle to where Obed, Maita and their families were concealed. Two other elders joined them, and Urco explained what he had seen and of his recurrent dream.

"They call us by name," Obed said. "The calling one sometimes speaks familiar words."

In whispers they debated until the *whup, whup, whup, whup* of a helicopter quieted them and drowned out the voice of the calling person. After a few minutes the helicopter left and the calling voice could be heard again.

"That was not a flying beetle," Urco said, confirming that the sound they had all heard several days earlier was different than this. "This is a dragonfly or grasshopper."

The elders resumed their debate. When he was certain he had heard everyone's opinion, Urco said: "They are calling for us and they know we are here. I do not think they will go away. I will go out and meet them. Obed, you will come with me because you understand the calling person. Maita, I want you to take five hunters with their blowpipes and hide at the edge of the forest, within range of the whiter-than-clouds people. I do not want you to shoot them unless they become hostile. If they want curare, I will give them one gourd and Obed can tell them to go away."

Urco went to his family and told them of his plan.

"If anything happens to me I want you to go deeper into the rainforest and hide," He said. "Take food and weapons. You will need them."

Making the sound of a marmoset, he signaled to the others. Obed joined him, as did the tiny monkey that was his pet. The two men stood, hidden at the edge of the forest until the warriors had taken their positions. Urco took a deep breath and stepped out into the open, twenty yards from where Starling, Moncrief and Garrido stood.

They stared in disbelief at the colossal physical specimen; blond hair, blue eyes, white skin, looking like he had stepped out of a book on Norse mythology, save for the tiny monkey wrapped around his right bicep. Obed followed, stepping out of the shadows and taking his place beside Urco, taller, a bit bent with age, but nevertheless an imposing creature.

Five human beings stood, transfixed, staring as if the first who blinked lost. Only the pygmy marmoset chittered at the foreign creatures standing in the grass. Urco's sharp gaze saw the boat in the middle of the river with silhouettes of several people, but the boat did not seem to be moving. He was relieved.

Garrido, who had stopped talking when Urco first emerged, now resumed with a new phrase: "Can you understand me?" Repeating it in the various dialects took several minutes. When there was no response, she started through them a second time. This time, halfway through, Obed took a step forward and answered. Garrido repeated the part she understood back to him:

"You are Obed. The man with you is Urco." She said it in three dialects until she found the one to which Obed responded.

"Are you of the Chilco?"

Obed responded affirmatively. For several minutes the two interpreters verbally probed to find the extent of their mutual comprehension. Garrido learned that Urco was the chief and shaman of the tribe and that they were on some sort of quest. Obed understood that the whiter-than-clouds people were of a tribe called "Amrkan" and that they came in peace to learn from the Chilco.

As the halting conversation continued, Urco said something to Obed which the elder tried to convey to Garrido. Language failed them. Urco, realizing his question wasn't getting through, twirled his finger in the air and uttered: "Wop. Wop. Wop." It brought laughter from the three Americans.

"Helicopter," Garrido said as she twirled her finger in the air in response. "Wop. Wop. Wop." She turned to Moncrief who was connected to the boat by radio. "Have them send a drone."

Garrido turned and pointed toward the boat, then followed the drone with her pointer finger as it lifted from the boat and flew across the water, landing at her feet.

"Drone," Garrido said, again twirling her finger in the air. "Whir."

Starling picked up the drone and carried it halfway to Urco and Obed where he placed it on the grass, then retreated. The two Chilco looked at the strange insect, then at each other. Urco's pet wasn't so cautious. The tiny monkey bounded down from Urco's arm and dashed to the drone. It investigated the contraption, twirling the propellers with one digit, and tried to lift it.

Emboldened by the little monkey, and seeing no signs of hostility from the visitors, Maita stepped from the forest, followed by another curious warrior. Moncrief and Starling recognized them as two of the three hunters in the video. Urco joined them as they poked at the drone, picked it up, turned it over, shook it. Urco tossed it in the air and it crashed back to earth. He stepped back, confused. Maita picked it up and was about to do the same when they realized that one of the Amrkans was standing beside them. Although all three towered above her, the three warriors jumped back.

Moncrief raised both hands, palms out, in a sign of peace. The naked white warriors stopped backing up. With one hand still extended in peace, Moncrief bent down where Maita had dropped it, and set the drone in an upright position. Then, changing her hand from palm out to raised index finger, which she hoped was a universal signal for "wait a minute," she radioed the boat to activate the drone. Slowly the propellers began to whir, and the eyes of the warriors grew big. Moncrief said "boat" to get their attention, then pointed out to the boat and told the operator to lift off. As directed, the drone slowly lifted from the ground. The warriors resumed backpedaling. Again Moncrief extended her hands to calm them. She pointed to the boat again and instructed the operator fly the craft up, down, in circles, using her hand with each command to show the Chilco what she wanted the drone to do.

An hour later, having cobbled together enough understanding so that both sides had agreed to meet again the following day, the Berrie University/National Graphic expeditionary force returned to the barge train to celebrate and file reports for the day. Dial and his copilot were already there with cocktails in hand, their mechanical "insect" bobbing on its pontoons beside the barges. Emails rocketed through the ether.

The word went out: The Lost Tribe had been located. History was happening in real time.

In the Chilco camp things were less ebullient. A fierce debate was transpiring: should the tribe retreat back into the forest, cross the river and continue their journey toward the mountains or stay and meet with the Amrkans the next day. The tribe was evenly divided, and it was up to Urco to make the final decision. He brooded for a moment, thinking of how Amaru would have dealt with the situation. Finally he rose. "They have found us," he said, "and they are peaceful. If we move they will find us again. They will not give up, and next time they may not be so peaceful. We shall stay here tonight and meet with them tomorrow and tomorrow night. In two days we shall continue our journey to the mountains."

* * *

"Have you found the curare? Remember," the email continued, "the reason the Days' paid for this trip was to find the curare!! Vikter."

"Not yet," replied Starling. "They are involved in some kind of migration, so this is not a village setting. That complicates looking for the curare. They carry everything with them and there is no permanent place for anything. I'm hopeful we'll find it tomorrow."

"That is your first and only priority. When—not if, but when—you find it, I want an immediate call," the reply email read. "Use your satellite phone. I have someone standing by to pick it up from you and transport it back here so we can start on the antidote for Dr. Castro immediately." Personally, curare and any antidote it might deliver were of little interest to Starling, but he understood the veiled threat contained in Glass's email. He put his satellite phone in his backpack so he wouldn't forget it.

Vikter dialed Dmitri.

"They've found them only fifty kilometers from your base, right under your nose. Don't fly tomorrow until you hear from me. When our person has the curare in his possession I will call you and give you the coordinates. You should be able to fly in and pick it up without using all that firepower you've got on those Mi-24s."

Dmitri sounded disappointed.

Chapter 43

When Leon and Mahogany stepped from the boat onto the shore of the Rio Maquia the next morning shockwaves raced through the Chilco community. Women came out of hiding to stare at the couple. Children, curious, innocent and unintimidated, approached the strangers, the more aggressive tugging at their clothes. The elders were stunned. Amrkans were not just whiter-than-clouds people. They were also blacker than oil birds.

Urco remembered them from his dream. He brought his family to show them, and Mahogany was instantly drawn to his wife. Even though Mahogany had no children of her own, pregnancy and childbirth gave them a biological common ground with a language all its own.

Unconcerned about the damage it was doing to her clothes, Mahogany sat on the forest floor with Urco's family and most of the women of the tribe. Using gestures, expressions and single syllables they communicated. One of the women offered a camu camu, cut in half. Mahogany took a tiny bite of the plum-like fruit and then made a puckered face at the acidic taste. Her expression sent the throng into peals of laughter, and she laughed with them.

Gilbert, a veteran of similar encounters with remote tribes, began by taking photographs of the expedition members and showing them to the Chilco so they could see both the person and the photo simultaneously. Then he did the same with the children, who had no misgivings about being photographed. When shown their own photos, they stared at the picture, never having seen their own faces before, while their playmates pointed and laughed and teased. Many of the adults were less willing, but when Urco and Obed both acquiesced, and then were delighted by photos of themselves, much of the reluctance fell away.

Moncrief, Starling and Garrido moved as a group, trying to communicate with members of the tribe, gleaning as much information as possible about the life and history of the Chilco. The elders were the primary source of information, but when a meal was being prepared, Moncrief found two women who were willing to show them things about day-to-day living.

With Mahogany immersed in Urco's family, and Gilbert busily shooting pictures, Leon wandered the patch of rainforest that had been home to the Chilco during the past forty-eight hours. The small horses interested him, and the children followed him everywhere, touching and tugging. The adults regarded him with respect, dipping their heads and averting their eyes when he passed. The irony of the situation dripped. His six-foot-two, two hundred thirty-five-pound physique had given him status in his world, while his skin color had taken it away. Here, he was smaller than even the smallest of the grown men, but the color of his skin gave him status.

Now he sat on the bow of the beached boat, his head moving slowly back and forth in wonderment at what he was seeing. Naked, primitive people and fully clothed, technologically advanced westerners, freely mingled without fear or embarrassment.

This is how the world is meant to be, he thought: the lamb lying down with the lion.

And above it all the spirit of Terry Castro watched, simultaneously proud and humbled that the two cultures of which he considered himself a part were proving to be compatible. Even the presence of Adam Starling did not temper his feelings. In fact, as he watched Starling interact with the Chilco, he was not sure he could have done as well. Had he been able, tears would have filled his eyes.

In a brief ceremony, Starling and Moncrief presented Urco with a tanned deerskin, soft and smooth as a baby's bottom, and with a coil of extremely pliable hemp rope, gifts chosen both because of their utility for the tribe and for their environmental friendliness. Urco gave the gifts to his mother for distribution among the women of the tribe, keeping for himself only one small square of the hide, which he would make into a new pouch to carry the amulets for summoning the shaman.

An elder appeared carrying a calabash gourd. A stopper was stuffed snugly in a hole in the top, and a rawhide cord was tied around its neck. Urco took the gourd from the elder and handed it to Starling. His words were unintelligible except for one: curare. Starling turned and held it out to Moncrief and for a moment they both held up the gourd as Gilbert snapped pictures. Through the interpreter they thanked Urco and the tribe for the gift.

The ceremony ended with vows of friendship between Garrido and Obed, loud enough for all to hear, and handshakes with Urco and the expedition party, accomplished after a fumbling start thanks to a little show and tell, and hands-on instruction, by Starling and Moncrief.

Within minutes all the Chilco children were shaking hands with each other and laughing.

Starling stepped away from the noisy throng milling about the grassy beach and made the required call to Glass, leaving a message when he didn't answer. He then delivered the calabash to Leon.

"This is the curare you came to find," he said. "Mr. Glass will be sending someone to pick it up so you can get it back to Day Pharmaceuticals as soon as possible."

A puzzled look crossed Leon's face. "How does Vikter know about this?" he asked.

"I've been giving him daily reports. He instructed me to do that before we left. He wanted to be kept abreast of the progress of the trip, and of your health. I assumed you knew."

Leon nodded his approval. Just like Vikter, he thought, to make sure we're okay.

"Funny, though," Starling added. "He didn't mention anything about picking up the curare until yesterday when I told him we had located the Chilco. In fact, he'd never mentioned the curare at all until then."

Again Leon frowned. National Geographic was prepared to transport the curare. Why would Vikter send someone to get it? His thoughts were distracted as the chef and kitchen crew from the barge arrived, along with containers of food and supplies. It had been part of the plan from the beginning, if the expedition found the Lost Tribe, to prepare a communal meal as a gesture of good will. The meal was planned to reflect the diet of the indigenous people of the Amazon basin so not to create gastric problems for the guests. The members of the expedition, on the other hand, ate at their own risk.

* * *

Castro, from his ethereal position high above the grassy beach, was the first to hear them, the unmistakable *wump, wump, wump, wump* of large helicopters, approaching fast.

They came in just above the treetops like fat, angry hornets, scattering the children and sending the adult Chilco scurrying into the forest. Sergei did a U-turn over the river and settled his chopper just above the beach. The downdraft flattened a hundred-foot circle in the grass and sent the meal supplies flying in all directions. The second helicopter suspended above the river, a hundred yards away, did a one-eighty so that it faced the beach and the rainforest.

Sergei hovered in place until they spotted Leon, crouched in the boat to reduce the blast from the rotors.

"Him," Dmitri said, pointing toward Leon. "He has it."

A door slid open and Dmitri dropped a ladder over the side. The third crew member, an AK-47 slung over his back, climbed out of the belly of the beast and began to descend. His feet hit the ground as the first volley of darts was launched from the tree line. The churning wind deflected most of them, but several clanked off the underside of the helicopter and one found its target.

Before they had seen the helicopters, the Chilco had reacted to the sound, racing into the forest to arm themselves. Urco's dream had foretold of the death the flying beetles could bring, and they were prepared to destroy the evil before it destroyed them.

"I've been hit," the Russian screamed through the headset he was wearing. He let go of the ladder and grabbed at the thing buried in his shoulder.

"We're under attack," Sergei radioed to the other chopper as he pulled up, leaving his wounded comrade on the ground. A warrior wielding a spear charged out of the forest toward the abandoned Russian. Dmitri fired wildly with his sidearm as Sergei turned the chopper. A burst of machine gun fire from the second helicopter cut down the warrior before he could reach his target.

At the first sound of a gunshot Leon dove over the side of the boat and swam down the shoreline. The warm green water and muffled sound of gunfire, now joined by the heavy blast of 23 mm cannons, firing from the nose of one of the helicopters, left him disoriented. This couldn't be happening. It had to be a dream.

When he came up for air he saw the carnage.

The cannon from the offshore helicopter raked the shore and the tree line, plowing dirt and tree fragments, blood and bone in its wake. A machine gun chattered, sweeping the beach area. Adam Starling, frozen upright in shock, was the first of the expedition to go down, two bullets tearing out the back of his body as they passed through him. One of the kitchen crew was cartwheeled by the impact of a cannon shell, dead before he hit the ground.

"Get over the boat," Dmitri shouted at Sergei, pointing to the beached craft and ramming another clip into his pistol.

Moncrief, on the ground next to the tree line, shouted into her radio: "Crocko! Crocko! We're being attacked. Two helicopters. Call Peru Air Command." Cannon rounds whizzed just over her head and exploded into the tree line amidst screams.

Gilbert ran, low to the ground, straight for the boat, focused on the helicopter over the river that was raining death on the shore. He rolled over the gunwale and crouched behind the drone monitor. Activating the drone, he flew it at maximum speed toward the helicopter. The heavy rotors of the Mi-24 swatted it away like a mosquito just as Dmitri emptied his clip into the top of Gilbert's head.

Maita raced out of the forest, coming up behind the wounded Russian who was trying to get the AK-47 off his back with his one functional arm, and deftly cut his throat, then ran toward the hovering helicopter. Dmitri had located the calabash gourd where Leon had stashed it and was starting down the ladder. Maita whipped the blowpipe off his back and flopped on the ground to steady his aim as machine gun fired sizzled over his head, cutting down two warriors that had followed him. Maita's shot was true, driving the dart deep into Dmitri's neck.

The hulking Russian hung on the ladder, hooking one arm through a rung, firing his pistol with his free hand. Maita resumed his charge, and took a slug squarely in the face. The back of his head exploded in a geyser of bones, brains and blood. Dmitri dropped the last few feet to the boat, lost his balance and fell on the dead body of Gilbert. He shoved Gilbert's body out of his way, then grasped the end of the dart with both hands and broke the shaft, knowing that if he pulled it out, he might bleed to death before they got back to Iquitos.

Free of his passenger, Sergei pivoted the helicopter and triggered the nose cannon in spurts, pouring shells into the tree line.

Over the wall of trees that separated the two rivers rose the little National Geographic Bell 220, half the size of the Russian gunships and armed with only a single rifle, wielded by Dial's copilot, Curt Turner, leaning out the side window. But they had the element of surprise. Coming in from behind the Russian behemoth they settled alongside the opening that housed a side-mount machine gun that was spewing death at the shore. Turner fired several rounds into the window until the machine gun fell silent. The Russian pilot, suddenly aware he was under attack, pivoted the giant war machine as the Bell 220 clawed for elevation. Dial knew that the Mi-24 was faster and more agile than his little craft. He couldn't run, and he couldn't fight. As the Mi-24's cannon barrel elevated and the first shell fired, Dial dove straight for the nose of the Russian gunship. A ball of fire erupted as the two came together and plummeted the hundred feet into the river.

Urco was only vaguely aware of the exploding helicopters as he charged toward Dmitri, intent on avenging the death of his best friend. The massive Russian rose from the bottom of the boat with the calabash in his hand just in time to see the maniacal face of the Chilco chieftain hurtling toward him. He fired, and the bullet caught Urco in the side, spinning him around and knocking him to the ground just short of the boat. Dmitri pulled the trigger again. Click. Again. Click. He searched for another clip but he had none. The huge Indian was up on all fours, trying to get up. Dmitri stepped out of the boat and kicked Urco in the ribs, causing him to collapse. He aimed another kick at the fallen chieftain but before it connected there was an explosion in Dmitri's back, folding him backward, popping vertebrae.

Later, Leon would say it was the best block he ever threw.

The Russian went down in pain. Leon's airborne body spun away and landed on the shoreline. Dazed, Leon lay for an instant, mentally checking whether there was anything broken in his seventy-five-year-old body. A sudden burst of gunfire brought him back to the moment. Bullets clanged off the hull of the helicopter hovering overhead.

"Get up here!" Sergei shouted into his headphone as he spun the helicopter and fired a cannon burst at the source of the hostile gunfire. The impact of the cannon shells sent the chef, who had been firing wildly with the AK-47 taken off the dead Russian, diving to the ground where he huddled, expecting to die.

Dmitri used the side of the boat to pull himself upright. His KGB training kept him functioning despite the excruciating pain that wracked his entire body. He grasped the calabash gourd with one hand and, as the ladder swung toward him, put one foot on the bottom rung and looped his other arm around a higher one.

"Go!" he shouted at the mouthpiece that still dangled around his neck.

Castro looked on in horror, silently screaming at the insanity of it all, as the helicopter with Dmitri dangling from the ladder, rose and banked to the northeast. He looked back at the beach and the shattered rainforest.

In his horror he felt himself slowly drifting upward, until the carnage was no longer visible, until the beach disappeared, until the rainforest was only a memory.

Chapter 44

The nine-millimeter soft nose had made a small hole upon entry but had taken a sizable chunk out of Urco's lower back as it exited. Leon pulled off his wet shirt and stuffed it in the hole, staunching the bleeding. He prayed nothing vital had been hit.

He crawled to the boat to look for the first-aid kit.

Moncrief, shaken but unscathed, rose from the grass. She radioed the barge train. The medical officer answered. Call for medi-vacs and get over here, she ordered. They would have to portage the other boat and the medi-vac would come from Tarapota. Both would take at least an hour, he explained.

She went to the chef, still huddled on the ground on all fours beside the discarded AK-47. She sat him up but saw vacant eyes. She laid him on his back, wishing she had something to elevate his feet.

She saw Starling, his eyes rolled back in his head, and knew there was no reason to stop. The Russian, a scarlet ribbon around his neck, lay in a puddle of blood. The bloody bodies of the two warriors that had followed Maita lay nearby, their lives ripped away by bullets. Farther on was Maita, his face missing.

Moncrief found Leon crouched over Urco, putting ointment on a bullet wound. In the boat next to them was her friend and colleague, Alain Gilbert, crumpled in the metallic stench of his own blood and brains.

"Help me roll him over," Leon shouted at her, snapping her out of her daze. Before she could react Urco rolled over on his own and levered himself to a sitting position. They both said, "stop," but the shaman did not understand them. He sat, waiting for the dizziness to clear. Leon squirted the antibiotic on a large gauze pad and then applied it to Urco's back, then wrapped a pressure bandage around Urco's middle to hold the gauze pad in place. The Chilco chief did not object, nor did he flinch when

Leon pulled the blood-soaked T-shirt out of the gaping wound.

People began wandering aimlessly out of the shredded forest onto the scarred beach, some with blood running from wounds, others with vacant expressions. From within the rainforest came wails of anguish, growing in intensity as the extent of the devastation was recognized.

Leon helped Urco to his feet, aware that it was medically stupid, but knowing he would want it this way. A chief had to be able to show his people that he was alive and able to lead them. Both men scanned the shore for their wives, but they were not among those who had come of the trees. Together they hobbled through the bloody, torn battlefield, stopping at the bodies of three Chilco, one a little girl whose blue eyes were still open in an expression that could only be described as peaceful. The lower half of her body was missing.

Leon stooped and closed her eyes as Urco steeled himself to hold back anger. Moncrief, who had steered them away from a path that would have led them to Maita, wept unabashedly at the sight of the dead child.

Farther on they found both members of the kitchen crew. They never got to serve their honorary meal.

Urco and Leon entered the butchered rainforest. The first thirty feet were shredded foliage and splintered trees spattered with body parts and blood. Dead and dying Chilco lay amidst the devastation. One, with no arm below his elbow, screamed in agony. At least a score of young warriors had died trying to defend their people with blowpipes and spears against weapons that killed before they were seen.

A child ran through the chaos. Urco staggered but remained upright at the impact of the sobbing youngster. It was his son, his middle child, whom he held and soothed until the youngster could communicate between sobs. Although they could not understand, Leon and Moncrief knew it was not good news. Urco's eyes flashed as he hobbled as fast as he could, following his son.

Beneath the shelter of palm branches, where Urco had warned his wife and children about the danger of the whiter-than-clouds people, lay his pregnant wife, covered like a protective blanket by Mahogany Day. Both women, and Urco's unborn child, had been pierced by a single cannon shell. They were all dead.

The two men fell upon each other, and crumbled to the ground, and wept.

* * *

Sergei set down in the first open area, minutes from where the slaughter had taken place. As gently as he could maneuver a thirty-ton helicopter, he lowered Dmitri to the ground, then landed next to him. He helped the big man into the helicopter and strapped him in a passenger seat. They were airborne in five minutes.

"We should be in Iquitos in an hour," he yelled over his shoulder at Dmitri. "We get you to a doctor."

Dmitri was not sure what had happened but the pain was overwhelming. He feared his back was broken. The arrowhead embedded in his neck was a nuisance, but it only hurt if he turned his head to the right. An extraction and a few stitches would take care of that.

Sergei kept the helicopter at full throttle, racing at two hundred miles per hour just above the treetops to avoid radar detection. He needed to get to Iquitos quickly, not so much for Dmitri's health but to hide the helicopter, get away from it. The mess they had left behind would reach authorities soon, and even the obsolete fighters of the Peruvian Air Force were too much for his Mi-24 to handle.

Even though the calabash gourd was safely strapped in one of the passenger seats, the mission was a failure. He had lost a man, Dmitri was badly injured and the other helicopter was missing. They had failed to dispose of witnesses and wipe out the evidence as ordered. Whoever had planned it had botched it, but he knew where the blame would fall. He would have to deal with that later. For now, he just wanted to get to Iquitos, get his money and get out of South America.

* * *

Immediately after talking with Dmitri, Vikter had booked a flight to Iquitos. The next day, at his stopover in Lima, he picked up Starling's message. He contacted the Russian with the final instructions.

He would be in Iquitos before the Russians got there. He liked that. It gave him control of the meeting.

Vikter reached Iquitos and taxied to La Casa Chacruna. He confirmed that the Wi-Fi was working and confirmed his return flight the next day. He called Dmitri, thinking that the pickup should have happened by now and that they would be on their way back. He didn't get an answer. Not surprising. Hard to hear a phone in a noisy helicopter.

He waited, something he was not good at. He checked the markets. Day Pharmaceuticals was up another point. He called his office to check in. There was nothing that needed his immediate attention. He tried the local television but there was nothing in English so he turned it off. He flipped through a three-month-old travel magazine. He tried Dmitri again.

After an hour his patience ran out. The taxi had passed a bar only a block from the Inn. Dammit, he thought, they can wait for me. He walked to the bar. A drunk on a chair, leaning against the wall in a back corner; a bunch of flies and an ex-pat bartender from Fresno were the occupants of the dirty, smelly establishment. A half-dozen tables with plastic tablecloths, all looking greasy, crowded the floor. Vikter elected to sit at the bar.

"We don't have scotch and the whiskey is shit," the bartender told him, "but I can make you a mean margarita."

Vikter consented.

An old television set with a blurry picture hung on the wall over the back bar. Vikter watched a soccer game that, judging by the haircuts of the players, had been played twenty years ago. The bartender came back with his margarita.

"I should have told you, no salt," Vikter said, staring at the heavily salted rim of the stout, stemmed glass.

"Just wipe it off."

Ordinarily Vikter would have demanded a new one, but, rather than piss off the only bartender in the area, he took a napkin and wiped the rim. He took a drink and immediately knew it was a mistake. The salt that had dissolved from the rim into the drink before he had had a chance to wipe it off bored into his canker sores like a dentist's drill.

"How is it?" the bartender asked.

"Can I have some water?"

"Better not. How about a beer?"

Vikter nodded, grimacing with the salt-induced pain. He took a pull off the cold beer and swished it in his mouth before swallowing. It gave him some relief.

"Can you make me another one without the salt?"

Vikter went back to watching the soccer game, until it was interrupted by a news flash. He couldn't tell if the breaking news was part of the old rerun or was live.

"What's going on?" he asked, nodding toward the television as the bartender delivered the margarita. Mr. Fresno turned and looked.

"Some helicopter crash, or something." He watched for a minute. "Sounds like two helicopters collided. Bunch of people dead. One of the helicopters was from National Geographic."

A chill ran down Vikter's back. He stared at the TV commentator, silently cursing his inability to understand Spanish. He threw a twenty-dollar bill on the bar and left without taking a drink of the second margarita.

How had that stupid Russian fucked up, he wondered as he walked rapidly back to the Inn. Two helicopters down. One had to be one of the Russians. The Days' group had only one helicopter. It should have been a simple pickup. What had that trigger-happy motherfucker done?

Vikter's thoughts shifted to self-preservation as he walked: could he be traced to the Russians? Vasiliev had arranged it, the men, the helicopters, the lodging. There was nothing to link him directly, and no one knew of the curare except his sister's brat, and no one would believe her. Vasiliev had taken care of that, and if she became a problem he could probably take care of her permanently. But there were the phone calls with Dmitri and the calls and emails with Starling. Shit!

He unlocked the door to his room. Sitting in the chair Vikter had specifically positioned for himself was Dmitri, looking ashen and in pain with something sticking out of the side of his neck. Standing, looking out the window, was Sergei.

Vikter shut the door behind him.

"What the fuck happened," he said.

"They were ready for us," Sergei said. "We got the stuff you wanted, but they were waiting for us." He pointed at the calabash gourd lying on the bed.

"How in the hell could they have been waiting for you? No one knew about this unless one of you got drunk and leaked something. Where are the rest?"

"I don't know. We lost Petr right away. There wasn't a big enough space to land, so we dropped a ladder. They shot him before he reached the ground."

"What happened to him?" Vikter interrupted, pointing to Dmitri.

"He went to get the gourd, but he got shot in the neck with an arrow and hurt his back. He thinks it's broken. He should see a doctor."

"Where are the rest?"

"I don't know. We were under fire and they were supposed to be hanging over the river, covering us. When Dmitri got his hands on the gourd, I pulled out with him hanging on the ladder. I thought they would be right behind me, but when I stopped to get Dmitri in the helicopter they didn't show up."

"They crashed, you dumb shit!" Vikter shrieked at the Russian pilot, sweat beads popping out on his forehead. "It's all over the news. They crashed into the National Geographic helicopter. All that fucking firepower and you motherfuckers can't do a simple pickup."

Sergei reddened, his anger boiling. "You got your shit," he shouted, pointing again at the calabash. "Just give me the money and we'll be out of here."

Vikter was tempted to negotiate, but thought better of it. The quicker they left the better. He handed Sergei a briefcase. The pilot opened it and looked at the bundles of one hundred dollar bills. He picked up a bundle and counted it, then measured it side-by-side with the other bundles. He counted the bundles.

"Okay."

Sergei got his arm under the hulk in the chair and helped him stand. They half-walked, half-stumbled to the door, and left. Minutes later Vikter heard a car in the courtyard. Looking out the window of his room he saw Sergei helping Dmitri into a taxi. He exhaled.

He pulled a fat, hard-sided suitcase out of the closet and opened it. Inside it was packed with foam rubber squares. He put the calabash on top and drew an outline, then removed the rubber squares so that the calabash fit snugly into a foam rubber cocoon. He shut the foam-lined lid. By tomorrow night it would be in a safe laboratory at Day Pharmaceuticals being analyzed and reverse engineered so that they could chemically duplicate the substance. There should be enough left over for experiments to see if it really had life-extending qualities.

It would be three in the morning in Moscow. A call to Vasiliev would have to wait for a few hours. He was hopeful that Bogdan would be able to take care of the incriminating phone calls just as he had taken care of Carrie. Feeling confident, Vikter went back to the bar. He ordered dinner and finally got to drink a salt-free margarita. It was very good. He had a second, and then one for the road.

Back in his room, getting ready for bed, he looked in the dingy bathroom mirror. Gray stubble was starting to appear at his temples. He needed a shave. He stared at lines on his face that he had never seen before. He was getting old. Just as he was about to become one of the richest men in the world he was getting old.

The tequila was talking, getting louder. His third margarita was still half full and he took another gulp. It talked him right to the suitcase and he opened the lid. Why should he get old when he had the stuff right in this suitcase to keep him young forever?

He worked the cork free and sniffed at the hole in the calabash. A pungent aroma made his face pucker. He wobbled to the bathroom and found a paper cup. He poured a shot of the curare into it, raised it in a personal toast to "the fountain of youth," and tossed it back.

Vikter gagged as it came back up. He managed to spew most of it into the sink, along with the contents of his stomach. He stood for several minutes, bent over the sink with hands on the countertop, sweating, his nose running and eyes watering. He spit for the last time, and filled another paper cup with water from the faucet. He shakily raised it to his lips and rinsed out his mouth.

Lesson learned, he took the calabash into the kitchen and found a spoon. He dribbled a few drops of curare into a spoon and then stirred it into the remainder of his margarita. This time he sipped it slowly. Still bitter, but potable.

How long, he wondered, would it take to work?

Part IV

Chapter 45

Four Months Later.

"I'm doing as well as can be expected under the circumstances. No. I should correct that. I'm doing pretty damn good."

Father Wyman sat in Leon Day's home office, listening. The visit had been long overdue, and this was not a fund-raising trip, just two friends commiserating.

"How's your health?" the priest asked. "You're looking pretty damn good."

Leon smiled. "You know, for all the awful things that happened, that trip gave me back my health...and I didn't even have to take the curare. Of course, it helps that Glass isn't poisoning me anymore."

"Tell me about that. I never did get the whole story."

"Glass was scheming to steal my company for years," Leon said. "From the time he took over operations when I had serious health issues. One of the things he did was sneak an overdose of vitamin B_6 into my drug regimen. It caused all sorts of crazy symptoms: aches and pains, gastric problems, weakness, memory issues. It made my real health problems worse, and they couldn't diagnose the source. When we decided to do the expedition, I knew I needed to get stronger so I made up my mind to stop taking most of the drugs that had been prescribed for me. I figured it would either kill me or cure me. Luckily, it did the latter. Go figure: a guy who owns a pharmaceutical company gets healthy when he stops taking his own products."

Father Wyman shook his head. "The world is full of irony," he said.

Sanjay interrupted, delivering iced tea and lemon cookies. "Is it all right if I leave now?" he asked Leon, who nodded his consent.

"I don't know what I'm going to do without him," Leon said

after Sanjay had left. "He does everything, trying to make up for Mahogany, I think. Even goes to the cemetery every day and puts fresh flowers on her grave. That's where he's going now."

"Is he leaving you?" Father Wyman asked.

"No. I'm leaving him."

The priest looked puzzled.

"When are you going to retire?" It was Leon's turn to ask the priest a question.

"I'm thinking next year or maybe the year after at the latest. Why?"

"Well, you've always liked this house. I'd like to give it to you as a retirement gift."

The priest sat back in his chair in surprise. "I couldn't..."

"Wait. Before you say no, you haven't heard the best part. Sanjay goes with the house."

Father Wyman was dumbfounded. After a lengthy discussion, he agreed to accept the gift but only on the condition that the home be given to Berrie University and not to him, personally. "You can put whatever limitations you want on its use, and, this way, you can get a tax deduction," he reasoned.

"I'll put money in an endowment to maintain the house, and to pay Sanjay and take care of his retirement," Day added.

"But what are you going to do?" Father Wyman asked.

"Now that I have my company back I'm going to give it to the employees, just like Mahogany and I planned before I got sick; before Glass stole it. Then I'm going back to Peru."

Leon's phone buzzed. "Sorry, I've got to take this." He walked out of the room.

Father Wyman, still shaking his head in amazement, looked at the mementos that adorned Leon's office: pictures of his football days at Berrie University and in the NFL, photos with celebrities and politicians, plaques honoring his community service, and, most recently, a blowpipe, a dart and a calabash gourd.

"Are you going to take those with you?" the priest asked

when Leon came back in the room.

"They'll go with me wherever I go," he replied.

"I'm a little surprised. Don't they bring back painful memories?"

Leon nodded, hooking his thumb under his chin and covering his mouth with his index finger. He paused to compose himself.

"They do, but there are also good memories and I don't ever want to forget any of them, good or bad."

"And that," Leon continued, nodding toward the calabash, "is a reminder of lessons that we all should learn."

Father Wyman cocked an eye. "Lessons?" he said.

"Do you know how Glass died?" Leon asked. The priest shook his head.

"He believed that the curare had the power to extend life. If true, then it also had the power to make the person who controlled it rich beyond imagination. That's why he sent those thugs to steal the curare. Plus, he not only wanted to be rich, he wanted to live forever. He drank the curare and it killed him. He had open ulcers, canker sores, in his mouth and the poison got into his bloodstream."

"It killed a lot of people."

Leon nodded grimly. "More than thirty Chilco, including an unborn child; Alain; Starling; the kitchen crew; the two pilots who gave up their lives to save who knows how many, Mahogany." His voice caught at the mention of his late wife's name.

Father Wyman rose and put his arm around his grieving friend. "She was a wonderful woman," he said. "One of God's real disciples."

They stayed that way for a few minutes until Leon nodded, letting Father Wyman know he was okay.

The priest sat back in his chair. "So, greed can kill you, is the first lesson," he said.

"There is evidence that Glass's belief about the curare is true,"

Leon said. "The Chilco in the video, the one that came back to get his dart from Dr. Castro, was over a hundred years old when he died of a snake bite. His name was Amaru. He was the tribe shaman and Urco's father.

"We learned all that from Obed, who is nearly fifty, himself, extremely old for a Chilco, unless you are the tribe shaman. According to legend, all the shaman of the Chilco lived to be over a hundred because they were the only ones of the tribe who made the curare. They tasted it for potency, and it was the tasting that gave them all long life.

"Obed said his first recollection of Amaru, when Obed was just a boy, was that Amaru had two grown sons. The sons grew old and died, but Amaru didn't seem to get any older. Years later Amaru and another woman had another son. That is Urco. Urco didn't want to become shaman because he didn't want to taste the curare and outlive his wife and children. Obed told us that Urco was actually Amaru's third family."

Leon stopped for a moment and took a drink of iced tea. He checked his watch.

"We'll need to leave in about a half hour," he said, and then continued his story.

"When they found Glass in the hotel room the Iquitos authorities also found the calabash packed in a padded suitcase. It was still full of curare, except for the little bit Glass had drunk. Terry Castro had passed away so the original reason we went looking for the curare was gone, but I still arranged to have the calabash shipped here. I was going to have the curare analyzed to determine its components. I was thinking like Glass, seeing big dollar signs.

"Then I began to think about what would happen if we developed a drug that doubled a person's life expectancy. It was as though I was having a conversation with Mahogany. We talked about what happens when you double or triple or quadruple the population of people over eighty; people who didn't plan or prepare to live to be that old. We talked about the burden it would place on society's infrastructure. How do you create enough jobs to accommodate everybody? How do young people get jobs when old people have to work longer? We talked about famine and disease and quality of life, and we talked about greed. What would happen if it fell into the wrong hands and it was made available only to the wealthy? Other than our own selfish interests, we couldn't think of one good thing that would come out having a drug like that."

"So what did you do?"

"We didn't analyze it. I had the whole contents dumped into one of our hazardous waste containers and then had it disposed of. I kept the calabash to remind me."

"Remind you?"

"Just because you can, doesn't mean you should. That's the second lesson. Did I do the right thing, Father?"

Father Wyman thought for a moment.

"Did you pray about it?"

"I did."

"And, after you prayed, you believe you did the right thing?"

"Yes."

"Then it is the right thing."

A half hour later the two men were seated in the back of Day's limousine, motoring south on Highway 101 toward Sausalito.

"What are you going to do in Peru?" Father Wyman asked.

"See Urco. See if there's anything I can do to help the Chilco now that they're back in the Andes, in the clouds. Hang with them for a while. After that, I'm not sure."

The limousine pulled off 101 onto Bridgeway, then angled south along the waterfront until it pulled to the curb in front of a refurbished multilevel building, a multitude of gray architectural cubicles stretching up the steep hillside that faced the bay. A cluster of people stood on the sidewalk. Above their heads a new polished brass sign read: "Mahogany Day Center for International Justice."

Father Wyman and Leon got out and paused long enough to read the bronze plaque just under the sign: "This Center honors the spirit and the bravery of Mahogany Day, Ben "Crocko" Dial, Curt Turner, Alain Gilbert and Dr. Terry Castro, all of whom died heroically while pursuing and defending humanitarian justice."

"Shall we go cut a ribbon?" Leon said.

The opening ceremony was short. Leon's brief words honored his wife, and Father Wyman's lauded the collaboration between Day Pharmaceutical Company, The National Geographic Society and Berrie University in the establishment of the new center. Then the ribbon was cut and the crowd moved up the steps to tour the facility.

"Pretty impressive."

Leon turned at the words and got a warm hug from Holly Bouquet.

"Do I get a hug, too?"

Leon stepped back and looked at his former medium standing next to Holly. "Is this the same person that taught me to believe in spirits? My goodness how you have changed." He enveloped Carrie in a bear hug.

"This is so special," he said after he let go of Carrie. "I didn't expect to see you two here. Thank you both for coming."

"We wouldn't have missed it for anything," Holly said.

"I wish Terry could have been here to see this," Leon said.

"Oh, he is," Carrie said with a twinkle in her eye. "So is Amaru. Those two hang out a lot together."

"Not that long ago I would have said you were crazy for saying that. Now I believe it," Leon said. "What are you doing now?"

"I moved to Chicago. I work for a private investigation firm."

Leon looked at Holly. "You?"

"Yup."

"Good for both of you. Did you fly out just for the grand opening of the center?"

"Well, it's one of the reasons," Holly said. "We've been hired to investigate a case of international human trafficking. We thought it might be a fitting first project for the Mahogany Day Center for International Justice."

Leon appeared to expand with pride, and a huge smile spread across his face.

"Oh," Holly continued. "Did I mention that it involves a Russian named Bogdan Vasiliev. I think you've heard of him."

About the Author

Rob Jung is a former newspaper writer and lawyer. He spent seven years as a sportswriter in Minnesota while earning his bachelor degree in sociology and political science from Winona State College, then moved to Massachusetts to attend Harvard Law School, where he received a Juris Doctor degree. After more than forty years of practicing law, Jung began a writing career. *Cloud Warriors* is his debut novel. He lives in Minnesota with his wife, Kathy, and Daisy, a cuddly King Charles spaniel. He has three children, four grandchildren and one great-grandchild, all of whom, to his delight, live in Minnesota. You can follow him on his website at http://www.Robjungwriter.com, or on Facebook at www.facebook.com/robjungwriter.

From Rob Jung

I hope that you derive as much enjoyment from reading *Cloud Warriors* as I had in writing it. If you have a few moments, please enter your review of *Cloud Warriors* at your favorite online site. If you would like a preview of future books, please visit my website: http://www.Robjungwriter.com. Coming next: *The Reaper*, a psychological thriller in which the disappearance of a famous painting entwines the lives of three people in an ethical and moral dilemma a century later—with deadly consequences.

Sincerely,
Rob Jung

Roundfire
FICTION

Put simply, we publish great stories. Whether it's literary or popular, a gentle tale or a pulsating thriller, the connecting theme in all Roundfire fiction titles is that once you pick them up you won't want to put them down.

If you have enjoyed this book, why not tell other readers by posting a review on your preferred book site.

Recent bestsellers from Roundfire are:

The Bookseller's Sonnets

Andi Rosenthal

The Bookseller's Sonnets intertwines three love stories with a tale of religious identity and mystery spanning five hundred years and three countries.

Paperback: 978-1-84694-342-3 ebook: 978-184694-626-4

Birds of the Nile

An Egyptian Adventure

N.E. David

Ex-diplomat Michael Blake wanted a quiet birding trip up the Nile – he wasn't expecting a revolution.

Paperback: 978-1-78279-158-4 ebook: 978-1-78279-157-7

Blood Profit$

The Lithium Conspiracy

J. Victor Tomaszek, James N. Patrick, Sr.

The blood of the many for the profits of the few… *Blood Profit$*

will take you into the cigar-smoke-filled room where American policy and laws are really made.
Paperback: 978-1-78279-483-7 ebook: 978-1-78279-277-2

The Burden

A Family Saga

N.E. David

Frank will do anything to keep his mother and father apart. But he's carrying baggage – and it might just weigh him down ...
Paperback: 978-1-78279-936-8 ebook: 978-1-78279-937-5

The Cause

Roderick Vincent

The second American Revolution will be a fire lit from an internal spark.
Paperback: 978-1-78279-763-0 ebook: 978-1-78279-762-3

Don't Drink and Fly

The Story of Bernice O'Hanlon: Part One

Cathie Devitt

Bernice is a witch living in Glasgow. She loses her way in her life and wanders off the beaten track looking for the garden of enlightenment.
Paperback: 978-1-78279-016-7 ebook: 978-1-78279-015-0

Gag

Melissa Unger

One rainy afternoon in a Brooklyn diner, Peter Howland punctures an egg with his fork. Repulsed, Peter pushes the plate away and never eats again.
Paperback: 978-1-78279-564-3 ebook: 978-1-78279-563-6

The Master Yeshua

The Undiscovered Gospel of Joseph

Joyce Luck

Jesus is not who you think he is. The year is 75 CE. Joseph ben Jude is frail and ailing, but he has a prophecy to fulfil …

Paperback: 978-1-78279-974-0 ebook: 978-1-78279-975-7

Tuareg

Alberto Vazquez-Figueroa

With over 5 million copies sold worldwide, *Tuareg* is a classic adventure story from best-selling author Alberto Vazquez-Figueroa, about honour, revenge and a clash of cultures.

Paperback: 978-1-84694-192-4

On the Far Side, There's a Boy

Paula Coston

Martine Haslett, a thirty-something 1980s woman, plays hard on the fringes of the London drag club scene until one night which prompts her to sign up to a charity. She writes to a young Sri Lankan boy, with consequences far and long.

Paperback: 978-1-78279-574-2 ebook: 978-1-78279-573-5

Readers of ebooks can buy or view any of these bestsellers by clicking on the live link in the title. Most titles are published in paperback and as an ebook. Paperbacks are available in traditional bookshops. Both print and ebook formats are available online.
Find more titles and sign up to our readers' newsletter at http://www.johnhuntpublishing.com/fiction

Follow us on Facebook at https://www.facebook.com/JHPfiction and Twitter at https://twitter.com/JHPFiction